The Woman Whose Marriage Broke

THE WOMAN WHOSE MARRIAGE BROKE

Cally Berryman (PhD)

Published in Australia by Marble Media

Email: callyberryman@hotmail.com
Website: callyberryman.com

First published in Australia in 2024
Copyright © Cally Berryman 2024

Berryman, Cally
The Woman Whose Marriage Broke

ISBN: 978-06454288-0-3 (pbk)
eISBN: 978-0-6454288-1-0 (ebook)

Cover layout and design by graphic designer: PizBee Design

Disclaimer
All care has been taken in the information's preparation, but
no responsibility can be accepted by the publisher or author
for any damages resulting from the misinterpretation of this
work. All contact details provided within this book were
current at the time of publication, but are subject to change.
The advice provided within this book is based on the experience
of the individuals. Professionals should be consulted for
individual problems. The author and publisher shall not be
responsible for any person regarding any loss or damage
caused directly or indirectly by the information in this book.

ABOUT THE AUTHOR

This book is the third published book by
Cally Berryman (PhD)
The previous books are:
The Accidental Gambler (Fiction) 2016
Calel (Non-fiction) 2017

CONTENTS

About the Author..v

PART 1: Before

Chapter One 2

Chapter Two 4

Chapter Three 11

Chapter Four 23

Chapter Five...27

Chapter Six..31

Chapter Seven..36

Chapter Eight..41

Chapter Nine...44

Chapter Ten 47

Chapter Eleven...52

Chapter Twelve...56

Chapter Thirteen...62

Chapter Fourteen...70

Chapter Fifteen 73

Chapter Sixteen 76

Chapter Seventeen..81

Chapter Eighteen 85

Chapter Nineteen...91

Chapter Twenty...95

Chapter Twenty-One 97

Chapter Twenty-Two 100
Chapter Twenty-Three 103
Chapter Twenty-Four...105
Chapter Twenty-Five 108
Chapter Twenty-Six 113
Chapter Twenty-Seven..117
Chapter Twenty-Eight..121
Chapter Twenty-Nine...123
Chapter Thirty...127
Chapter Thirty-One 129
Chapter Thirty-Two..134
Chapter Thirty-Three...135

PART 2: After

Chapter Thirty-Four 138
Chapter Thirty-Five 143
Chapter Thirty-Six..144
Chapter Thirty-Seven 149
Chapter Thirty-Eight 159
Chapter Thirty-Nine 164
Chapter Forty...169
Chapter Forty-One 172
Chapter Forty-Two..174
Chapter Forty-Three...179
Chapter Forty-Four...188
Chapter Forty-Five 194
Chapter Forty-Six 201

Chapter Forty-Seven 206

Chapter Forty-Eight 208

Chapter Forty-Nine 210

Chapter Fifty 212

Chapter Fifty-One...213

Chapter Fifty-Two 215

Chapter Fifty-Three 220

Chapter Fifty-Four 223

Chapter Fifty-Five...225

Chapter Fifty-Six...229

Chapter Fifty-Seven...233

Chapter Fifty-Eight...238

Chapter Fifty-Nine...241

Chapter Sixty...244

Chapter Sixty-One 246

Chapter Sixty-Two 248

Chapter Sixty-Three...251

Chapter Sixty-Four 254

Chapter Sixty-Five 257

Chapter Sixty-Six 264

Chapter Sixty-Seven 266

Chapter Sixty-Eight 268

Chapter Sixty-Nine 270

Chapter Seventy...276

Chapter Seventy-One 279

Chapter Seventy-Two...283

Chapter Seventy-Three...285

Chapter Seventy-Four 288

Chapter Seventy-Five 292

Chapter Seventy-Six 296

Chapter Seventy-Seven 298

Chapter Seventy-Eight 300

Chapter Seventy-Nine 303

Chapter Eighty..310

Chapter Eighty-One 315

Chapter Eighty-Two...318

PART 3: Later

Chapter Eighty-Three 322

Chapter Eighty-Four..326

Chapter Eighty-Five 334

Chapter Eighty-Six 336

Chapter Eighty-Seven 344

Chapter Eighty-Eight 348

Chapter Eighty-Nine 349

Chapter Ninety...352

Chapter Ninety-One 360

Chapter Ninety-Two...362

Chapter Ninety-Three..369

Chapter Ninety-Four 375

Chapter Ninety-Five 383

Chapter Ninety-Six 388

Chapter Ninety-Seven 391

Chapter Ninety-Eight 399

Chapter Ninety-Nine 403

Chapter One hundred...405

Chapter One Hundred and One............................407

Chapter One Hundred and Two 409

Chapter One Hundred and Three 411

Chapter One Hundred and Four............................413

Postscript...416

PART 1

Before

CHAPTER ONE

Tuesday, the man slams the door to the decaying caravan which hides in the long grass and trees on the edge of the city. He is thin, has brown greasy hair, a hard mouth and shiny arrogant eyes. He wears a soiled, dark blue tracksuit. Rubs his hands together, sniffs, looks around for a long time, finally steps down the three steps to the thick grass, drops when he hears a police siren go past on the highway, does not move until the police car is gone. A plane roars overhead, looks up, shades his eyes from the sun. Searches through his pockets for loose change, finds a folded $20, has enough for a piece of fish, flake is his favourite with chips. The man walks the beaten track through the matted grass of the paddock to the vicinity of the local fish and chips shop. He peers around the shop before he gives his order to a pimply youth. It is a day since he last ate, the smell of the fried seafood cooking makes his mouth moisten.

"Do you want salt with the chips?" said the youth.

"Yes." He licks his lips.

When the food is cooked and wrapped, he takes the fish and chips in the warm paper parcel, tears a hole in the top of the paper, pulls out chip after chip, scoffs them greedily. He rips a piece of paper and holds the hot fish in it, sits on the wooden bench outside the shop, eats his fill. When he is finished, wipes his hand over his greasy mouth and swipes it over his tracksuit pants. He strides to the nearby liquor shop, purchases two cans of beer, sculls both cans, crushes the cans, throws them under the bench, belches, wipes his mouth again.

One thing is missing from his day. His pulse quickens, peers at his watch.

The time is right.

CHAPTER TWO

On the same Tuesday, the Dunfield household in East Brunswick started like hundreds of other mornings. A sunny, cloudless day, a cool summer breeze puffed on the leaves of the poplar trees. Small bright insects buzzed overhead. A waft of jasmine lingered in the air.

"Bye sweetheart, have a great day at school," Nancy gives daughter Millie an expansive hug.

"Love you."

Nancy is a slim, energetic woman with shoulder-length wavy red hair, a handful of freckles over her nose and cheeks. She wears dark blue stretch jeans and a bright red shirt.

Mother and daughter stand at the front door to say goodbye, the coloured lights from the tinted glass on the open front door blink red and green. The renovated federation home is in an inner-city suburb of Melbourne. The neighbourhood used to be multicultural, with simple homes and poor European families escaping the war. East Brunswick is now upmarket and expensive. A broad mix of professionals, wealthy retirees, and groups of younger renters fill expansive homes. Cars politely edge down their street. There are no blaring sounds of hectic horns and impatient drivers. There is a peacefulness, a serenity in the air. Large over hanging plane trees hang from the nature strips like a protective green canopy, casting a soothing shade over the surroundings, and droop languidly towards the middle of the street. The trees create a cool green canopy to the surroundings. The nature strips in the street are meticulously mowed, almost look manicured, reflecting the lush house gardens and creating a serene environment. Paid gardeners work tirelessly to create house gardens with English themed plants of roses, lavender, peonies, hollyhocks and geraniums in individual gardens.

"Don't forget we're shopping for a dress to wear it to Angie's party after I come home from school. Make sure you have your credit card ready," said Millie. She is a bright extroverted twelve-year-old with brown hair who sees the world through a positive prism.

"Credit card at the ready," Nancy kisses Millie on her head.

Millie slips her school backpack over her small shoulders. Her best friend, Angie, is already at the front gate.

"Angie's here," said Millie. She adjusts the backpack on her shoulders again; is heavy with textbooks, notebooks, and lunch. The plastic lunch box contains two rounds of ham and cheese sandwiches, cut into triangles, a slice of homemade carrot cake, a ripe peach and a small box of sultanas.

Millie walks to the front gate. "Hi," said Millie. "What's new?"

"I couldn't sleep, have been panicking about the maths exam," said Angie, a deep frown on her forehead; has dyslexia and experiences difficulties with schoolwork.

"I can help you with revision," Millie said. "Maths is easy for me."

"Not for me." Angie said.

"How are the plans for your party? Kirsty has a cute brother, you could invite him, said Millie."

"Mum has already sent out the invitations, she said no boys for this birthday party," said Angie.

They walk step by step, side by side. Their similar brown hair, both tied back with green ribbons, sway in unison. They wear matching green and gold school blazers.

Angie listens more than she speaks, occasionally glancing at her friend with a smile that does not quite meet her eyes. Her gaze falls on her pleated skirt, fingers tracing the fabric, a habit she has whenever she thinks of her parent's separation, although the parents are more friendly with each other now. She lives with her mother Tessa and her new partner Monday to Friday and stays with her father and his latest girlfriend on some weekends. Angie hated her parents separating but has become accustomed to the new living arrangements.

Millie checks on Angie to see if she is struggling and regularly helps her with schoolwork. She knows

Angie's problems with dyslexia and the effect on her academic work.

"Are you okay?" Millie's voice cuts through Angie's reverie.

Angie forces herself to grin. "Yeah, just thinking about the maths exam."

"Don't worry, I will help you," said Millie.

They arrive at the crowded tram stop, blend into the sea of students, climb the steps into the tram. Angie leans closer to Millie, comforted by her presence in the cramped tram.

Nancy watches the girls until they are out of sight. She has worked hard at creating a happy family, in part to compensate for her own childhood. Her parents had died in a car accident when she was a baby and brought up by two aunts, Aunt Stella and Aunt Ruth and Aunt Ruth's husband, Uncle Jack. The aunts were sisters of her mother, Elizabeth. Although Nancy has been raised in a poor but loving home, she has always felt she was a motherless daughter, and this has marked her self-esteem.

Nancy recalled her country school days, where she had been bullied and called nasty names by two boys at primary school.

'You were so ugly as a baby that when your mother and father saw your red hair, they dropped dead,' the bullies chanted in the schoolyard.

Nancy had covered her ears and cried.

'Shut up, leave Nancy alone,' her best friend Dianne said to the boys. She was taller than the boys, would swing a punch at them that sometimes connected. The boys complained to the teacher, who ignored them.

Even now, although they live far apart, Dianne and Nancy have kept a strong bond and stay connected, taking turns to ring and gossip each week. Dianne is now a busy school principal at a country school, is a widow, was married to Joe, a farmer until he died of a heart attack last year. Nancy plans to take Millie to see where she lived and show her the old school and the route she used to take on her bike to Dianne's.

Today, Nancy enters her newly renovated kitchen. It has the warmth and style of a traditional federation style with white cabinets, deep brown polished floors. A white marble kitchen island takes pride of place in the centre. She loves to cook elaborate meals; her dinner parties are legend amongst their friends. There are two large double door refrigerators, one packed with elegant cuts of meat, fish, and cheeses. The second fridge contains fine wines and mixer drinks.

Robert, her husband of 15 years, works long hours as a successful accountant. "I won't have to work such long hours when I have my accounting firm," he tells Nancy.

The Dunfields have two cars: Robert's navy BMW 335 series, is his pride and joy. He pays to have it cleaned and polished each week. Nancy has a small blue Toyota Yaris, not only economical on fuel but is easy to park in the city. Robert hates riding in Nancy's car. His large muscular body is cramped and foolish in the small car. Their combined salaries enable them to live a carefree life with a private school for Millie, restaurant meals, and frequent parties. They travel often, usually on brief trips interstate.

Nancy works as a registered nurse and is a team leader in the accident and emergency department of a large teaching hospital in Carlton.

Her phone buzzes, it is another close friend, Gloria. They have been firm friends since they studied nursing at university. They are opposites in character. Nancy soothes situations, creates harmony, is neat and controlled. Gloria is short, has brown hair, wears glasses, plump, opiniated, assertive, and messy and is the Nurse Unit Manager of a surgical ward. Whereas Nancy is polite and lacks assertiveness, Gloria is brutally frank and does not suffer fools at all. She has chastised junior doctors on her ward who have not done the right thing by the patients under her care. When they are rostered on similar shifts, they debrief after work at the work cafe on the ground.

Gloria is married to Chris Vella, who owns a fruit shop and who loves Gloria's rounded curves.

"What are you doing?" said Gloria, her three sons can be heard arguing in the background. "Be quiet … I am talking on the phone." The boys keep shouting. "Hang on, I will go into the other room, as I can't hear myself think here."

There is a loud crash and a howling child. "I will

ring you back later. Timothy has fallen off a chair and I need to play nurse," said Gloria.

Nancy turns to look at the back garden. The lemon, orange, and apple trees hold masses of fruit, which she shares with friends and neighbours. Although they can easily afford a gardener, she prefers to garden herself, finds it relaxing. She beams at three bright-eyed, tiny brown sparrows who twitter as they peck the seeds in the bird feeder that hangs from the apple tree. Parsley, basil, Vietnamese mint, oregano, and thyme thrive in the herb patch. The vegetable garden has a good crop of beans, carrots, tomatoes, and silver beet and pumpkins. Yellow roses form an arc over the sturdy mental gazebo. The garden is as an extended family to Nancy; she worries if a lettuce wilts in the vegetable patch or if a shrub dies. Is excited with each perfumed rose that blooms.

Her life differs vastly from her previous life as an orphaned child when she lived in the country with her aunts and uncle. She moves around the kitchen, putting the washed breakfast crockery away. The open window brings a slight breeze and an aroma of lavender. She takes a flowered China cup from the cup stand, drops an Earl Grey tea bag in the cup and switches on the kettle.

"I will weed the vegetable patch and spend a couple of hours working on my master's assignment and then ring Gloria."

CHAPTER THREE

The same Tuesday, at 3.30 p.m., the school bell rings at Millie Dunfield's school. The courtyard buzzes with girls in green and gold uniforms. High-pitched feminine voices reverberate through the courtyard, along the corridors and onto the street. Mothers, some in tennis outfits, wait nearby to whisk daughters to after-school activities. The afternoon has been stressful for the students. At the general assembly, the Head Mistress had again emphasised the need to study and do well in the oncoming exams to be worthy of the school.

"You must work extra hard to achieve excellent grades expected of the school community. The competition to enter university is tough," said the Head Mistress.

The girls nudge their friends and pull faces of discomfort.

"Ring you later," Millie waves at Angie.

"Don't ring before six. I have piano lessons," said Angie.

"Come on, Angie," her mother beckons her into the open Audi car door. She is a tall dark-haired woman who is wearing tight fitting black Nike gym gear.

Millie pulls her blazer tight as she walks out the school entrance, the heavy school backpack now heavier with more books. Adjusts the straps again and places the headset over her head, which connects to her mobile phone. She sings along with Christina Aguilera *Fall into Line.*

Millie's phone rings.

"Hurry, don't dawdle, I am waiting," said Nancy.

"I am hurrying," said Millie.

The day is warm. She wants to remove the blazer but might be in trouble if she does. There are strict rules for wearing the full uniform, including the hat in public. She walks to the tram stop, waits ten minutes until the number nineteen tram arrives. Gets off the tram at her tram stop and takes a shortcut through the local park to go home faster. Children usually play in the playground at this time of day. But not today. No one sways on the swings. No children are on the slides, nor on the roundabout. Millie sings as she walks, takes in the smell of eucalyptus trees and grass smells. Large clumps of dense native hibiscus and prickly grevilia bushes grow in clusters around the barbeque and picnic tables. The park is familiar to Millie; she has been coming to this park for years, knows each tree and bush.

I hope the lavender dress is still in the shop.

The man with the soiled navy-blue tracksuit has been watching Millie, shadowing her movements from a distance. He glances over his shoulder to see if he is being watched. There is no one around. The man walks faster, catches up to Millie.

"Can you help me?" He said in a gruff voice.

Millie removes the headphones.

"What ..."

"My puppy Benny has run into the bushes." He points to the Hibiscus bushes. "I called him, but he won't come out."

Millie has a tightening in her chest, knows she must not talk to strangers. But a puppy needing rescuing is different. She will help the man and leave.

The stranger and Millie call out "Benny... Benny... Benny."

Millie bends down to look in the bushes. "He's not there."

Without warning, the stranger in a practised manoeuvrer wraps his dirty elbow around Millie's throat in a headlock, choking her.

Millie shrieks, tries to pull at his elbow, scratches his skin with her nails.

"You little bitch!" He punches her repeatedly in the face with his fist while keeping his elbow around her neck.

Millie squirms and tries to kick the man. "Help... help...," she shouts, at the same time trying desperately to pull his arm away.

"Shut up, or I'll kill you now," said the attacker. His voice slurred, reeks of stale beer and fish. His steel like grip stiffens around Millie's throat. He drags the struggling, screaming girl towards a large clump of native hibiscus and prickly grevilia bushes.

Millie kicks the man, bites hard on his elbow, drawing blood.

"So, you want to fight?" The stranger slams his grimy fist over and over into her face, releasing a torrent of blood from her nose.

"No... no...," screams Millie, she struggles to release his grip around her neck but is powerless.

The stranger drags Millie into the thick bush, one arm around her neck, the other ripping at her underpants.

"Stop... no... no... get off me... don't ...help... help," Millie shrieks.

At that moment, Alan Brody jogs past. He hears a young girl screaming for help. He turns his head to investigate where the noise is coming from, moves towards the bushes and pulls them back. Alan Brody sees the stranger crouching over the girl's body, her terror-stricken face streaked with blood and dirt.

"What the hell are you doing?" Alan Brody's voice booms. He drags the man off Millie.

"Bastard," said the stranger. He scrambles to get up, catches his hair on the branches, drawing blood. He pulls his pants up, runs away.

Time stands still. There is no sound, a vortex of nothingness, an alien town. No one can speak the language of assault.

Alan Brody is unsure of what he has witnessed, or

what to do. He is a thin, tall, blond-haired man with a deep voice. The attack has shaken him.

"You are safe now," he said, helping Millie up and out of the crushed thicket of plants. He gasps when he recognises Millie's school blazer. His daughter Juliet attends the same school and often walks home using this shortcut through the park.

Millie is mute, in shock, unable to make the words in her head come out of her mouth.

"I notice by your school blazer you attend the same school as my daughter Juliet. She's in year eight." He speaks in a soft, measured tone, aware of the girl's distress.

Millie stares past him, unable to understand what he is saying. Bright red blood trickles from her nose. She shivers, and her teeth clatter. Millie looks down, sees her underpants around her ankles, yanks them up.

"He tried to kill me," Millie's eyes hollowed out with terror.

"I did nothing to him." Millie's voice grows louder and echoes in the park.

"He tried to kill me." She eyes Alan Brody, unsure if this man might harm her. A hundred ideas run through her mind. She gulps air as though submerged in mud. Her hands shake.

A magpie sings in the distance.

"Here, use this to stop the blood from your nose," Alan Brody hands her a clean folded handkerchief. He takes his mobile phone out of his jogging pants.

"I'm going to call for an ambulance and the police."

Millie gapes in the direction where the attacker fled, her breathing comes in gasps. Her backpack lies open on the ground; school hat, books and a left-over sandwich from her lunch box lie in the dirt and dried leaves, nearby are the broken phone and headset. The sun glimmers on the shattered phone screen.

"You are safe now," Alan Brody repeats. "I will stay here with you and travel in the ambulance to the hospital. No one can harm you now," he repeats.

Millie looks away. "My phone's broken... my wrist hurts... I must be a mess." She smooths the skirt, pulls twigs off the blazer, wipes the blood from her nose again with the clean handkerchief. Her hair matted with dirt and plant muck. "I shouldn't have taken the shortcut." She puts a hand to her throat.

"It is not your fault." Alan Brody does not know what to say. He wants to comfort the terrified girl but is fearful of frightening her further.

"What's your mother's phone number? We can ring her."

Millie stumbles over the numbers.

He rings Nancy, "My name is Alan Brody. An incident has happened. A stranger has attacked Millie."

"Oh, my God, no, not Millie." Nancy's voice is a shriek. "Is she all right? Can I speak with her?"

"We are waiting for the ambulance. Here, you talk to Millie." His hand trembles as he hands his phone to Millie.

Millie takes the phone and struggles to find the

16

words to say. "Mum, a horrible man dragged me into the bushes... He hit me... he tried to kill me... dragged my pants down... I screamed and bit him. He hit me again."

"Oh, my God." An icy chill runs through Nancy's body, covers her mouth.

"This man saved me." Millie turns to Alan Brody. She cannot speak any more, hands the mobile phone back.

Somewhere in the distance a dog barks.

Alan Brody tries to soothe Nancy. "My daughter Juliet goes to the same school as Millie. I will stay with Millie until you arrive at the hospital."

"This can't be happening." Nancy grabs her bag, and races to her car.

Six ambulances are lined up outside the emergency department hospital in central Melbourne. On the nearby roads, bumper-to-bumper traffic slows drivers. Trams clang as they stop at the hospital, and overhead, the roar of a helicopter landing at the helicopter berth on top of the hospital building.

Twenty minutes after the phone call from Alan Brody, Nancy gasping and flustered, rushes into the emergency department. She uses her employee swipe card to enter the department. The ward clerk informs Nancy of Millie's cubicle, she rushes to the cubicle and envelops Millie in her arms.

"My poor darling."

Millie was unrecognizable from the girl who left home earlier in the day. Her hair dishevelled and ragged with dirt and twigs, face and body covered in blood and soil, visible scratches and lacerations over her face, body and arms. She groans in pain.

"My hand hurts." She breaks into deep sobs, clings to Nancy.

The curtained cubicle is an outstation on planet Mars to Nancy. Although she works here, it is now foreign and unreal. Today, she is no longer a health professional in control, now one more distressed and powerless parent.

The emergency department is in chaos. Two hours earlier in the day, a terrifying bus crash occurred, creating bedlam in the emergency department, with incoming wounded. It is still crammed with patients, ambulance officers, police, doctors, nurses, and family members. Multiple phones are ringing and beeping. People cry out in pain and call for relatives. Trolleys rattle past, carrying patients to X-rays and other areas in the department. Sounds of running feet, a babble of excited communication rises and falls in waves.

Millie puts her hands over her ears. "I can't stand the noise."

Alan Brody stands by Millie's bed. "The doctor has completed an assessment of Millie. We're waiting for the police and a forensic doctor to take the required swabs... and do the interviews." His voice sounds apologetic.

Nancy stares at Alan Brody. She has a vague recollection of meeting him at a school function.

"I cannot thank you enough ..." Nancy shakes Alan's hand over and over.

"It could have been Juliet," his voice cracks.

"If you hadn't intervened...," Nancy's voice trails, her mind fills with images of Millie murdered. She shakes his hand again.

"I will leave you with Millie, and wait in the waiting room," Alan Brody's voice breaks. He coughs, "I have a fair description of the attacker to give to the police," he coughs again.

Nancy is afraid to hold Millie's hand, as any touch makes her startle in pain.

Millie makes strange noises in her throat, swallows hard. She looks at the cubicle ceiling, trying to make sense of where she is and what has happened, shuts her eyes. A nurse yanks back the cubicle curtains and startles Millie. A few minutes later, a trolley arrives to take Millie and Nancy to a quieter space to be interviewed. Ten minutes later, a thin policewoman and female doctor arrive to interview her and take samples from Millie's clothes and body.

"Sorry Millie," said the doctor. "I know this is unpleasant for you, but it has to be done."

Millie is deeply embarrassed by the intimate examinations. She does not know where to look. She hides her face under a sheet. Takes a long time to answer the policewoman's questions. Overuses "um" and "ah." Millie keeps putting her hand to her throat where a thick red mark has developed. Blood is caked in her hair, face, and hands. The school uniform skirt has patches of muddy brown.

Nancy stands back, bites her lips, trying not to cry out, holds her elbows, her heart beats like an express train.

After the doctor and police leave, Dr. Sam Edwards returns and orders diagnostic tests, which include blood tests and x-rays. The results show a fracture on Millie's left cheek, head injury where she had been thrown on the ground by the attacker, a broken nose, fractured wrist, and extensive bruising. She has sustained multiple lacerations on her face and arms that require suturing. Millie clings to Nancy's red shirt, twisting it and holding it like a life rope, the shirt an anchor of normality that she once had. She is still dazed and unable to comprehend her surroundings. Pain medication is administered through an intravenous line.

A nurse materialises to clean Millie's wounds. "Is the patient your daughter?" the colleague's eyes are wide-eyed.

"This is my daughter Millie."

The nurse looks intently into Nancy's eyes, puts her hand on Nancy's shoulder. There is an unspoken connection and concern. She wraps Nancy in a quick hug.

"Notify me if you need anything at all."

The nurse removes Millie's school uniform and helps her into a white hospital gown. She carefully cleans the dirt and grime from the lacerations and assists the doctor with the suturing of the wounds and the plaster cast on Millie's wrist. She provides Nancy with a cup of tea and sandwiches. They both know that Millie will have to wait a long time before being admitted to the trauma ward.

Other nurses rush in and out of the emergency department's cubicle, checking the intravenous line, taking observations, doing their duties. Colleagues say comforting words to Nancy, then run to respond to a patient's buzzer or emergency code.

Nancy stares at the equipment and monitor. She watches the intravenous drip pulsating into Millie's arm, the blood pressure machine automatically doing its job. She recalls past images of patients she has nursed in this same cubicle. Bloodied victims of crime, road accidents, asthmatic attacks. Unthinkable ... now her child is involved. Nancy is invisible, no longer the professional, stripped of power and position. She steadies her shaking hands.

Millie dozes on an off from the effects of the analgesic. Serious black and navy bruises are spreading across Millie's face, neck, and body. Later, the nurse will wash her hair, which is caked with grime.

Nancy checks her mobile phone for the twentieth time, no message back from Robert, who is in the USA attending a work conference. She checks the intravenous, scans the monitors repeatedly. Shivers, wraps her body in the white surgical blanket that a nurse has provided. Nancy checks her phone again.

An hour later, Robert rings, speaks first to Nancy and then Millie.

"Stay strong, Princess; I'm catching the next available flight," his voice quivers.

"We will get through this together." The connection fades and is gone.

Nancy calls Gloria to explain the situation. "I need you. Please come."

"I will be there in 30 minutes," said Gloria.

Nancy slumps in her seat, watches Millie sleep, and experiences the dank loneliness of the emergency room. The assault has tipped Nancy into unfamiliarity and turmoil. In one moment in time, her life has stopped going in the normal safe direction and is now a slow-motion move in a zigzag, making no sense.

CHAPTER FOUR

It is twelve months since the attack on Millie. She has been changed. The East Brunswick family dynamics have been permanently altered. The home looks the same from the outside, with its coloured glass doors and lush garden. But everything has changed within.

Millie now recoils from touch even from a goodnight hug before she goes to bed at home. "Don't touch me," Millie pushes Nancy away. She hates physical closeness unless she instigates it. Touch is triggering and threatening.

"Leave me alone. Stop babying me." Then later, "Can I sleep with you?" Millie wakes from a nightmare, snuggles into the four-poster bed between her parents, holding both their hands. Falls asleep, later wakes in terror, screaming, "No, no, get away from me."

Millie's moods have become more erratic; emotions erupt without warning. She has reverted to younger childlike conduct with frequent outbursts of anger and disruptive behaviour. The panic attacks continue. She freezes when she remembers the attack and the smell of the attacker and beer or fish. This brings on nausea. "I am going to be sick."

Over time, Millie's physical injuries from the attack

heal, but her mind does not. She continuously replays the assault over and over, her brain stuck in a groove. The emotional effect remains deep. She develops post-traumatic stress disorder (PTSD) with severe flashbacks, panic attacks, terrifying nightmares. Millie's personality changes: she had been bright and extroverted, now is on guard, afraid of strangers. She locks the door as soon as she enters her home. Clicks the car door to lock when she puts on her seatbelt. Is afraid to travel on public transport alone, anxious of being in the open, terrified of being alone, unsafe all the time. Her brain stuck on red alert. The odour of fish and beer and anyone who resembles the attacker triggers Millie into deep anxiety. She trembles at loud noises and shouting. She cannot go near any park. Has not returned to school.

Nancy took leave from work to stay home and care for Millie, and as a result, Nancy experienced the worst of Millie's frustration and anger.

Millie has extensive trauma counselling with her psychologist Alice Parker, who has ten years' experience treating young assault and rape victims.

"It will get better," said Alice. She is in her forties, short, wears black-rimmed owl glasses, has shoulder-length blonde hair. She has used a variety of treatment modalities, including cognitive behaviour therapy and art therapy. Millie attends a support group for girls with PTSD, takes judo lessons and learns self-defence.

Robert is involved but at a distance, he is out of

his depth emotionally, unsure how to help, keeps busy with his accounting work.

"I don't think I have had a proper night's sleep in a year," Robert tells his brother Dean.

The emotional pressure on the family is immense.

Nancy and Robert have family counselling to learn how to assist Millie, and Aunt Stella, Gloria, and Maxine- Robert's mother, do what they can to support the now dysfunctional family.

Today, Nancy is in the white walled kitchen of her home. There is an expired parking voucher clipped on the left side. She has used it as a bookmark. It has dropped out of a recipe book she took out of the bookshelf this morning. She picks it up, turns it around this way, and that, stares hard at it, places the voucher on the marble island in the centre of the kitchen. Her face is pale, looks out of the window. When Millie was an inpatient in the trauma ward, Nancy had parked her car in a dusty, open-air car park near the hospital. She drove early to the car park and left late at night. Had held herself tight, kept her emotions in check, waiting for Robert to return from the USA. It took several days for a panicked Robert to get a ticket home to Australia.

Nancy held the voucher in her hand, can almost hear the parking attendant's thick smoker's voice in her head. He had seen Nancy at the car park each day; she had explained the reason for going to the hospital.

"I saved a spot for you near the lights, so you can have the lights to guide you when you leave at night," the burly man had said when Nancy collected the parking receipt.

The importance of his action did not resound at first.

"Thanks." Nancy parked the Yaris in the spot he had shown her under the lights. He had made sure she had a safe place to park. In a world where an evil man had created so much damage to her beautiful daughter, this unexpected kindness showed her there were still good people around.

Nancy picked up the parking ticket and replaced it back in the recipe book.

CHAPTER FIVE

It's hot and airless in the psychology department room. In a corner of the room, a forlorn rubber plant sits. Along the back wall there are four office chairs, and a desk pushed there to make space. Alice, the psychologist, sits on a green corduroy bean bag in the middle of the room with three girls aged between twelve to fourteen. The girls are part of the support group for young girls suffering from long term PTSD. They are stretched out on matching bean bags around Alice.

A young girl with anxious eyes and luxurious blonde hair said, "I cannot block the flashbacks of my trauma. I tried, but they sit on replay in my mind."

Alice signals for her to continue.

"I'm trying to quieten my nerves. Hours can pass without me remembering ... then unexpectedly, something will trigger me, and I relive the images of my mother being stabbed by my father. I can hear my mother's screams in my mind and see the blood spurting." The girl places her hands over her eyes and cries.

Alice and the other girls form a pyramid of support

around the blonde girl, holding her until she settles. They have supported her like this before.

Outside, the force of a wind burst rattles the windows, causing everyone to look up.

The girls return to their beanbags.

There is a comfortable silence.

A clear voice breaks the silence. It is the girl with thick brown plaits. "I am not safe anywhere outside our home. Even coming to this support meeting is upsetting." She shakes her head. The plaits fly out in two directions at once. Her face crumples with anxiety. She is about to cry, bites her lip, picks a speck of fluff from her jeans. "Even though it is good for me to know that I am not the only one struggling with PTSD. My anxiety level is sky high during these meetings." She plays with her hair, twisting the plaited hair in circles until it is coiled tight, and then releases it, watching it spin. Twists it again and lets it go.

"I am super cautious, am afraid to go out alone," said the pigtailed girl. She twists her hair into a ball and watches it unravel. "I avoid anyone and any place that reminds me of the horrible time. The image of the road accident that killed my father and sister always stays with me." She looks up. "If I close my eyes, even now, I can touch the cold metal of my father's car seat pushed against me when the drunk driver smashed into our car. The nightmares are the worst part. I am terrified of the dark. I always sleep with the bedside light on."

"You are doing fine. It takes time to heal," said Alice, her voice reassuring.

The room is hushed once more.

"My brain goes into horror, replaying the physical attack. One moment walking home from school listening to music and the next being dragged to the bushes and assaulted." Millie stares at Alice. "You said it might take months to stop the brain replaying what happened."

The group murmurs in agreement.

Millie thinks of Alan Brody, her rescuer. She recalls the softly spoken female police officer who interviewed her at the hospital, her mother being there. It has blended into one scene, overlapping a quilt of horrible memories.

"When I was in the emergency department, I had to climb onto a metal tray that was shaped like a large pencil case—the MRI machine. They had to exclude brain bleeds. Someone placed a soft pillow under my head. I had to remove my shoes," said Millie. "All that happened that day is stuck in my brain."

The wind outside gathers intensity, thunder explodes in the sky nearby.

No one speaks.

"I know I am a pain to my parents. They are unsure how to handle me," Millie sighs. "I'm unsure how to handle myself." She nibbles on her nail. "In one moment, I want a cuddle."

"The next moment, hating anyone to touch and I push them away." She holds up her left wrist.

"My wrist still hurts at the fracture point." Millie looks around the room at the other girls. "You guys know what it is like."

The group murmurs their support.

The blonde girl said, "I vowed not to let PTSD win." She twists the pen she is holding. "I scribble words on paper, spew words from my head into my journal. I call it my hate book. Everything that I despise is in it."

"I've started art therapy and read the story of the artist Van Gogh. He used art to heal," said Millie.

"French fries stuffed in my mouth stop me thinking," said the pigtailed girl.

The group laugh.

CHAPTER SIX

It is two years since Millie's assault; she is now aged fourteen. It is 7 p.m. at the Dunfield's house in leafy East Brunswick. The house's interior lights shine yellow.

Robert drives home from work. The garage door does not open.

"Damn remote." He removes the batteries and reinserts them in the remote. The door rolls up after three attempts. He drives the navy BMW into the garage. Slams the car door with such force that the car windows shake. He checks the mailbox, collects the letters jammed inside and walks towards the house. The gate creaks when it is opened. Blue-slate sturdy steps lead to the house entrance. Blooming white rose bushes edge a well-watered lawn, stand like white sentinels from the fence to the front door. The thick, wooden panelled front door has stained-glass decorations in the shape of exotic parrots embedded in it. Robert had organised a large mortgage to pay for the remodelling of the house to its original Federation style.

"I'm home." His voice reverberates through the large house, his sturdy footsteps pound on polished floorboards. He takes off his navy-blue jacket, hangs it on the hall stand, straightens the jacket sleeves, looks in the mirror, and fixes his hair. Throws the keys to the car into the drawer in the hall stand, shoves the drawer shut. Robert is forty-six, is motivated to rise to senior accountant within two years. Colleagues see him as a sharp accountant who makes good money for clients.

Nancy sits at the end of the long mahogany table in the dining room, head arched over a laptop. She is surrounded by open textbooks, peers at the scribbled handwritten notes on a thick yellow pad and returns to typing.

"Hello, darling," Nancy said without looking up. "I will be with you in a minute." She is forty-four years old, the red hair cut in a trendy, bob-style hairstyle, which she flicks from side to side as her head moves. People who know Nancy imply she is a compassionate friend.

"The house is a mess," said Robert Dunfield. He places the brown leather briefcase with *Robert Dunfield* embossed in gold onto the floor; drags a chair to the wooden table where Nancy is working. "I hate coming home to this mess," he pushes the textbooks and notes to the end of the table.

"What are you doing?" said Nancy, looking up from the laptop.

The grandfather clock in the hall makes a metallic sound.

"Why can't you study in your office?" He has a sharp voice.

"The dining table is the only place wide enough for me to spread my textbooks and notes," she said. "Sorry, I forgot the time." Nancy heaps the notes and textbooks into a pile, closes the laptop.

He shakes his head.

Nancy turns to Robert, eyes shining. "I have been on such a roll today. The thesis interviews are coming together." She gives a high-five sign into the air. "It's like a gigantic jigsaw puzzle; each step leads to another piece." The light from the lamp in the ceiling above Nancy's head projects a halo over her face. "Today I completed the last interview. The interviewee and I met at The Coffee Club." She is aware he is not listening to her but keeps talking.

"I took heaps of notes. I am typing them now while they're fresh in my mind." She holds pages of scribbled notes on a yellow notepad for Robert to see. He does not look up. Robert has unrolled *The Age* newspaper, is reading.

"I interviewed a woman whose eleven-year-old boy who was admitted to the emergency department after breaking his left femur from falling off his skateboard." Nancy makes a sad face. "The negative comments by this mother related to the nursing staff were hard to take. The mother implied the nurses were too busy to support and keep her informed about the son's progress."

Robert looks up from the paper. "Have you started dinner yet? I'm starving."

"No, but I can make you a quick snack. Would

you like a toasted cheese and tomato sandwich?" She holds her hands out in a questioning manner.

"I work long hours for this family and do not want to come home to a sandwich." He turns the pages of the newspaper.

"My thesis is coming together," her voice flat.

"Organise your priorities. My meal comes before your studies." He glares at her.

Nancy bites her lip.

He sees Nancy's deflated face and sighs. "I'll get take away." He folds the paper, slams the door on the way out. Robert returns 30 minutes later cradling two enormous pizza boxes containing pepperoni pizza, chips, and garlic bread.

"Sorry, I didn't mean to be snappy. Work has been a pain." He gave her a half-hearted kiss on the cheek.

"Millie," Nancy calls "pizza."

Millie bounces into the room. She still suffers from periodic episodes of PTSD and still has panic attacks. Is back at school, and caught up with the missed schoolwork, continues counselling with Alice.

"Hi, dad. Pizza, good job." Millie sits at the table, opens one of the pizza boxes, takes a piece, and grabs a handful of hot chips.

"How was school?" Robert watches Millie intently, looking for any signs of anxiety.

Millie relates the rotten egg experiment in science class. "The stench was dreadful."

Robert has his back turned to Nancy.

Nancy nibbles on a slice of pizza. "What's the matter Robert? Do you have an issue with me?"

Robert shakes his head. "Don't take it personally. I told you; it has been a rotten day at work."

"Do you want to talk about it?"

"Definitely not," he said. "I want to forget the day, not rehash it over and over." He eats, collects his plate, throws it into the sink, goes into the lounge room, clicks the remote and watches the rest of the 7:30 report on ABC.

Millie disappears into her bedroom and the internet.

Nancy stays at the dining table.

What has gotten into him? He was the one who encouraged me to do something with my life.

That night, Robert wants sex and pushes against Nancy. She pretends to be asleep. He does not stop. "I love you." His words hang in the air.

How can he speak of love when he has been horrible?

She rolls over, turns her back to him, hugs the doona tightly.

CHAPTER SEVEN

It is afternoon on a warm autumn day. The passengers on the crowded bus stand and cling to the straps that hang above. It is simpler for Nancy to take a bus to the Victoria market than struggle to find a parking spot. Near Nancy's feet, there are two hessian shopping bags with an assortment of fine cheeses and nuts from the market. No matter where she places the bags, the man next to her slides his foot over her bags. She glares at the man, but he ignores her stare. The bus speeds through leafy green suburbs, taking with it the passengers who attempt to regain their balance. Nancy looks at the other passengers, packed closely together like sardines on the bus. They remind her of actors waiting to step out onto a stage, dressed for a distinct part. Men in smart suits, university students wearing T-shirts and torn jeans, young women in flowery dresses. One woman clutches an enormous bunch of pink chrysanthemums. The bus smells of sweat and gym shoes, giving off an unpleasant rubbery odour, unclean. Passengers stare blankly out of the window. A woman is talking loudly on her mobile phone. Two dark-haired women converse in an unknown language. The woman in the seat in front of Nancy rubs her ankles and grimaces. Nancy glances at the woman's shoes, comfortable flats. Shoes convey information related to a person, flat shoes for sore feet.

Nancy remembers another bus trip when she and Robert spent some time in Malaysia. Robert had appointments with clients in Kuala Lumpur and demanded Nancy accompany him. She did not want to go.

～

"Come on. It will be fun. Just the two of us in Malaysia," Robert had said.

"You go on your own," Nancy had tried to get him to see reason. She knew he would be too busy to spend time with her. But he wouldn't listen. Robert got his way as usual. Aunt Stella stayed with Millie at their house.

They landed in hot and steamy Kuala Lumpur and checked into the Grand Hyatt hotel. Each day, Robert left the hotel early in the morning and did not return until late in the evening. The humidity and appointments with the clients exhausted him. When he returned to the hotel, all he could do was eat dinner and fall asleep.

During the day, Nancy toured the city on her own. She visited the Petronas Twin Towers with eighty-eight floors and a sky bridge on the forty-first and forty-second floors. Explored the spectacular Kuala Lumpur Bird Garden. Visited the Butterfly Park and

Bukit Bintang shopping district. She spent too much on souvenirs for Millie, Aunt Stella, and Gloria and visited a hawker's centre. A young woman with jet black hair, an apron covering her cropped jeans. The woman twisted and turned the fried rice that was cooking in a pan, added soy sauce, red sauce, sliced chillies, mushrooms, eggs and vegetables. The aroma intoxicating, Nancy bought a serve and ate with enthusiasm.

She remembers Robert's one free day; they had booked a trip to the Elephant Sanctuary, a long bus journey out of town. Excited tourists swayed with the bus in rhythm. An assortment of languages bubbled to the surface. At the back, a petite blonde girl sang in German. Sleepy couples rolled towards each other. A toddler ran up the aisle, followed by his father, who grabbed the child, who fussed and howled when forced to sit on the father's lap. A woman in the seat opposite pulled the thin flowered cotton curtain across the window, rolled into a ball, and fell asleep. The tropical sun shone through the windows, the humidity intense, with only an overhead fan on the bus.

Robert's face was beetroot red, sweat dripped from his face, his T-shirt grew damp patches around his neck and armpits. Nancy fanned herself with a travel brochure. The air was thick and hot; the temperature climbed further. They sped past tropical rain forests, green palm forests, ivy creepers that formed a canopy over vegetation, and small wooden houses. The road snaked around ridges; the engine roared as it ascended the slope, strained at the steep climb. They passed electric towers which resembled giant caged metal monsters waiting to escape and run.

Nancy had patted Robert's thigh and stared into his eyes. "Have you enjoyed the trip to KL?"

Robert did not answer, peered out of the window. He pointed to the stabilisers on the side of the mountains. "They must have problems with soil erosion," his voice muffled by the bus noise.

"Is something the matter?" Said Nancy.

"This is the first time I have had you to myself for weeks. You are always busy with Millie, work, or your studies."

"Don't start. Let's enjoy today," she said.

He pulled away, moved to the far end of the seat, faced the window.

The passengers burst into loud cheers and clapping when the rickety bus crept into the gates of the elephant sanctuary. The guide ushered the group into a cinema complex to watch a film of elephants being captured, given injections of tranquillizers to make them calm. Another clip showed stressed elephants shifted from one place to another by truck. The video's sound uncoordinated by the film. Nancy was horrified by the cruel way the animals were beaten and tied to posts.

It's heartbreaking to see those elephants in such a state.

The bus group walked to where six large grey elephants were penned behind a wooden slat fence, their trunks swayed in the air. Children squealed with excitement, begged to pat the elephants. Robert held a banana to one whose trunk waved near him.

"He likes me," Robert said. The elephant's trunk reached to take the banana.

Nancy could not watch, pulled her hat over her face, witnessed the animal's distress, identified with the elephants. The heat of the sanctuary felt like an oven. It hurt her head. She moved to the shade of a nearby tree.

Robert came over to her. "Have a sip," said Robert, offering his water bottle.

She wanted more than water from him.

CHAPTER EIGHT

Millie and Nancy are stretched out on the white cane chairs at the back patio of the East Brunswick house. Above, a purple wisteria vine cascades from the patio roof, and the scent of lemon blossoms drifts through the air. It is growing dark, yellow lights inside the house give off a warm glow. Black birds call to others, hungry insects buzz by. Robert is at work.

Millie gives off small snorting noises, which she did when stressed.

Nancy glances at Millie, whose eyes dart from side to side of the backyard as if to make sense of where she was, gives off small fluttering hand movements, opens and crosses her arms, her left leg taps incessantly on the ground.

"What's up?" Nancy attempts to keep her voice light, unintrusive.

"Get off my case," Millie's eyes flash, avoids Nancy's gaze, pretends to take a sip of water from the glass she is holding. Her hand quivers, drops the glass, spilling the contents over the cane chair. She grabs the glass and tosses it towards the garden, leaps up, slams the chair back, storms inside. The back door made a loud bang.

Nancy shakes her head.

Here we go again.

Nancy picks up the glass, waits twenty minutes in the merging darkness, goes inside. She is outside Millie's room, wills herself to be strong. She taps hesitantly on the door, waits, no answer, taps again.

"Millie."

"Come in," said a small voice.

Nancy edges into the room, which smells of paint and turpentine. Most days, the room has its own female vibrational energy, not today. It has a heaviness that permeates the shining satin curtains, the princess bed festooned with three brown, sad -eyed teddy bears.

Millie stands at her paint easel, paintbrush in hand. Her face has blue paint streaked over her cheeks and nose. The painting is an ugly, chaotic jumble of blue shades, colours blurring into each other.

Nancy concentrates hard to make a remark, to connect with Millie. And not set Millie off on a barrage of shouting and abuse when she is in this type of mood.

 "Your painting reminds me of an abstract image. The blue might show uncertainty." She said the words cautiously, not to antagonise her daughter, unsure whether she will again be the butt of Millie's anger and frustration.

Millie looks wild and haunted, as if someone has cornered her. "I can't get out of this black hole. I am doing what I have been told to do. But I can still see his angry eyes and... and his stink."

"Maybe you should go into those emotions, gain mastery over them by painting him." Nancy was unsure whether it was the correct answer. The words poured out unplanned.

"Turn around and face him. Do not close your eyes to the images. Use them."

Millie replaces the paper on the easel, mixes oil paints of brown, black and red. Slaps the paintbrush as though possessed by an inner demon. The image springs to life, a huge grotesque monster's eyes, bloodshot, pure, evil, cruel.

Nancy looks away, the eyes frighten her. For the first time, she has a visual image of her daughter's deep anguish. "Repaint the eyes until you have power over them."

She goes to the kitchen; shudders, she has been privy to her child's inner nightmare. She looks out at the garden—it is now pitch-black outside.

I have been on the wrong track, trying to encourage Millie to forget the assault and get on with her life. She must face her demons.

CHAPTER NINE

It is mid-afternoon at the East Brunswick house. Nancy is in the garden, wears old stained blue jeans and one of Robert's old shirts. She pushes the heavy wheelbarrow laden with weeds and dried plants towards the compost bin. She returns to digging and turning over the soil in order to plant the vegetable seedlings. Nancy rolls down her gardening gloves, checks the time.

One hour before I collect Millie from school and take her to the dentist.

She pulls out a small notebook from her jean's pocket, scribbles details of plantings and when to fertilise. Three black and white magpies peck at the seeds in the bird feeder. A black crow comes to join them, the magpies chase him away. The weather is overcast. Black storm clouds grow darker in the distance. Nancy rests on the wooden bench, watches bees buzz around the lavender bushes. Masses of perfumed yellow roses form a dense canopy over a metal arch.

"I love the smell of my roses." She inhales deeply, takes the scissors and clips the dead roses.

～

For fifteen years, Robert and Nancy had been a contented couple. They accepted and were tolerant of each other's differences, in step with each other. But since Millie's assault, there was a widening gap between their togetherness. He has developed a habit of criticising Nancy, finds something to complain about her studying or the rushed meals.

"You are always studying," Robert said, his voice reproachful and annoyed.

Nancy said nothing.

"I am an outsider in my family," he said, his face like thunder.

She tried to argue the point, but he had already closed her down by switching on the television.

I will not stop studying.

Nancy is destabilised and uncertain about her next steps. At first, she assumed work pressure produced Robert's unpleasantness. He often apologised after an outburst. She was walking on a field of unexploded bombs. Anything she said or did would make him flare up.

"I am unsure what to do," she later told Gloria over the phone.

"He is a selfish man. He would find something to complain, even if you weren't studying." Gloria said.

"Why don't you organise a party of family and friends? It might soften his irritability."

~

A few weeks later, Nancy organised a party for their wedding anniversary, invited a mix of close friends and family. She cooked Robert's favourite food; lobster, salmon, eggs, bacon pies, and bought seven fresh cheeses. She had decorated the lounge room with red and gold streamers, gold balloons swayed overhead. Someone turned the volume up as Pink sang *Get the party started.* The noise was deafening; the room resounded with gyrating dancers and flickering lights. Nancy moved through the crowd, found Robert in the kitchen arguing with his brother, Dean.

"The trouble with you is you don't know what you don't know," said Dean. He held a beer with one hand and jabbed Robert's chest with the other.

"I know more than you will ever know," said Robert, grabbed hold of Dean's hand.

"I leave you two alone together for one minute, and you fight," said Nancy. She places the silver tray of empty champagne glasses on the kitchen bench. "Come and join the party." Nancy drags Robert to the dance floor.

After five minutes of dancing, he pulls away, waves to a man in a corner. "I need to have a word with my boss." He releases Nancy's hand.

At that moment, she knew her marriage was in trouble.

CHAPTER TEN

Students hassle for seats at crowded tables at the university food hall. Trays clang, chairs screech, voices rise and fall, every so often a burst of laughter echoes throughout the building. Dim sims, potato cakes, and chips are cheap and popular, as well as hot Asian curries and rice. The cheap meals are drying under the heating lights. International students hang out in groups. The local students wear hoodies, ripped jeans, and shirts.

Nancy and two colleagues are eating at the university's food hall before evening classes for the Masters lectures.

Rebecca, an edgy student in the same Masters class as Nancy, chews the ends of her long brown hair. "I think I will bail out of the course."

"Don't leave. Accept it is a distressing day," Nancy said. "Tomorrow will be better."

The other student, Marlene, her blonde hair pulled back, a grey silk scarf knotted at her neck, has a laugh that resembles a hyena. Each sentence ends with a laugh. The hyena laugh annoys Nancy.

"I was a child who trusted in Santa Claus and fairies," the laughing student said. "Now I believe in tattslotto, Keno, and lottery tickets. If you believe, good luck will follow."

Rebecca gave her a pained look. "It will take more than just believing to pass the course."

"I am visualising success," Marlene said.

"I had a terrible meeting with my thesis supervisor earlier. He wants the thesis analysis finished." Nancy has a frown on her face.

"I have run out of excuses for my supervisor," said Rebecca. "Work is messy and desperate; I can barely drive home. The last thing I want to do after work is study."

"I hear you loud and clear," said Nancy.

"Our ward is short staffed, people off sick. I crash when I get home. My husband and children complain about eating take-away meals," said Marlene. She does not laugh.

They sip their coffee in silence.

Nancy has worked the early shift at the hospital, has not slept well. Last night, Millie had another of her terrifying nightmares.

"No ...no... get away from me," Millie had screamed, woke with sweat pouring down her face, crying hysterically.

Nancy rushed by her side, held her. "I am here. Nothing can harm you," she said over and over until Millie was fully awake. By the time Millie was settled, it was time to get ready for work at the hospital.

Today at the cafe, Nancy hides a yawn behind her hand. She wants to go home but is afraid to miss the important lecture. One part of her brain maintains attention, the other half asleep. She searches for a barley-sugar sweet in her bag, pops it in her mouth, tastes the sugar rush.

How to get through the evening class.

Once bathed in grandeur, the old university building had been more than a classroom, lofty ceilings, ornate light fittings, drapes. The lecturer Dr Clark is unapproachable, her replies to students' questions are critical and judgmental. The students are fearful of her knife-point sharpness. "You should know this," Dr Clark said. "If you paid attention and studied the material I told you to read, you wouldn't ask such stupid questions."

"In emergency nursing, it is about issues of life and death. Every second is crucial." Dr Clark writes on the board in large letters. *Life and death.* She turns to face the class, glaring at the students. "Nothing more so than a patient admitted into the emergency department with signs of anaphylaxis. Remember the steps—get a full history from the patient or relatives. Do a thorough assessment, observations, check conscious state, urticaria rash, abdominal pain, nausea, vomiting. When advised by the doctor, administer Adrenalin 1:1000 0.3 mg or whatever dose or drug the doctor orders. Monitor the patient, if poor infusion, insert an intravenous line."

The students struggle to take notes and keep up.

Registered nurses of different ages and experiences are together in this evening's class. They have a common goal to learn and improve their qualifications. The air in the lecture room is thick with anxiety as students scribble notes. Pens fly over notebooks, students in intense concentration. Their attentions appear to bounce, become airborne and transformed into scribbles onto pages. Glowering faces stare at the whiteboard, littered with overlapping words.

"There's an excellent chance you will have questions on the exam related to anaphylaxis. I suggest you learn this section well." Dr. Clark aggressively wipes the whiteboard with wide swipes, as if erasing the day.

The class is hushed. Students turn to each other. "Did you get the notes on the board?"

"Can you please distribute a copy of your notes to the class?" one student asked.

Dr Clark gives a curt reply. "If you have read the pre reading, you wouldn't be asking."

The student blushes bright red and sits down.

"What's wrong with your leg?" Nancy whispers to a student sitting next to her. The student's crutches propped on the wall.

"I fell from a stool. Nothing broken, just painful to walk," she said.

"Are you having trouble keeping up with the lecture?" Nancy said.

"I will have to hit the textbooks tonight while the topic is fresh in my head," said the student.

"Me too," said Nancy.

"Perhaps I can come over to your place and we can compare notes," the student said.

Nancy nods.

CHAPTER ELEVEN

Robert waits for his eleven o'clock client—a successful hairdresser who owns four salons. The client plans to minimise his tax. Robert has arrived early, needing time to himself. He glances out of the long windows of the upmarket restaurant in High street. He considers the classical garden outside with Roman urns and statues of young naked boys in muscular poses. The restaurant had once been an elegant home of a wealthy grazier who later became a successful politician. The familiar essence of privilege surrounds him. This is his world. He grew up in a household mirrored in what he sees. His father's wealth produced an indulged life; his current life is nowhere near what he wants. He turns to look at the entrance; the client is not there. Robert removes his jacket, the blue silk tie hangs over his white linen shirt, he unbuttons the top button of his shirt. The ongoing problems at home are wearing Robert out. Millie's behaviour has been hard to deal with. He loves his daughter but is powerless to deal with Millie's ongoing issues. Her regular nightmares overwhelm him.

His phone rings. "Hi Maxine, this is not a suitable time to talk. I am waiting for a client."

"I have a professional question about my investments." Maxine does not trust anyone with her finances, not even her accountant son. She checks on her portfolio at least once a week. She wants to tweak this or that and improve her income. "I want to sell some of my shares and need advice." Her voice was loud.

"Why do you need the money?" he closes his eyes.

"None of your business," she snaps.

He lets out a sigh of frustration. "As your accountant, I should have some rights of knowledge."

And as your son, I have rights as well.

"Don't get sharp with me" she is loud and aggressive.

The couple at the table in front turns towards Robert. He puts his hand over the phone.

"I am busy now. I will come to your house after work, and we can discuss your share portfolio." He clicks off on the phone and exhales.

That woman will be the death of me.

He gets up and goes to the window again, takes another look at the classical garden of neat lawns and clipped shrubs. Returns to his seat, sips the chilled water, taps his fingers on the table, combs his fingers through his hair.

"Do you want to order now?" The server wears black pants and a white cotton shirt with a black bow tie.

Robert shakes his head. "I am waiting for someone.

When he comes, I will let you know." He checks his mobile for messages. There is nothing.

I must calm down.

He has worked hard to get where he is in his career, has gained the trust of his boss Nick, who has recently assigned him two of his wealthier clients. Robert has plans to one day own a company like Masters and Smith himself. He has always had detailed plans for each part of his life and plans to be as rich as his father. His personal life is not going to plan. Millie and Nancy were unsettling. He understands Millie's issues but finds her behaviour bizarre, is powerless to assist his child.

Nancy has changed. She is not the sweet natured, sexy, easy-going woman she used to be. The woman who used to make him laugh and brighten his day. Her studies and desire to perform well academically distract her from her other obligations. It annoys him she wants to do her own thing and wishes she would smarten up her appearance. The more she studies, the sloppier she becomes. He sees the women at the office and knows how women should look.

Her studies are taking over our marriage.

The mobile pings, the absent client, tells Robert he is stuck in traffic, will be late.

Robert signals to the server, orders an apple tart, which is brought on a small silver tray. He uses the silver fork to eat the tart. He checks the time again. Stares darkly at the elegantly dressed older woman on the table next to him, who has droned on and on, telling trivial details of an encounter with a friend. The older man with her stares out at the garden.

I hope the new client is a 'keeper' Nick would be pleased.

"Robert," said a man—he turns around, not him, another Robert.

After rechecking the phone, he found no new messages.

Ten minutes pass; he spots the client striding towards him.

"Sorry I'm late," the client said.

"No problem," said Robert, smiling.

He pulls a chair out for the client.

CHAPTER TWELVE

The steam train puffs and hisses as the air pump builds up pressure. A burst of steam ejected through the stack, along with soot and smoke and the puff of the engine. The steam train carriages have wooden panelled interior and green leather seats which reflect a yesteryear when train travel meant dressing up for the event. In those years, the gospel of steam affected work and travel. Today's tourist steam train ride is a renewal of older times that once were available only to the few.

Aunt Stella leans out from the train's window, grey hair streams behind her head, cool air blowing on her face.

"I love this," her words muted by the steam whistle. "It brings me back to my girlhood days," another whistle.

The children in the carriage stomp and scramble from window to window, taking turns to hang out of the window and wave to each other. Whenever the train whistle blows, the children squeal and mimic pulling on a cord.

Sunlight is reflected on the dancing dust particles in the carriage. Two women dressed in thick black puffer jackets gossip. A woman sits tight-lipped, a silk scarf covering her hair, wears heavy makeup and has manicured long pink nails. It appears as though she is not enjoying herself, dragged along to complete her partner's idea of enjoyment.

The male rail enthusiasts aboard the vintage train are excited as they eagerly look out of the windows, clutching their cameras and phones, capturing images of another billow of smoke and steam. There are serious discussions of engine types among men wearing caps and beanies.

"There's the old gold mine we spoke about earlier," said Nancy, pointing to the horizon.

Aunt Stella peers out of the window. She jumps when the train whistle blows. "It's coming back to me." She sits back in her seat. "Father saved for a long time to take us girls on a steam train ride." She said. "The trains were something we enjoyed. We always had a wonderful time, chattered, and giggled all day. I prepared lunch, usually cheese and tomato sandwiches, and orange cordial to drink." Grey hair flutters around Aunt Stella's glowing face.

"Elizabeth and I lived in the town with father. The poor man struggled to look after us after mother died." Aunt Stella's face was sad. "Ruth had to live with a relative as father could not look after a baby."

"You are a dear to celebrate my birthday this way," said Aunt Stella again, giving Nancy a hug.

"We still have lunch to enjoy at the Castlemaine Railway hotel," said Nancy.

Smoke from the steam engine fills the carriage. Aunt Stella coughs. Nancy pulls the wooden window shut.

"The paddocks are so dry. We need rain. I hope there aren't bush fires this summer," said Aunt Stella, her voice again muffled against the train noises.

"Father said- when he was young, grandfather used to take him to town to buy flour and provisions in a horse and cart. The journey took two hours. Women in my grandmother's days had a tough life. They stayed at home to do the household chores and care for children, garden, cook, look after animals, milk the cows and deal with any emergency."

Aunt Stella watches the woman with the silk scarf powder her nose and apply more lipstick, looks at Nancy. "In my grandmother's day, there were no doctors nearby. The women only had folk remedies and each other, and sadly little babies often died. They ran the farms and did all for the family and had to deal with snakes and pestilence while their husbands fought in the war or were away working." Aunt Stella's face is downcast. "Nowadays, it is much easier for women in rural areas with the internet and cars."

The train slows, the whistle blows again. Aunt Stella jerks forward. "Did I ever tell you I had an uncle who was a steam train driver?"

"No," said Nancy, patting soot particles from her clothes.

"Henry had the Melbourne to Mildura train run until he died... I shouldn't be telling you this," she leant closer, lowered her voice. "Henry had a lover, her husband shot him dead. The family pretended a heart attack that killed him." She smooths her hair. "He was an old rogue; had girlfriends at the overnight points between Melbourne and Mildura. His big mistake, getting involved with the wife of another train driver. The husband came home unexpectedly after his train derailed and found Henry in bed with his wife." She adjusted the cameo brooch on her dress. "Bang. He shot Henry through the heart. He died immediately, but the man spared his wife. She begged for mercy; he couldn't bring himself to kill a woman."

The carriage quiet, the other passengers eavesdrop.

"At Henry's funeral, two women came to pay their respects. One woman had a baby boy she said was Henry's son."

"What?" Nancy puts a hand to her mouth.

"Henry's wife had no choice but to take the woman and the child into her home... People did those things then.... It was Henry's child, and she always wanted children but couldn't conceive." She said.

"What happened to the boy?"

"Ted stayed with Henry's wife and his mother. They became a team and brought him up together. In those days, people did what they could to survive. Ted grew tall and wiry like Henry, the image of his father. He has grown into a lovely man. A relative told me the full story at Ruth's funeral."

The train ends at Castlemaine's yellow and brown

painted railway station. Nancy has questions to ask. They will have to wait until after lunch.

The passengers from the train disembark and stroll to the Castlemaine's Railway Hotel. The meal of the day is roast lamb with mint sauce, served with roast potatoes, pumpkin, and green peas. Dessert had been a large piece of apple pie and ice cream. Aunt Stella and Nancy agreed the meal was in keeping with the vintage train adventure.

The steam train's return trip convivial, with passengers in the carriage exchanging family stories and secrets. The woman who wore the silk scarf disclosed her DNA test resulted in the discovery of unknown stepbrothers and sisters in England. "I found out my grandfather had two wives," she said. "He had one wife in England and one in Australia. I found out when I did our historical chart."

～

"Thank you for the steam train ride today. I had a marvellous birthday," said Aunt Stella.

Nancy edges closer to Aunt Stella. "Can you tell me more about my parents? I know they died in an accident when I was young, and you and Aunt Ruth and Uncle Jack looked after me," Nancy said, her head tilted to one side.

"It's late. I am unsure you need to hear the story tonight." Aunt Stella yawns and turns to watch the cuckoo bird as it pops out of the clock. She has a frightened look on her face. "Let's not spoil a wonderful day. We can talk about them another time." She yawns again.

"Promise?"

"Yes, I promise," said Aunt Stella, her face deadly pale.

∾

Nancy and Gloria are sitting on Nancy's back veranda, enjoying the sunshine. The aroma of honeysuckle is soft in the background.

"It has been weeks since we had the anniversary party. Nothing has changed between Robert and me," Nancy said.

The wind rustles the trees.

"I thought Robert would realise many people in his life care about him and he would settle down," said Gloria.

"Robert and I share a home and bed. That's it, we have become strangers to each other," she said.

"What is worse is Millie takes her frustrations out on me. What can I do? Millie sees her father as the shining light in her life, in part because of his frequent absences for work. He has become like an absent god to her. If I say anything harsh to Robert, she leaps to his defence."

Gloria takes a bite of the cupcake. "It is hard for you."

CHAPTER THIRTEEN

Nancy stands in front of the air-conditioning vent, cooling herself at the East Brunswick house. It has been hot; she has watered the garden, given each plant a good long soak, covered the delicate vegetables with an old sheet to protect them from the scorching sun. At twelve noon, she pulls on her navy nurse's scrubs for her afternoon shift at the hospital. It has been arranged that Angie's mother will collect Millie and Angie from school and bring Millie home. Nancy has prepared a beef casserole for Millie and Robert's dinner. It only requires heating for five minutes in the microwave.

Nancy sets out for work, drives past small children running through garden sprinklers on front lawns. She smiles, remembers how she and Dianne did that on hot days in the country. When she arrives at the hospital, there is a line of ambulances ramped at the entrance of the hospital.

It is going to be a long night tonight.

She scans her identification tag into the parking machine. The new concrete parking building has four floors. Each floor appears to be full, no parking spaces, drives to the top floor, finds a lone parking spot, parks her car.

A small group of people are huddled near the lifts. As soon as they see her in uniform, they run over to her, eyes filled with fear and apprehension. "Can you tell me which way to the emergency department?" said one with a turban.

"Follow me. I am going there," Nancy said.

The group follows, another man joins them. They arrive at the emergency department waiting room. She gestures for the group to approach the triage nurse standing at the counter.

Once masks were for robbers hiding their identity, now all in the waiting room wear masks. The waiting room is a babel of noise and anxious humanity, a strong odour of sweat, mixed with antiseptic and cleaning products, coupled with faint traces of the odour of vomit. Two men have bloodied bandages wrapped around their heads. A man hobbles with crutches and winces as he moves. A woman dry retches and holds a sick bag to her mouth. There are no empty seats in the cramped waiting room, the plastic seats offer little comfort. While some people cough and wheeze, others groan and moan. A large, robust man spreads out wide on the waiting room floor, refuses to move so others have to step around him. The tension in the room is palpable, anxiety mixed with fear. Three security guards dressed in black hover in the background, ready to pounce if there is a disturbance.

A toddler cries, "I want to go home now."

"We have to wait just a little longer," said the mother.

"The doctor must see my father now," shouts a pink- haired woman to the triage nurse. "Look at him, he is vomiting again... he is eighty and too old to wait out here," she points to the old man.

The triage nurse checks on the old man, takes his blood pressure and pulse. Speaks in a practised tone, "Please be patient. The doctor will see you as soon as he can."

The pink-haired woman glares at the triage nurse and sits back in her plastic seat. The old man is bent over, retching into a sick bag.

In the background, a game show plays on the television, the sound muted, descriptive words run across the bottom of the screen. No one in the room watches the screen. A heavily tattooed woman in ragged shorts and a cropped top catches sight of Nancy in her uniform, runs to her. "I must see my sister. No-one will let me in," she said.

"Go to the triage nurse. She will help you," Nancy said.

The woman runs to the nurse in the triage booth, pleads to be allowed in the emergency ward. "My sister has special needs. I must be with her."

The Triage nurse rings the ward, signals to the woman in shorts, presses the button that opens the doors into the emergency ward. "Your sister is in cubicle six."

The door opens, the woman runs in.

An intense argument escalates into a shouting match between two men in the waiting room.

'Code Grey' is called.

The security men escort the men outside.

Nancy swipes her identification tag and the automatic sliding doors open into the emergency ward. A familiar sight greets her. Bloodied patients on trolleys and rushed nurses and medical staff. Paramedics wait next to trolleys waiting for their turn to hand over to the ward staff.

"What happened?" Nancy asks a familiar face.

"An explosion in a picture theatre," said Dr Tom Ferris. "It is like a scene from a horror movie," he hurries off.

At the nurse handover, the nurse unit manager (NUM) assigns Nancy to *special* a young man who is a *at risk*, to special a patient means Nancy will only care for the one patient during her shift, she will address all his nursing care and treatment. The youth and his girlfriend had been in the movie theatre when the explosion occurred. His girlfriend died in the blast. The youth sustained severe burns and head injuries and is unconscious. The NUM states that as soon as a bed becomes available, the youth will be transferred to the intensive care ward.

Nancy completes the neurological observations on the patient, shines a torch in his eyes to check his pupil reaction, asks him if he can hear her and to squeeze her hand. He does not respond. She speaks to him as if he could hear, informs him of the day's date and her name, adjusts the beeping monitors which continuously track the youth's observations. She adjusts the rate of the intravenous line, administers intravenous drugs as per the doctor's orders, checks the monitors repeatedly.

Nancy recalls other young men with severe head injuries she has nursed. Some were paralysed, or wheelchair bound, others did not survive and died.

Millie had been in one of the nearby cubicles after her assault, the event forever stamped in Nancy's memory. Whenever she nurses a patient in the cubicle, she thinks of Millie's assault.

Nancy turns her attention to the parents of the young man, speaks comforting words to reassure them. The parents stand mute and statue- like next to their son's bedside. She explains what the monitors show.

"Never give up hope. It is possible for the young to make a remarkable recovery."

The mother places her hands in the pockets of her green cardigan, retrieves a tissue and wipes her nose. The father, a short stocky man, wears paint-stained overalls, remains silent.

Nancy signals to the volunteer in the red t-shirt who is on duty in the emergency department. "Can you please bring a round of mixed sandwiches and white tea for the parents?" The volunteer hurries to the food trolley and comes back with the food on a tray. The father unwraps the plastic around the sandwiches, offers one to his wife. She shakes her head.

"Is there anyone I can ring for you?" Nancy said.

The father said, "We've informed the family. They will be here soon."

"Although it looks hopeless now, the latest research shows that the brain can heal and adapt to trauma." Nancy said. "Neuroplasticity is the adaptation of the brain with stimulation." She lets the words sink in. Writes out 'neuroplasticity,' on a post it note, hands it to the mother. "Google the phrase. It will give you hope."

The mother breaks into sobs, throws herself into Nancy's arms. "It is so unfair..." she said.

Nancy holds the woman until the husband pulls her away.

"Come on," he said. Sits his wife on a chair.

A younger brother and sister join the parents. They sit wordlessly on the chairs provided, their red eyes wide and swollen.

At the end of her shift, Nancy provides the handover to the night staff. She checks on the youth before she leaves. They have a bed in the intensive care ward for him. The porters arrive, the patient and equipment can be transferred into the lift. The night staff *special* squeezes into the lift with the patient, manages the intravenous and drainage containers, places the patient's file on the trolley. The youth's parents and siblings press into the lift.

"Thank you for your wonderful care of our son," said the youth's mother. "And thank you for giving us hope."

"Yes." The father said.

"Take care, look after yourselves," said Nancy, watches the lift door as it closes. She finds her vehicle in the parking lot. It is 10 pm; gets in the car, locks it, joins the stream of traffic onto the main road.

Blue lights flash ahead, a police Random Breath Testing Unit.

"Pull over here," a police officer said, pointing to Nancy, who joins a queue of drivers waiting to be breathalysed. The young officer passes Nancy a breathalyser. "Blow into this."

She blows into the container.

He reads the breathalyser. "You're clear," he said, waves Nancy on.

Nancy thinks the police officer reminds her of a boy she had a crush on when she was at school. What happened to him? It is raining, the windscreen wipers push against the torrents of water. At the level crossing, a line of car headlights reflect in her rear vision mirror. A train zooms past, carriages packed with men and women going out for a fun night in the city. Another train rushes by in the opposite direction. The image of the young man she nursed earlier stays in her mind. She hopes he will survive, realises the trauma will affect the entire family, mother, father, and siblings, even cousins, aunts, and grandparents, as well as school friends, will all experience radical grief and pain. Eventually the train barriers open, cars swish through the rain and puddles. Nancy turns her car into the street, past factories, shops.

She never planned to be a nurse, had drifted into it.

"Nursing is a wonderful career for a girl," Aunt Ruth had said a long time ago. "You can travel and see the world as a nurse. And learn how to take care of your own family when they are sick."

Nursing had changed her life and widened her opportunities, from living in a small country town to the excitement and drama of the city. A good friend, Suzanne, had organised a blind date for Nancy with Robert. He was handsome, intelligent, attentive at first, buying her expensive presents, ringing often, taking her out to fancy restaurants and weekends away. Without warning or argument, Robert pulled back and was unavailable. Nancy broke off the relationship, but he pursued her, and eventually they married. Their union became a strange dance with no clear rhythm. Robert moved one way. Nancy tried to keep up and work in concert with his wishes, his plans, his ideologies, a push and pull element to their relationship. These days Nancy is less inclined to follow his dance, wants to do her own thing. She knows something is wrong with the marriage but does not know how to fix it.

I wonder if all marriages are like this.

CHAPTER FOURTEEN

Maxine Dunfield's lounge room in South Yarra exudes an elegant charm. Huge brass lamps with fringed beige edges sit on small marble tables, large bunches of fresh carnations and roses burst out of vases, perfuming the room. The open fire crackles with potent energy and force, an impatient flame rushes up the chimney. *The New Yorker, Better Homes and Gardens* cram the bookshelves. Large ornate rugs lie languid on polished floors. The weak afternoon sun beams through the long wooden windows. Bach's music soothes in the background. Beige silk curtains hang from the tall ceiling and fall to the floor. Gold-framed portraits of long dead relatives hang on the walls, giving the room a sombre touch.

Maxine has a few wrinkles around her eyes and mouth, short silver hair cut in a flattering style, wears a tailored blue linen dress. Two gold bracelets slide up and down her left arm as she knits. She sits bolt upright in the velvet armchair, concentrating on her knitting, face flushed, feverish, voice husky, every so often gives a small cough into a cotton handkerchief.

Nancy is with Maxine, is awkward in this room, the mother-in-law in a command position. A tight-lipped smile is on Nancy's face, is nervous, knows Maxine disapproves of her. She couldn't decide what to wear, changed outfits three times. The beige slacks and black jumper now seem wrong. Maxine intimidates her; knows she was against Robert marrying her.

"I came to see if you needed anything, since you were sick." Nancy said.

"I am managing" is the lukewarm response.

"How is the fever?... I brought homemade chicken soup for you, and a couple of wholemeal buns...."

"That was kind of you," said Maxine in a tone that belies her words.

"What do you think of this jumper for Robert?" said Maxine, holding it up.

"It is nice," Nancy said but knows Robert will never wear the hand-knitted jumper. He is more invested in designer clothes, more in keeping with his rising position at the firm.

"Do you need me to do anything? I can water the garden later if you like," Nancy said.

"No, the gardener will do that on Wednesday when he comes."

She watches Maxine, notices the significance of how Maxine pulls the wool tight and has to struggle to push the knitting needles through the loop. The usual sound of the click-clack of knitting needles is missing. In its place is a quieter tone of wool gripped. Maxine yanks the yarn harder, then unwinds a small section of yarn.

"Nancy, take the washing off the line, will you?

Fold the sheets into squares, edges to edges," said Maxine.

Nancy does not move.

"What...?" Maxine puts her knitting down.

"Nothing," said Nancy. "Just thinking."

"Bring in the washing." Maxine's voice rose.

"It can wait. Let's talk first." Nancy tries to keep her voice measured.

Maxine gets up and walks in front of Nancy. "Bring in the washing as it might rain."

"I can do it later... I brought you the soup and ... We could talk awhile first."

Maxine points her finger at Nancy. "Bring in the washing now, and I will watch you do it."

Nancy reluctantly collects the washing basket and walks to the clothesline. She has a flash of insight. She recognises the symbolism of the knitting—how Maxine has jerked the family hard so they could not move, controlling them to suffocation. Maxine's power came from holding others back so they could not flourish on their own. Powerless in herself, she manipulates others.

Nancy understood Robert and his brother Dean have been pulled tight.

CHAPTER FIFTEEN

The evening started badly in the East Brunswick house. The trees outside swayed against the backdrop of a darkening sky. Nancy was working on her thesis on the highly polished table in the dining area, her books and notes fanned out on the table. She knows Robert disapproves of her studying in the dining space. But it is convenient for her. The desk in her office is too small.

Robert comes into the room wearing an unpleasant scowl on his face. He peers over her shoulder. "You should change the format of the icons on the computer desktop," he said. His voice was crisp as a teacher's speaking to a small child. "You should alphabetise them."

The overhead lights in the dining room shone golden, muffled sounds filtered in from the television next door.

"I want the icons the way they are." She would not cave into him tonight.

"My way is better," he said.

The argument had grown to something she could not comprehend.

He stood too close to her. "You have a fixation

on your studies. It's not healthy," he smelt of whisky. "Face the facts, you don't have the skills to complete a thesis, no matter how hard you try."

"Leave me alone," she said, pulling away from him, determined to finish typing the paragraph.

"I could destroy your work," said Robert. He hisses the comment through clenched teeth, a menacing look on his face.

"Why are you so angry? I have done nothing to you," she said. Anger rises, mixed with fear, examines the room, wondering where to run. She is aware they are arguing over something insignificant, but it seems more substantial. She is afraid. Should she call out to Millie? Decides against it, doesn't want to upset her. Anyway, Millie always takes Robert's side of any argument.

"Do you realise you have obligations to me, to Millie?" He towers over her, his voice loud.

"I'm going to the library," she said, grabs her notes and the laptop, bangs the door on her way out.

Ten minutes later, Nancy is at the local library. It is an alternative universe. She calms in the library's peacefulness. A group of men and women are moving towards a room for creative writing classes. In another room, students recite Spanish verbs. An assortment of secondary students work on the library computers. A steady stream of individuals walk up and down the aisles searching for particular books or cluster around the librarian's desk.

Nancy sets her laptop on a table, is too rattled to

write anything, reads over her notes. There were red flags in their relationship before they got married. She should have heeded them, but he had begged for a second chance. But despite her misgivings, she married him. She regrets that now and blames herself. An hour and a half later, she drives home.

Robert was sitting outside on the back patio sipping another whisky. "You should listen to me. I know computers; you don't."

Nancy said nothing, could not trust herself to discuss it further.

CHAPTER SIXTEEN

Robert's work office is secluded from the main road. There is little traffic noise from the busy street below. He watches people move around in the building opposite; he is taking a break, stretching his legs, has been working on a complicated tax report for a wealthy client. The sky is changing, dark clouds are rolling in, heralding more rain. It always seemed to rain these days.

A quick knock on the door, and Nick Masters bursts into the office. Nick is Robert's boss, a thick, solid man who walks with studied confidence, is used to getting his own way. It is unusual for the CEO of Masters and Smith to come to Robert's office.

"Meet you in ten minutes at the new coffee bean shop," said Nick.

"What's up?" Robert pops a peppermint in his mouth.

"Tell you later." Nick sounds mysterious, closes the office door as he leaves.

Five minutes later, Robert strides to the elevator and meets Monica Appleby, a loud, opinionated client of Nick's. She has been flirting with Robert for years.

"Hello Robert; you look nice," she said. "We should have lunch one day." She touches his arm.

Robert plays the game, taught by the master—Nick. "Most definitely, soon." He said, "I would love to stay and chat, but I have an important meeting."

Robert dashes out the front door, sidesteps a large puddle of water near the entrance, bumps into Clarissa, Nick's personal secretary.

"Whoops," she said, steadying herself by grabbing his elbow.

He inhales her perfume.

"You seem to be in a hurry." She said.

"Nick and I have a meeting at the new coffee shop."

"Don't be late, he hates to wait," she touches her blonde hair.

Robert watches Clarissa as she walks back into the building, she knows he is watching. She gives a small wave. He waves back.

His phone buzzed. The phone ID shows it is his wife. He ignores the call; lets it go to voice mail. He strides into the modernistic shop, with white walls and ceiling, plain wooden tables, and functional white chairs. The pure while effect appeals to the young professionals that frequent the shop. He sniffs, the delicious coffee aroma permeates the room. Robert looks around.

Nick is talking on his mobile when he sees Robert and clicks off. "I've ordered for us." He gestures for Robert to sit. "I have news."

Robert wears a small frown on his face, fears where the conversation is going.

"The intelligent way you managed two of our more demanding clients impressed me. The feedback about you from the clients has been complimentary," said Nick.

Robert raises his eyebrows.

The server brings the refreshments.

"You could take Wilson's senior position when he retires next month." Nick leans back in his chair.

"That is very generous of you, thank you," Robert exhales.

～

Later that afternoon, back at the office building, Nick calls a meeting of senior staff and tells them of Robert's promotion. The meeting room has wide, sweeping windows. Senior executives of the company are grouped around a large oblong table. Nick is in a large swivel chair at one end. "I'm nervous Robert might end up taking my job. Robert is rising the career ladder so fast." He laughs and the group laugh on cue.

The accountants know Nick is a shrewd operator; he knows the right thing to say in any situation. He has a sixth sense about the business, which clients are in for the long haul and the temporary clients who have their tax issues fixed and disappear. Nick pampers the wealthier clients who hold large portfolios, most have been long term. Nick makes them think they are part of the company. He plans to throw a dinner for Robert's promotion and expects the senior staff and their partners to attend and mingle with the clients and their partners.

～

The Masters and Smith function is held at The Melba Restaurant at The Langham in the South Bank of Melbourne, which boasts of floor-to-ceiling views of the Yarra River and Melbourne city. The heady smell of roast chicken, lamb and beef greets customers at the restaurant. Guests can request specific food cooked on the spot. The chefs prepare a variety of English, Asian, Indian, rotisserie and seafood dishes. Cold meats and twelve kinds of cheeses and salads are piled on giant dishes. The dessert display has thirty types of choices, including cheesecake, jellies, cakes and assorted fruit.

Robert wears his best black suit, and white shirt. He sees Clarissa and grins; she acknowledges him. Clarissa has a long, dark blue dress with a deep cleavage, her blonde hair piled carelessly high on her head. Nick signals to Clarissa, and on cue she moves to the wealthy clients, calling them by name and maintains a light flirtatious air.

Robert studies the wives of the partners, they are formally dressed in tasteful, fashionable clothes. He is annoyed that Nancy did not make a greater effort to sparkle and wore the same black cocktail dress she wore at a previous Masters and Smith function.

"Let me pay for a new dress," he had said to Nancy.

"This one is still newish," Nancy said. "No one remembers who wore what."

Later in the evening, Nick makes a speech welcoming the clients and announces Robert's promotion. The guests clap politely as servers refill their glasses.

During the evening Nancy and Denise, Nick's wife, engage in a lengthy conversation. Denise is a short, plump woman, and does not seem to fit in with the stylish crowd. She wears an elegant black dress with masses of pearls around her neck.

On the drive home, Robert asks, "What did you talk about with Denise?"

"Denise mentioned their son, Grant, has a disability and is in a wheelchair. She knows I'm a nurse and asked my opinion on short-term holiday relief programs for her son. Nick dotes on his son. He will do anything for him."

"What happened to Grant?"

"Grant's birth had been complicated. It left him with physical handicaps."

"Nick has never mentioned that his son had a disability," said Robert.

"People open up to nurses, they trust us," she said.

CHAPTER SEVENTEEN

A giant peppercorn tree shades the entrance to the red brick building in the front of Alice Parker, the psychologist's office. Millie arrives for her appointment, squats on the front steps, waits five minutes, and walks up the steps to the front door of the building. Opens the door; a wave of fear triggers her, lets the door slam and returns to the steps. The voice inside Millie's head says. *Run away, run away.*

Nancy has been watching from the car, her eyes riveted on Millie, wants to jump out of the car and comfort her daughter, but knows it is a journey Millie must do over and over until she masters it, or will never cope in the world. Nancy glances at her watch; it is ten to three—early; she is always early.

Millie opens the front door again, peers insides, glances up and down the hall. She sees a dark-haired man pushing a floor polisher; he works the end of the corridor, pushes the polisher back and forth and in circles, comes closer to Millie. He gives a quick glance at her as he passes. Millie looks away, trembles, walks to the end of the hallway, goes to the door, which has *Alice Parker Psychologist* etched in black lettering.

There is a seat outside, falls into the chair, leans to one side, covers her eyes with her hands.

I hate this.

When she removes her hands -the man has gone - she knocks on the door.

"Come in." Alice jumps up when she sees the state that Millie is in. "What's going on? Talk to me."

"The man, the man..." Millie cannot say the words.

"He reminds you of the attacker?" Said Alice.

Millie bends her head. "When I see strangers, I think of him. I hate this. I want to be my old self before..." Millie's voice is a whisper.

Alice blows the long fringe from her face, pushes the thick fair hair behind her ears. Behind her are wooden bookshelves stuffed with textbooks pushed in the shelves indiscriminately. Other books pile on her desk, others stacked on the floor. A half-drunk cold cup of coffee sits on the desk.

"It distresses me to see you are still being triggered by anyone who has a resemblance to the attacker." Alice takes a sip of the cold drink, pulls a face, places the cup on her desk. "Are you still afraid of walking near parks, being in open spaces and the smell of fish?"

Millie turns her head, pretends to read the title of a book on the bookshelf. "Yes," Millie said, her voice almost inaudible. "Sometimes I go for days, and I am fine. Then boom—something triggers me, and I am back. All I want to do is run away."

"It's time to try something new," said Alice, a worried expression on her face. "We've explored cognitive behavioural therapy." Alice writes sentences on the yellow pad. "Medications can help, but I am loath to get you started on benzodiazepines or selective serotonin reuptake inhibitors."

"I have been trying to do the things you told me to," said Millie, pulling at her jumper sleeves.

"I know, you have worked hard," Alice said. "There are other treatments we can try that are more complex. One is Eye Movement Desensitization and Reprocessing, known as EMDR. You focus on sounds and movements while we discuss the trauma. It can change the way you remember the assault."

Millie pulls the jumper cuffs further, so they cover her hands.

"We haven't tried Prolonged Exposure Therapy, also known as PE." She gets a book from the bookshelf. "There are other therapies we haven't tried yet. One of them will work." Writes on the pad.

"Is your mother in the car? Bring her in. I want to discuss PE therapy with her."

Later that evening, Nancy calls Gloria. "Millie is still in the PTSD straitjacket; she still has terrible panic attacks."

"Poor kid, it has been hard for her... and for you and Robert."

Nancy heaves a sigh. "I am helpless to fix Millie. It

has been a long time. It breaks my heart to see Millie tortured by the memories of the attack."

CHAPTER EIGHTEEN

Robert and his boss are meeting in Nick's office. Nick pulls two dead leaves from a large spider plant that sits on his desk. He looks up at the ivy plant curling around the light on the ceiling. The ivy plant hangs like a green serpent from the ceiling above his desk. "Look at you," Nick points to the plant. "They always go to the light."

Nick's office is a greenhouse of luxurious plants, has a large monstera settled in a bright red pot in a corner. A silver, long-necked watering can is resting on the windowsill.

"Is your house like your office?" said Robert, turning to stare at the plants.

Nick takes off his glasses, gives them a polish with a cotton handkerchief. "More so," he said. "Not sure how it started, but whenever Denise and I go shopping, we always come back with a stack of plants. We love a green environment. Denise does an exceptional job of keeping the plants healthy. I do the heavy lifting, repotting the big guys, and moving them around." His usual gruff voice has a soft edge to it. "It's our shared obsession," he said.

"Nancy is a gardener," Robert said.

"I'm glad to hear that. Gardening is an activity that shows a person cares for the environment." Nick leans closer.

"A piece of advice regarding the client, John Curtis, he requires a light touch, or he will drop us and go somewhere else, if you dictate what he should do or not," warns Nick, leaning on his desk,. "The man is a pompous prick, but I put up with his nonsense as he brings good business to our company. The best clients that provide the most profit for us come from Curtis. Now and then Curtis tries a dodgy request, but as long as we stay on the right side of the law, we are all right. We aren't the police." Nick opens his desk drawer, takes two chocolate bars, offers Robert one.

Robert shakes his head.

"How is your Millie?"

"She's up and down, some days good, other days triggered by something." Robert is uncomfortable speaking about Millie. "Nancy has had to deal with the worst of Millie's explosive behaviour."

"It's a cruel world," said Nick, but does not elaborate, drops his voice. "All work and no play makes for dullness. It would help if you had a diversion... Have a sweet discrete affair."

Robert crinkles his eyebrows. Cannot believe what he heard. It is not the conversation you have with a boss. He never understood men who cheated on their wives, never been interested in complicating his life further, but the idea has now seeded in his mind. On one level, Robert thinks the conversation is absurd, on another, excited by the notion.

"That's what I did." Nick's heavy frame is squashed against the desk; his bulging stomach hangs over his belt buckle. "I have a word of warning for you. Don't leave your wife or you will regret it." He reaches for his gold fountain pen and taps it three times. "I would never leave Denise... never... not for any shining new woman. I love my wife." He uses the handkerchief to wipe the dust from the picture of his wife on his desk. "Keep the wife, or it will cost you dearly."

Nick takes the call from his wife. "Denise, do whatever you think best; don't worry about the cost. Grant is worth it."

Robert opens his mouth to say something, closes it.

Nick turns to Robert. "Divorce is expensive. Do not stay with the girlfriend for too long, either. It ends up as another marriage of sorts and she will want kids."

The conversation turns to clients and how to use psychology to bond the clients to the company. Nick slaps his thick hand on his desk. "I think it is time we should have a male bonding session with the new accountant." Nick picks up the phone.

"Clarissa, tell Simon to come to my office now. Robert and I are taking Simon out for lunch. Cancel any afternoon appointments for him." He puts down the phone and grins. He rubs his hands together. "Here we go."

Simon arrives in Nick's office. He is a weedy, thin

man, looks as though he has recently graduated from university, is unimpressed about the plan. "I have a girlfriend," Simon said. "She would not like this type of male bonding."

"No need to tell her," Nick said.

An hour later an excited Nick, curious Robert, and miserable Simon take their seats at *The Men's Town*. The room is dingy, dark, has strange black vinyl padded walls. It is hard to see clearly as the overhead lights are red and dimmed. The room is jammed with older men—they squirm in their seats like agitated children. The seats surround a central square, which has two large poles secured from the ceiling to the floor.

Nick nudges Simon as a tall, curvaceous brunette struts onto the stage. "You will love Big Brenda," he said.

Simon shrinks in his seat, an exasperated look on his face of resignation. He shakes his head.

Robert leans forward in his seat.

Big Brenda is tall, has long legs, is a buxom brunette, wears high-heeled pink plastic shoes, a tiny orange bra covering her nipples and a bright orange G-string pants. She does a provocative dance routine. Opens her legs, gyrates up and down the pole—the room erupts with male voices shouting encouragement. Three hostesses mingle with the crowd taking alcohol orders–they wear red G-strings with tassels on their bras and walk around in high heels. The assembled men order expensive drinks and openly gawk at the scantily clad women. The room stinks of male sweat and stale tobacco while pulsating piped music thumps loudly. Jimmy Barnes belts out *Working Class Man*.

"Up next is the sexy Carmel," says a man with the microphone as Tina Turner sings *Simply the Best*. Carmel is a long-legged blond-haired woman with thick hair to her waist. She wears three layers of flimsy lingerie, which she removes to the beat of loud music. The men clap in unison, rising to a crescendo when she throws off her last garment and stands naked in front of them.

"Time for me to go," said Simon, taking his jacket and creeps out of the room.

Nick and Robert do not see him go as they stay transfixed. Lap dancers move around the men, sit on men's laps, and press their almost nude bodies against the men for a fee.

Robert has never been to a club like this and cannot keep his eyes off the women.

"Nick how are you honey?" said a thin strawberry-blonde woman who was taking orders for drinks.

"Hello sweetheart, you look amazing," said Nick and places a $100 bill down her G-string pants.

The woman gives Nick an open-mouth kiss and moves on.

Robert swallows hard.

Those sexy women.

∼

It is late when Robert returns home and unlocks the door. A light shines in Nancy's office down the hall. He does not go to her; removes his jacket, hangs it on the hook. He goes to the kitchen and searches in the fridge. Takes a slice of leftover rhubarb pie, warms it in the microwave. The women from the strip club are still on his mind. Robert had entered a world he never realised existed, and it excited him.

I deserve to have some fun.

CHAPTER NINETEEN

It is evening at the Dunfield home. A month has passed since Robert attended the Men's Club with Nick and Simon. Robert is watching television in the lounge room of their home.

Nancy has worked the 7-3 shift at the hospital, collected Millie from school, cooked a meal of steak and vegetables. Robert ate his dinner, barely speaking to Millie and Nancy, then plopped in front of the television, channel flicking, a nervous habit he had when he was upset.

Nancy had asked, "Robert, could you please put the dishes in the dishwasher? I have to take Millie for her orthodontic appointment."

"I am tired," he said with a sarcastic tone, turns his back to her.

"It's your mother's birthday; give her a ring," she said. "Maxine would appreciate a call from you. I sent a card and a present."

He ignores her.

"You should be grateful to have a mother to acknowledge on her birthday," she said.

"Nancy, the poor little orphan girl." The killer blow, it hit home. He closed his eyes, does not want to engage anymore. His face flushed with anger. "I'm exhausted by your nagging." He glares at Nancy; the look suggests he has been wounded as though shot in the leg.

"Come on Millie, we don't want to be late," Nancy calls for her daughter.

Robert does not look up. He keeps flicking the remote. Flashes of programs come and go - a kaleidoscope of colour.

Why did I marry Nancy? She is such a bore.

～

"Why do you argue with dad?" Millie said when they were in the car. "You know, it only makes him angry."

"I wasn't arguing," Nancy said.

"It sounded like arguing to me," said Millie, staring at Nancy.

In her eyes, her father is the hero, and I am the monster.

When they return home, Robert is contrite. "I rang mother. She said to tell you she loved the multicoloured scarf." He does not face Nancy, his eyes fixed on the television screen.

"Good." Nancy's voice is flat. To be a better wife, she has been preparing Robert's favourite meals— steak, roast beef, and cheesecake for dessert. She had her hair styled into a flattering new fashion, has been wearing makeup and perfume, dressing in nicer clothes. She gives Robert her full attention when he is home. Despite her best efforts, he is critical of whatever she does. The neat, even pieces of her life are unravelling.

"Why are you so bad-tempered? What's the matter?" She said.

"It is your fault," his voice rises.

"I have turned my life inside out for you." She clears her throat.

"Stop the damn studying," he said.

No way.

The next day, after work, Nancy and Gloria meet at the hospital's coffee shop. They are both wearing the navy scrub tops and pants. Gloria has a thick blue cardigan over her scrubs. She removes her glasses and huffs on the glasses to clean them.

Nancy has explained the situation at home.

"I have tried to connect with Robert. He denies there is anything wrong with our marriage... 'It is all in your head,' he said."

"You could try marriage guidance," Gloria said. "Both of you have been under a great strain with Millie's problems."

"I don't think he will go to marriage guidance," Nancy said.

After dinner at the East Brunswick house, Nancy suggested marriage guidance to Robert.

"We have been through a lot ...in the last few years... perhaps we need counselling... to sort things out," she said. Her voice was thready and uncertain.

"There is nothing wrong with my marriage," he avoids her eyes.

After dinner, Robert disappears to meetings with clients dressed in his good suit and comes home late.

As soon as he leaves, Nancy works on the thesis.

CHAPTER TWENTY

Robert stands outside Nick's office; holds three thick folders in his arms, has been making excuses to go to Nick's office to speak with Clarissa. Her desk is in front of Nick's office. Nick's suggestion of a discreet affair has Robert intrigued and excited. Previously, he prided himself on being a family-oriented person. Nancy, Millie, and Robert were once a team, moving in the same direction.

Robert watches Clarissa. Her long blonde hair sways in rhythm with her body movements. She wears a form fitting black skirt, and a bright pink silky blouse which emphasises her rounded breasts.

"Hi," he said.

"Do you have an appointment to see Nick? He is terribly busy today," Clarissa said.

"I don't have an appointment. Just want to check something with him related to costing. I will only be a minute."

She presses the intercom for Nick's room, passes on the message. "He said he only has a few minutes, so be quick," she said.

Robert knocks on Nick's office door.

"Come in," Nick's voice booms.

Robert discusses the costs and billing for the new client. When he finishes, he stands up. "Does Clarissa have a boyfriend?"

"How would I know" Nick's eyes narrow. "I know she likes men," Nick returns to his work.

∾

When Robert returns home, Nancy has been gardening, her hair messy, dirt on her face. She wears old jeans and an old t-shirt. He compares her to the well-dressed elegant Clarissa he has spoken to earlier.

Nancy looks like something a cat dragged in.

"Is dinner ready? I'm starving," Robert said.

"Not yet," Nancy huffs, takes off her gardening gloves and moves inside.

He glares at Nancy. He has come to the realisation that he is getting old and hasn't lived his genuine life. A part of him wants the stability of his marriage and relationship with Nancy. Another part desires excitement. He envies the single male colleagues and their freedom. Even his brother Dean is dating a woman who is young and alluring.

CHAPTER TWENTY-ONE

It is early morning at the East Brunswick house. Robert lies on his back, looks up at the four-poster bed's canopy. Once the bed felt luxurious and romantic, now it appears silly. He remembers when he was at university his classmates had voted for him '*Most likely to succeed in business.*' It was true he was moving towards that goal but has a gaping emptiness in his personal life. The emotional connection that was part of his relationship with Nancy was gone. They used to stay up all night sharing their thoughts and life. Things have changed. Nancy is distracted by other things. Since Millie's attack, he understands the fragility of life and is impatient for his own life to sparkle. It is not sparkling now.

Nancy calls from the kitchen, "Robert, your eggs are ready."

He pulls the covers back, puts on his black dressing gown, goes to the kitchen, sits at the table.

"Hello, princess," he said to Millie, kissing the top of her head.

"Hey, dad," she makes a smacking kiss noise.

He does not greet Nancy.

Nancy places two fried eggs and three slices of

bacon onto his plate, pours the freshly brewed coffee into his cup. She holds the coffee pot, unable to move.

Robert looks up, senses her anxiety, has a scratchy sensation in his throat, humbled, he makes small talk.

"Have you made any special arrangements for your day off?"

Taken aback, she was startled by his words and acknowledgment of her presence. Discovering a crumpled tissue in her pocket, she wipes her eyes. She remembers when she was ten and lived with the aunts and uncle in the country; she had slipped away to the farm dam, remembers crunching twigs on the ground as she walked. The ground had been moist and slippery; it had been raining for days; the dam had overflowed over the sides. Two cormorants had flown past overhead. She had been bullied at school again. Today Nancy felt the same hopelessness.

"I might visit Aunt Stella." She knows Robert is not listening as he has opened the newspaper, reading.

Millie finishes her breakfast as the doorbell rings. "Angie's here."

"Bye, sweetheart," Nancy kisses her.

"Be good," Robert said.

～

Later that morning, Robert arrives at Masters and Smith. He steps into the elevator at the same time as Clarissa. She grins at him; her musky perfume fills his nostrils. He sniffs. "What's the name of your perfume?"

"Chanel N° 5. Marilyn Monroe, the actor, wore it when she went to bed... naked," she said.

Robert's eyebrows shoot up. He adjusts his tie. "We should have coffee together one day," he said.

"We should...." Clarissa waves to him as she steps out of the lift.

Her perfume lingers in the lift, filling the spaces, permeating his brain. He thinks of the possibilities that may be open to him.

CHAPTER TWENTY-TWO

Robert and Clarissa made a date to meet for coffee at the old cafe around the corner, the one with few patrons. They left the building separately not to be seen leaving together. He arrives early. His face has a slight flush of excitement. When Clarissa enters the shop, he calls her name and points to the table.

"I am glad you could get away," he said and smiled.

"How long have you got before you need to return to work?" Said Clarissa. She wore a black dress, with a single layer of tiny pearls around her neck, blonde hair piled carelessly on her head, held with a clasp. Wisps of hair fell over her eyes.

Here we go again, another man looking for a fling.

"I have forty minutes until Guthrie, my next client," said Robert.

"How are you going with the Guthrie account?" She moves her chair closer to his, leads the conversation, knows what interests him, has done her homework.

Robert bends closer. Chanel N° 5 fills his nostrils, remembers what Clarissa said in the elevator the other day about Marilyn Monroe and the perfume. He has an image of Clarissa naked in bed.

"Guthrie has been coming to us for years, even

before I finished my commercial law degree." She turns to glance at Robert, takes the clasp out of her hair, letting it fall over her face, then rearranges the hair clip.

His face develops a redness that creeps from his chin to his cheeks.

"Are you surprised to hear that secretaries have a brain?" she said. "Nick demands we have relevant degrees. I could have branched out into accounting myself, but I am too lazy." She rubs her arm. "Guthrie told me he's pleased with what you are doing to reduce his taxable income."

He stretches in the chair, pleased to receive the compliment.

She leans forward, this time rubs her hand over his arm, removes a single blonde hair from his shirt sleeve. "Oh, I'm shedding over you."

The touch electrifies Robert.

They gossip in a friendly manner; light talk full of hidden meaning. He looks at his watch. "We should go back now."

They return to work independently.

The last thing Robert wants is to see the dreadful Guthrie. He struggles to focus on Guthrie's demands for him to break a corporate tax rule, to benefit his taxes, His mind is on Clarissa. They plan to have lunch tomorrow at the Italian restaurant nearby.

On the way home from work, Robert buys a bunch of red roses for Nancy. He opens the door to his home, checks his face in the mirror, heads to the kitchen where she is cooking.

"These are for you," he said, hands her the flowers, gives her a peck on the cheek.

"What are these for?" a puzzled look on her face.

"Does a man need an excuse to give his wife flowers?"

"Thank you," she sniffs the roses. "They smell divine." She watches him as he walks down the hall to the bedroom. He is humming.

CHAPTER TWENTY-THREE

It is dark outside. Sleepy birds call to each other in the garden of the East Brunswick house. Crickets increase the volume of their nightly singsong. Inside the house, the Dunfield family is eating dinner. A discussion between Nancy and Millie is increasing in velocity.

"You are so old-fashioned," shouts Millie and leaps up from the dinner table, hands-on-hips. She glares at Nancy.

"I don't care what you say," Nancy said. "Even if Angie is allowed, I don't think you should go to a nightclub at fourteen." Nancy collects the dirty plates, places them in the dishwasher.

Robert looks up. "What has gotten into you?"

"Mum is an old fossil," Millie said.

"On this point, I agree with your mother. No daughter of mine is going to a nightclub at fourteen," he said.

Millie storms off to her room, and the door slams shut.

"Watch it." Robert hates the arguing and fighting. It frightens him. He recalls his parents' fights and sniping before his father left the family home. At some level, he knows he has caused some of the stress because of his irritation with Nancy. She has become something he does not like. He watches Nancy as she turns on the dishwasher. "We should have friends over for dinner."

She gives him a strange look.

"We could have a dinner party like we used to... invite a few friends," he said.

"When and who to invite?" she said, sitting down next to him.

"I will look at my commitments and we can organise a date," but does not get his diary.

"Let's make a date. I need to plan. I have an assignment due," she said.

"That's the trouble with you, always thinking of yourself. Never what I want." He is shouting now, losing control again.

"Why can't we make a restaurant reservation and organise to meet our friends there?"

He gets up, leaves.

She goes to the garden and sits in the gazebo, rocks back and forth.

CHAPTER TWENTY-FOUR

It is ten pm. Nancy peers out of the lounge room window of the East Brunswick home as Robert drives up. She watches the garage door open. He is wearing his navy work suit, his shirt open, tie hangs from his pocket. She holds the front door open for him. He drops his briefcase, hangs his jacket on the hall stand.

"Is there anything to eat?" He follows her to the kitchen. Nancy places two cooked roast potatoes and a large Chicken Kiev in the microwave. He sits at the table.

"You're home late tonight," she said. "I thought you might have been in a car accident. I tried to ring you, left you several messages."

"During a meeting, I put my phone on mute and completely forgot to unmute it afterwards." He avoids her eyes.

"Remember those clients I had appointments with when we were in KL? They have flown here and searched me out to work on their projects." He rambles on, giving too many details. His voice measured. "They asked me to join them for dinner and drinks after the late meeting, but I told them I want to go home." He does not look up at Nancy.

The microwave dings in the background as she places his meal on the table, sits next to him, watching him eat.

~

There was no meeting with the clients from KL. Robert had been at Clarissa's apartment of a luxury complex in Northcote. Robert and Clarissa left work in separate cars. He met her at the Northcote apartment. The main bedroom has a queen-sized bed, navy blue silk sheets, multiple-coloured cushions. He carried her to the bedroom; they had energetic sex. Afterwards, he showered, dressed, and headed home. It felt like a secret switch had been switched on in Robert's head; he felt euphoric, powerful, excited.

It was a letdown to come home to Nancy.

He does not feel guilty, told himself Nancy has a pleasant home, a child and is not missing out on anything.

~

Tonight, in her apartment, Clarissa stirs the tall glass with brandy and dry ginger. She plans to make this man a keeper, wants to marry, have children; does not want to work anymore. Is tired of having affairs with married men. Clarissa knows Robert is from a wealthy family and is potentially marriage material, except he is currently married. The fact he is interested in her suggests he does not love his wife.

I could persuade Robert to leave his wife.

CHAPTER TWENTY-FIVE

Gloria and Nancy are in the kitchen of Gloria's brick three-bedroom home in the leafy suburb of Moonee Ponds. The house is an old-fashioned sturdy brick house that once belonged to Gloria's parents, both of them dead. Gloria's boys are at school and there is a moment to have a break. Lego men and assorted pieces of colourful Lego buildings lie as traps on the floor for the unwary to step on at Gloria's house.

Nancy has been careful not to tread on the superhero toys, Maverick masks, and Star Wars laser figurines.

A small brown and white mixed breed dog rushes in holding a black leather lead in its mouth, gives frantic barks.

"No walks now Betsy. Be a good dog and wait," said Gloria, patting the panting furry head.

Betsy whines her unhappiness, takes the lead to a corner of the room and chews it.

The kitchen table is a jumble of cereal boxes and milk containers, plates with half eaten vegemite toast and dirty plates piled on the kitchen sink bench. Gloria clears a space for them on the wooden table.

"You sounded upset when you rang," said Gloria,

switching the kettle on and placing two mugs on the table.

"I'm so confused. I don't know what to do." Nancy takes off her jacket, hangs it behind a chair, runs her hands over her jeans.

Gloria, still in her blue dressing gown and bunny slippers, pours hot water over the coffee bags, sets out a plate of chocolate Tim Tam biscuits.

"Robert is gaslighting me, driving me insane. He runs hot and cold all the time." She waves her hands in the air. "He tells me he loves me but doesn't have the time for Millie and me. He is now a separate person from us. No, that is not right.... he has been detached for a long time." She cradles the hot mug in her hands.

Gloria makes a scoffing noise. "Robert is a fool."

Nancy taps her foot on the floor. "He brought me red roses the other day."

Gloria takes a bite of a biscuit. "Sounds like a guilty man."

"It started as a click. I told myself I was foolish," Nancy looks away. Picks up a Lego man from the floor, plays with his head, turning it this way and that. "But the darn idea dangled in my mind."

She said in a quiet voice. "Robert is having an affair. And there is nothing I can do to stop it," her voice trembled. "I ignored it at first. Robert has never been the sort to have affairs." She regains her composure.

Gloria reaches for another biscuit.

"I plucked up the courage to confront him as he left for another meeting. 'Where are you going? Do you have a girlfriend?' I said. He denied it, straight-faced, without blinking. Robert said, 'Stop talking rubbish. You should be grateful that I am working so hard for you and Millie.'"

The dog barks again, sits at Gloria's feet with the lead still in her mouth. "I know you want your walk Betsy... be patient." Gloria picks up the panting dog, places her on her lap. The dog reaches over and steals a biscuit.

Gloria shakes a finger at the dog.

"Last weekend, I booked us into a motel, an overnight, at Williamstown Beach, thinking we could talk things out. Millie stayed with Angie." Her eyes flash.

There is a knock on the door. Gloria gets up, returns with a parcel, places in on the table. "Sorry, go on," said Gloria.

"It was a bad idea. Robert spent his time avoiding me and going off on walks alone." She blew her nose.

Gloria takes a call. "I will call you later," she said. "It's my sister-in-law," she said to Nancy as a way of explanation.

"Go on, I am listening."

"So, there I sat on this so-called romantic weekend, clutching a glass of champagne by myself, waiting for him to return from his solitary walk. He didn't want me to go with him. He said he needed space to think."

Gloria pulls a disgusted face. "He is a piece of work."

Nancy looks around the kitchen. "I'm ashamed to

say I snooped; I checked his mobile phone while he was in the shower." She stumbles over the words. "He had several calls from a person named Clarissa."

"The beast," said Gloria.

"Who is Clarissa?" I asked Robert.

'She's Nick's secretary, and she has to ring me for work issues,' Robert said.

"During the weekend?" I said.

'Something had come up at work that I had to know to attend. Don't be suspicious. It makes you look pathetic,' Robert said.

Gloria shakes her head, places the dog back on the floor.

"Our marriage is in trouble. Let's fix it," I said to him. "Finally, he agreed to go to a Relationships Australia Marriage Guidance appointment." Her face was devoid of emotion.

Gloria got up and gave Nancy a hug. "You poor girl. It has been hard for you. Did he go to the counsellor?"

"Robert impressed the counsellor, turned on his charm offensive." 'My wife is the only woman I love,' Robert said, at the counsellor's office. 'There is no one else.'

'Robert said he has no one else. Are you a wee bit insecure?' said the counsellor.

"The counsellor eyed me as though I was an idiot," said Nancy.

"What do you want to do?" Said Gloria.

"This is all new to me. How to deal with the madness when I know something is wrong, but I am met with denial and anger?" Nancy crosses her arms and uncrosses them.

"Men can be such fools. What you need is an excellent solicitor."

CHAPTER TWENTY-SIX

It is Saturday afternoon at the East Brunswick house. Nancy finds an old bottle of Marveer polish in the laundry cupboard, opens the Marveer bottle, inhales the polish deeply. The woodsy aroma of the polish takes her back to her life on the farm. Nancy leans back against the washing machine and is transported to a previous life.

She remembered Aunt Stella used the Marveer polish to clean and shine the wood furniture at the farm. The home developed a pleasant aroma. The wooden table and chairs radiated love and care. Aunt Stella hummed as she worked, wore a floral apron with pockets stuffed with cleaning rags.

Nancy recalled the green and white Kooka gas stove which had pride of place in Aunt Stella's kitchen. In those days early in the morning, Aunt Stella would set out the flour, sugar, eggs, cake tins, baking paper out on the bench ready for the day's baking. By afternoon, a pot of a delicious soup bubbled on the stove, something delicious cooled on the cake rack, often Anzac biscuits and gingerbread men. While the yeast rose for the bread, Aunt Stella rolled the pastry for the meat pies, sliced apples for the apple tarts. She had relentless energy, never still.

Nancy could see herself as a young girl coming home from primary school.

"How was school?" Aunt Stella would say setting out two cupcakes covered in raspberry icing and coconut, placing a glass of homemade ginger beer next to the cupcakes. "I cooked the cupcakes just now. You can be the official taster."

"Yum," said Nancy.

∼

Nancy takes the Marveer polish container into the kitchen. The memories have shaken her. She knows she was loved in those days, not now. She gazes out of the window at the garden, not seeing the greenery. Her mind is on the past.

∼

On those farm days, Nancy's best friend Dianne lived nearby. They rode their bikes to the local country schoolhouse. The school had thirty students of different ages, two classrooms and two teachers. One taught the prep to grade three classes, the older teacher taught grades four to six. One teacher was gentle, while the other was prone to shouting at the students for any misdeeds.

Lola, another friend, had a miniature Shetland

pony called Scotty. She rode him to school. He was a hardy brown horse with a stocky body, four short fat legs and a long, thick shaggy mane. Lola harnessed Scotty to the fence during class. He was king of the children during the school day. Most children shared their lunch with the horse, who was partial to peanut butter sandwiches. The horse allowed the squealing children to pet and stroke him. But no matter how much they begged, Lola refused to let anyone ride Scotty. "I am the only one who can ride him. He bites anyone else who tries to ride him," Lola said.

Nancy remembered her bedroom window faced the hen house. She had names for each of the twelve Rhode Island Red hens; they were excellent layers. Her job was to collect the eggs. The ones with fluff stuck to the side of the eggs were *the lucky eggs*. A neighbour who had a rooster gave them fertilised eggs for when the hens became broody. After some time, one by one, the golden balls of fluff pecked out of the shells. The mother hen clucked, and the chicks hid under her warm brown fluffy feathers.

'The chicks are here,' Nancy had called to Aunt Stella.

Aunt Ruth's responsibilities were the farm itself, the sheep, and the vegetable patch. She always had food scraps for her magpies. They followed her around like black and white feathered *puppies* as she dug into the garden. The magpies gobbled the grubs she threw to them.

At night, they all sat by the fire. Uncle Jack regaled

them with funny stories about his day. Sometimes sneaking in stories related to the aunts.

'Remember the time Stella and Elizabeth went swimming in the river instead of going to Sunday school?' He said. 'Your father had a fit when he found out.'

'Oh, Jack,' said Aunt Ruth. 'Don't put ideas in Nancy's head.'

Nancy never knew whether the stories were true, but loved to hear them, especially tales about her mother, Elizabeth.

In those days, they all worked as a team, knowing their roles and obligations.

Nancy had planned to marry a man like Uncle Jack, instead she ended up with Robert.

CHAPTER TWENTY-SEVEN

Aunt Stella and Nancy are at The Pink Tea Shop. The wallpaper behind them has tiny red and pink flowers scattered on it. The teacups carry the same motif and are gold-trimmed. They sip on English breakfast tea, nibble on fat scones with cream and strawberry jam. Nancy has been speaking about her recollections of living on the farm as a child.

"I remembered how you used the Marveer polish on everything wooden," said Nancy.

"I still use the polish," said Aunt Stella.

The conversation turns to Johnny, Stella's fiancé, who died in the Vietnam war. Aunt Stella's face crumbles, she sniffs into a white lace-edged handkerchief.

"I never married," Aunt Stella said, voice unsteady. She coughs and touches the hand-painted cameo brooch that is on her neck. "I only fell in love once in my life and that was with Johnny." She smooths her printed green and white dress, stares ahead.

"I can still remember the dreadful day when I was told that Johnny had died." Her eyes moisten. "Some things never leave you." She looks at her hands.

"Johnny and I had such big plans. We planned to

marry and live in Echuca. He had dreams of being a country schoolteacher." She wipes her nose. "My Johnny was special."

Nancy squeezes Aunt Stella's hand.

"I could never love another man after Johnny died," said Aunt Stella.

"I am here for you," Nancy said.

Aunt Stella pats Nancy's hand.

"After he died, I worked for a dressmaker making clothes for rich ladies and I lived in a cold room in a boarding house. One day, Ruth visited me and said, 'Come and live with Jack and me. You can be the cook and cleaner, leaving me time to work on the farm while Jack goes to the bank.' That's what I did."

Aunt Stella sips her tea. "My great aunt told me how she learned about the passing of her husband in World War One. It was horrible. A telegraph lady would ride her bicycle and ring her bell to deliver the news. The great aunt said that the women in the street froze with fear. The woman hopped off her bicycle at the gate of the soldier's home." She touches the brooch again. "The other women instantly understood what that meant." Aunt Stella was silent. "The telegram informed my great aunt that her husband had died in the war. All wars are the same innocent men and women suffer. It is such a waste of the beautiful lives of young people." Aunt Stella's eyes glisten.

"I expect it had been a terrible shock for you when you heard both my parents died in an accident," said Nancy.

Aunt Stella drops her cup, the contents spill onto the white tablecloth; she mops the area of the spill with her serviette. Her cheeks are blazing red.

Nancy helps mop the spill, notes Aunt Stella's reaction.

"Your parents died when you were a baby, and the authorities would have sent you to an orphanage. But Aunt Ruth would have none of it. She suggested you could you live with us instead of an orphanage." Aunt Stella said. "The court agreed. You were to live with us." She stopped, wordless for a few moments. "We had to buy all the baby things, cots and blankets and learn how to pin a nappy. Aunt Ruth organised a roster system to make sure you were fed on time. Uncle Jack gave you the first bottle before he went to work. Then Ruth's turn before she worked on the farm. I fed you through the day and night. You were a happy baby."

She opens her bag, rummages around in the bottom. She pulls out a small square box, hands it to Nancy. "I found this the other day. This belonged to Elizabeth. I want you to have it as a keepsake of your mother."

Nancy opens the small jewellery box. Inside, there is a gold chain with an intricate design. The clasp has a small pearl embedded in it. She takes it out, fingers the chain before putting it on. "It's so delicate," said Nancy. Touches the shiny chain.

"I polished the chain, so it is like new. Remember, a mother's love never dies." Aunt Stella looks out of the window, a deep frown on her face. "Even if the mother is not around."

Nancy runs her hand over the chain. Was it her imagination, or was something warm coming from the chain?

CHAPTER TWENTY-EIGHT

It is night. Nancy sits at the dressing table at the East Brunswick house, ready for bed. The room smells of lavender from the oil burner. Nancy learned lavender's positive effects from a weekend aromatherapy course. Robert is at another meeting tonight, something related to his work. Nancy has stopped asking. They are living separate lives, communicating only when it is necessary.

Behind Nancy is the four-poster bed; it has a canopy roof, solid oak base with tutor style carved panels. Ten years ago, Robert and Nancy hunted speciality antique shops until they found the perfect bed for their bedroom. A local dressmaker sewed the crimson drapes that surround the bed. Millie used to snuggle into the bed between them when she was younger. Her face peeked from under the white duvet.

The bedroom windows face the back garden. Nancy can watch the birds move around the garden from the bedroom. She knows the bird families— the strong magpie mother and her two babies. The sparrow mother keeps her family close, the wattlebird family shy, fluttering off when a noise disturbs them. The blue wren family is nervous around humans. Mr

Blue Wren, proud in his majestic blue, keeps watch, Mrs Wren a quieter brown colour but courageous. One year, Mrs Wren brought her two tiny baby wrens to peck at the food. Nancy beamed all day.

She touches the gold chain that belonged to her mother. It seems to have developed its own momentum, is curious to learn all she can relate to her parents, intends to ask Aunt Stella questions about the chain. Did her father give it to her mother for a wedding or birthday gift? What sort of person was her mother, was she gentle and kind, like Aunt Stella? The gold chain has created an urge to know more about her mother.

She looks at her face in the mirror. Small wrinkles have formed around her eyes. She pulls her skin back to erase the laugh wrinkles. She does not laugh like she once did.

.

CHAPTER TWENTY-NINE

It is the beginning of a soft evening. Maxine switches on the lamp next to her chair. It gives off a warm amber glow. Maxine adjusts her position by the lounge room window. She gazes briefly out of the open window and the smell of freshly mowed lawn. Earlier in the day, the gardener had mowed the lawns; the garden is as she likes it. The garden bed near the window is filled with red and white roses in bloom. She returns to her knitting, is on the last sleeve of Robert's cable jumper, she plans to give him the jumper next week. She has always enjoyed knitting for her boys, likes the complicated knitting patterns that test her skills.

Millie rings, "Hi Maxine, I am inviting you to my birthday party on Saturday," said Millie. "It will be a low-key affair, mum and dad, Aunt Stella, and a couple of my friends. No raucous music, I promise."

"Mmm," said Maxine, puts the knitting down. She does not want to attend, does not like birthday parties.

"I have something on for Saturday," she lied.

"Please come. I want you at my party," Millie said.

"Here is an idea. You have your birthday party, and on Sunday, Robert, Nancy, and you can come here for a special afternoon celebration," her voice measured, trying to sound reasonable. "I want to see your face when you open your birthday gift. Remember the Apple iPhone you said you wanted? I bought it for you."

"Wow, that is too generous of you. Thank you," said Millie. "I will miss you on Saturday."

"I have to go. Someone is at the door," said Maxine and clicks off.

At the front step is a delivery man with a parcel. She signs for the parcel, pulls the iPhone from the packing.

The iPhone's expensive, $1,500. Robert will give me a lecture related to spoiling Millie.

She returns to her knitting, checks the pattern, counts the cable pattern stitches.

I can cope with Christmas parties. But children's birthday parties are too painful.

Maxine shudders as she remembers birthday parties when she was a child. Her parents insisted they celebrate her birthday with a boozy family party. Her mother invited relatives from both sides of the family. Most were heavy drinkers. Maxine never invited her friends. No musical chairs or pin the tail on the donkey games. Instead of fairy bread and sweet treats that children like, there were crates of beer, crisps, and nuts. Her mother bought a cake from the supermarket.

Maxine gets up and closes the drapes. Goes into the kitchen and gets a glass of water. She goes back to her chair. Sips the water.

She remembers her parents began drinking early in the day. Fights and arguments marred the party by the day's end. Often the neighbours called the police. She had been to other children's parties and understood how they should be.

There was never enough money for food, her parents drank whatever money father brought home. Maxine remembers the humiliation when she was told to ask the next-door neighbour for money to buy sausages for a meal, as they had nothing to eat. The neighbour gave her the money, aware of the drunken parties and the growing stack of beer bottles against the fence.

Maxine escaped the misery of her childhood. She has kept her past a secret and vowed never to be vulnerable again. And married the first prosperous man who asked her. Reginald came from an extensive line of notable high society linage and was captivated by Maxine's beauty and enthusiasm for life. Their wedding heralded in the daily papers and women's magazines. Maxine learnt to be the woman what Reginald desired. But tensions surfaced several decades later. Reginald became infatuated with a much younger woman who later became his fourth wife. Despite their divorce, Reginald and Maxine remained on good terms, and she fared well financially from the settlement. Reginald's money enabled Robert and Dean to have a different life and education to hers. Robert didn't like the boys' school, hated the school's striped blazer, and didn't like the endless rules.

Dean did better at school, captain of the cricket and football teams.

CHAPTER THIRTY

A roar erupts from the crowd at the local sports hotel. The mostly male attendees are glued to the football match on the enormous television screen. The place is filled with male sweat and powerful male voices. Robert and Dean are at the hotel drinking beer.

"I can't pretend anymore," Robert said. "Nancy bores me to shreds." He sighs to emphasise his point. "The emotional connection between Nancy and I has gone. She does not care what I do, and I don't care about her."

"Maybe it is you who's boring," said Dean.

"Clarissa is the best thing that ever happened to me," Robert said.

Dean shakes his head. "You are an idiot."

Robert ignores the remark. "Clarissa and I are in love. I told you we have been secretly dating for months." He adjusts his shirt collar. "I hate the sneaking around. We have plans... In the next few weeks, I will separate from Nancy and move into Clarissa's apartment." He stares at the television screen. A footballer kicks a goal and the pub crowd cheer.

"We will have to sell the house. Nancy and I will

split the proceedings fifty-fifty." He speaks as though the event has already happened.

Dean stares at him.

"Clarissa will sell her apartment. We will pool our money and buy something together." He refills his beer glass from the jug on the table.

"And you think Nancy will agree to all of this and the sale of the house? You have got to be kidding." Dean munches on a potato chip from the dish.

The hotel crowd goes wild as the football siren sounds at the end of the third quarter.

"The only thing that upsets me is leaving Millie," said Robert.

"You are mad, stark raving mad," said Dean, pours another beer. "It's lust, not love. It won't last." Dean stuffs more potato chips into his mouth.

CHAPTER THIRTY-ONE

Robert is in his office, looks out of the window at the buildings opposite. He checks his phone. His desk is piled high with manilla folders but cannot start working on them. It is a strange day. The wind swirls in the trees, causing leaves and twigs to cascade over the footpaths and roads. The force of the gale upends rubbish bins, pushing them over, scattering the contents on roads and nature strips. He hates the wind.

Tonight, I will tell Nancy I am leaving.

He looks at his watch, pulls his navy jacket on, collects his briefcase.

An hour later Robert arrives home, is accosted by the powerful smell of disinfectant and soap. He shudders.

Nancy is in the kitchen on her knees, scrubbing shelves, wears thick blue rubber gloves. Crockery and saucepans are stacked on the kitchen benches.

"You're home early."

He does not remove his jacket and does not hang it on the hall stand. Robert stands holding his briefcase, looking at Nancy with distaste. He strides from the kitchen to the hallway, and back to the kitchen.

"What is the matter with you? You are acting like a caged lion, ready to pounce," she said. "Has something happened?"

"You're a wonderful person, an exceptional mother," He mouths the words as if he is an actor in a play. "We haven't been getting on for a long time." He stares at the kitchen floor as though looking for his missing words. "I have changed. You have changed. Millie is the only thing keeping us together."

The wind shakes the windows.

He stands facing Nancy, his height towering over her. He adjusts his voice, drops it so it is softer. "I think it would be best if we took some time apart."

She stares at Robert, not sure about the meaning of his words. Heat spreads over her body. "What are you saying? Are you leaving me?" She gets up from where she has been cleaning.

"We never agree on anything. You are going in one direction, and I in another. It is not the way marriage should be."

They stare at each other. No one speaks.

"Are you leaving me to be with someone else?" she said.

"I told you; we need a break from each other for a while," he sits at the table.

"Is there anyone else? Tell the truth." She raises her voice.

"Of course not," Robert's voice rises again. He is shouting, bangs his hand on the table.

"Tell me, I must know." She grabs his shirt and will not let go. "Tell me now," she yells in his face, twists his shirt.

Robert uncoils her fingers from his shirt, fury in his eyes. "Yes, there is someone else, a beautiful woman who puts me first in her life."

Nancy blinks.

The wind outside blows harder, shaking the trees.

"You disappoint me," he said.

"How do I disappoint you?" she said.

"For a million reasons, you are not the woman I married." His voice has a cruel edge.

"Neither are you the man I married. You've changed," she said.

He marches to the bedroom, pulls two suitcases from the closet, opens the drawers where he keeps his underwear and socks and throws his clothes into the suitcase. He rolls the cupboard doors back and forth, pulling out shirts, ties, trousers, and jeans. Throws them on the bed, folds them in the suitcase. He retrieves the good suit from the cupboard.

She follows him into the bedroom, is an outsider watching a horror movie, cannot speak. She can see what is happening, but her brain refuses to come to terms with the reality, is in shock. "Are you leaving me now?" She does not know how to stop him. Should she grab his clothes and put them back in the cupboard? Should she kick him?

The timer pings in the kitchen where she has prepared beef stroganoff for dinner. "Will you at least stay for dinner?" She said.

"I will not need dinner from you tonight." His voice was sharp like a dagger.

She opens her mouth to speak. No words came out. There is a buzzing in her ear.

Outside, the wind blows harder.

She brushes the hair from her face, is aware she is still wearing the blue rubber gloves from scrubbing the cupboards in the kitchen, removes the gloves.

"Please stay. We can work this out. Our marriage is worth fighting for," she said.

He snaps the suitcases shut, carries them to the front door—his good suit over his shoulder. "I deserve to be happy," he said. "I will collect my other things later," strides out of the door carrying the suitcases, throws them in the car boot and drives away.

He drives to Clarissa's apartment, where she is waiting for him, hangs his clothes in her wardrobe, places his toothbrush and toiletries next to hers.

～

At the East Brunswick house, Nancy sits motionless.

She heard the front door close, the car start up and roar down the street. She wills him to return. It is dark outside when she realises he is not coming back. Goes to the kitchen, switches off the oven, replaces the saucepans and dishes on the clean shelves.

A heaviness comes over her.
How long had Robert planned his escape?

CHAPTER THIRTY-TWO

Nancy is at the kitchen table, thinks of dear friends who loved each other, held each other tight in bed. One day, their love evaporated, and they parted. She never expected it would happen to her. It occurred to Nancy he had stopped kissing her when he left and returned from work. A small thing, but it heralded something larger.

They used to tell each other their secrets. Be so close. Was it her fault he had found someone else? What had she done wrong? He was unhappy about her studying, but he seemed to have adapted to that. Did she miss the cues of his leaving? If he had told her, she would have changed. All she ever wanted was to have a happy home, her only dream.

Again, she was the powerless orphaned girl, bullied and taunted.

Her eyes burn, her nose is blocked and feels she is dangling on the edge of a cliff, about to slip down. Her mouth tastes foul, a distinct taste of failure.

CHAPTER THIRTY-THREE

It is late at night. Robert listens to the sound of traffic outside, stretches out on the bed in Clarissa's Northcote apartment. He watches Clarissa sleep, her long blonde hair spread over the pillows, bends over and gives her a tender kiss on the neck. Deep happiness flowing through him.

Gets out of bed, finds a pad and pen, he has many things to organise; his snail mail to be delivered to a post office box, notify the bank of his situation and separate his bank accounts from Nancy's. Inform the Road Traffic Authority address change and who to notify in an accident. He should meet with his solicitor to discuss a formal separation.

I will ring Millie tomorrow and explain things to her. She will be upset for a while but will get over it.

PART 2

After

CHAPTER THIRTY-FOUR

Two weeks have passed since Robert left Nancy and Millie to live with Clarissa. The East Brunswick house is quiet, as though smothered in a blanket and no vibrations of sound can enter.

Nancy tries to make sense of what has happened. Her husband has turned his back on his family and left them just like that, a turning of a page, the cutting out of people in his life. She wraps Aunt Stella's Afghan rug with its brightly coloured squares around her body and hides on the chesterfield in the lounge room with the television. Nancy watches old black and white movies and cries over the heroine's accident or loss of love and drinks many cups of English breakfast tea. Robert's leaving has been the undoing of her safety. She misses him, is numb, mute with pain; has not opened the laptop since he left. Each evening, she switches on the outdoor lights, looks out of the window looking for Robert's car, wishing for him to come back. But he does not return.

"Get a grip, mum," said Millie, her face tight like a guitar string.

"I...." Nancy clears her throat, coughs. "I can't." She rubs the back of her neck. She has lost the ability to act intelligently. Is a stranger in an unknown land, cannot speak the language of loss. The words come out gibberish.

Gloria comes to the house. "Let's go for a walk."

"I cannot." Nancy is leaden. Cannot entertain the idea of leaving the house. A part of her life has died, is full of grief. She is not working at the hospital at the moment, has taken time off, used her sick leave. Only three people know Robert has gone: Millie, Gloria, and Aunt Stella. She is ashamed to tell her other friends, views his leaving as a personal failure.

Aunt Stella calls every day. "How are you today, dear?"

"I am all right, I think...." Nancy makes small talk attempts to be bright. Aunt Stella can see through the pretence.

"Robert is not worth getting upset about," Aunt Stella's voice is soft.

Her mobile rings, but she lets it ring out, only answers if she knows it is Millie, Gloria, or Aunt Stella. She doesn't answer the door no matter who's knocking. She has shut the outside world out, is a wounded animal hiding away from life. Nancy wears her old black tracksuit, forgetting to shower some days. She shakes off her lethargy to cook dinner for Millie and herself. Still places three sets of cutlery on the table, puts out three plates.

"Dad's not coming home for dinner." Millie throws the extra cutlery in the drawer, shakes her head.

Nancy hangs three clean towels in the bathroom.

Millie grabs one and tosses it back in the linen press, gives her mother an exasperated glance.

Now and then she ventures outside to the garden to replace the seed in the bird feeder. It is peaceful in the garden with the plants and birds.

~

It is a school morning, Angie and Millie are a part of a mass of moving students on their way to various schools. They climb onto the tram.

"I miss dad. The house is a morgue without him," Millie said.

"Yeah, I know what you mean. It's hard to be neutral when your parents separate," said Angie.

A grinning student seated behind them knocks Millie's school hat off her head.

"Cut it out." Millie grabs the other student's hat and hurtles it to the back of the tram.

"Dad and I have met for a movie and hamburger a few times," Millie said. "He looks cool, wears new jazzy clothes." She flips the watch band around her wrist.

"Mum is going nuts," she said. "She hangs around the house all day. I don't know what she does. Sometimes she is still in her old tracksuit when I return from school," Millie blinks.

"She's not working at the hospital."

She stares out of the tram window. "I don't need

this extra stress in my life." Millie searches her pocket for a tissue, wipes her nose.

"Why don't you come and stay with me," Angie said, an anxious look on her face.

"I want to, but I can't. Mum might top herself or something." She checks her fingernails.

They join a mass of similar uniformed students moving in their school's direction.

"My mother acted weird after dad left," said Angie. "It takes time, but your mother will get over your dad leaving."

"I am sick of her behaviour," said Millie. "I hate dad has left us to be with Clarissa. Dad and I talk on the phone, and I see him at the weekend, but it is not the same."

At the East Brunswick home, Nancy pulls out the old family photograph albums and tortures herself with the blowtorch of remembering. The photos of their wedding depict both of them in love, holding hands, enjoying holidays, going on camping trips, and embracing each other with radiant joy. She was the skinny heroine, he the mighty hero. The two of them sought to change the world. When Millie was born, they became a three-person team

How could Robert forget those years?

She cannot tap into her anger, lives on a dank, smelly raft of sadness and blackness. The day Robert left, she removed her wedding ring and placed it in the drawer. A part of her said throw it in the rubbish, another part said he might come back, and she would wear the ring again. They were having marriage troubles, but no one leaves a family because of problems. Most find a solution. Some of Robert's clothes are in the cupboard. She cannot throw them away. He may return and will need them. She buries her face in his old jacket, inhales the musty aroma and traces of his aftershave. At night she rolls over in bed, wanting to wrap her legs around his body, forgetting he is somewhere else with Clarissa.

Robert's coming and going from the house had become a sturdy clock she had built the rhythm of her life. "He will be home soon," she used to think, defrost the meat and chop the veggies. Now Robert is eating with someone else, feeding each other from the same spoon, kissing between morsels of food, sharing secrets and stories of their day. Making love, snuggling together, watching a movie on TV, heads on each other's shoulders. As they used to do.

She tries to toughen up and grow a new membrane but cannot; her skin is too raw.

CHAPTER THIRTY-FIVE

Millie is at the East Brunswick house, lying on her bed staring at the ceiling when her phone rings.

"Hi dad." Millie sits up.

"How are you?" Robert said.

"Usual," she said.

There is an awkward silence between the two of them.

"Is it still okay to watch a movie on Saturday? Anything special you want to see?" Robert speaks quickly, as though he needs to get the conversation over.

"When am I going to meet Clarissa?"

"Now is not a suitable time," he said.

"Why can't I meet her?"

There is a pause.

"Do you want to talk to mum?" Millie said.

"No," he said.

"I miss you. When are you coming home?"

Robert can hear Millie crying.

"I will see you on Saturday. We can talk more," he hangs up.

Millie holds the phone for a long time before throwing it on the bed.

CHAPTER THIRTY-SIX

Six months have passed since Robert left. Nancy waits in her car outside Alice Parker's tree-lined Parkville office. She watches Millie as she goes up the steps of the building, wants to go with her, to give support, but holds herself back. Alice said to be overprotective was more harmful than helpful.

Millie had a triggering episode on the anniversary of the assault; the date forever stamped on her subconscious. She woke in agitation, terrified, all the improvements gone. She relived the attack as though it were yesterday.

Today, she cautiously edges down the corridor, looks back and forth, listens for sounds of footsteps. There are no strange men around today. She taps on the door of Alice's office.

"Come in," Alice said. The office is in semi-darkness. A small shaft of light is shining through the half-open curtains.

"I have a headache. The brightness makes it worse," Alice covers her eyes.

"Why didn't you cancel my appointment if you had a headache?" said Millie, falls into the chair.

"I wanted to see you. I was afraid your father's leaving may have been stressful for you," she said.

"It has been horrible," Millie's voice fades, she hangs her head.

"I noted the date. Yesterday was the anniversary of the assault." Alice drags a chair closer to where Millie is sitting. "It's normal to fall apart during any traumatic event, whether it's an assault, death, divorce." Alice opens a textbook and shows Millie the relevant chapters. *A meltdown is normal on the anniversary of any disturbing event.* Alice looks intently at Millie, taking in details of her distress.

Millie slumps further into the chair.

"In the future, you need to prepare for the date, so it doesn't upend your life. Make plans to go out with friends. The last thing you want is to sit at home and relive the events alone." She wants to comfort Millie but has to maintain a professional distance. Alice writes a note on her files.

"How are you managing since your father left?"

"I hate him not being home. When dad and I meet up, he is not himself. He is on guard, keeps me at a distance," she said. "But he seems happy," she squints at Alice. "I pleaded with him to return." Millie turns to the bookshelves, places a hand over her mouth, bites her lower lip. "I miss him so much." She bites her nails. "He told me he wouldn't be returning home."

"Mum has been acting weird... It has been awful." The tears Millie had suppressed slipped down her face. "I want him to come back," Millie's voice a whisper.

Alice hands her a tissue.

She wipes her eyes with the tissue. "Dad has forgotten us, now he loves Clarissa." Millie holds her hands in her lap. She looks down at her knees. There was a long pause. "I am scared things will get worse."

"You seem overwhelmed." Alice scribbles numbers on a Post-It note. "This is my after-hours phone number. Leave me a message if you want to talk to me."

Millie stuffs the note in her pocket.

"Is your friend Angie helpful?" Alice said.

"Angie wants me to stay with her, but I can't." She looks up at Alice. "Mum has been acting creepy. I'm frightened to leave her alone."

Millie watches a fly land on the table.

"Your first responsibility is to yourself." Alice makes direct eye contact with Millie. "Your mother will survive. It is normal to be unhinged when a husband leaves the marriage for another woman. Your mother is going through a period of grief."

The fly lands on Alice, she swipes at it.

"I have booked a space in my appointment book to see you later this week. I have more homework for you." Alice goes to the window and pulls back the curtains a little. "I want you to jot your deepest ideas in a notebook, what your impression related to what has happened, even angry ideas. It will help clarify your emotions." Alice rubs her eyes. "I have kept a journal for years. It helps me to unwind." Alice opens a drawer and pulls out a blank exercise book, hands it to Millie.

"Use this and bring it with you next time we meet," she said. "When my beloved dog, Mitzi, was too frail to walk. I kept her alive for as long as I could. I used to scribble things down in a notebook... how it felt to see her suffer... how it felt to sit next to Mitzi when the vet euthanized her... She was my best friend...." Alice's voice cracks. "Writing my true thoughts helped me to process the loss of Mitzi," Alice's voice tapered off to a whisper.

"I want you to write your deepest thoughts in your journal. Don't concern yourself with spelling or grammar, just get it down. The only rule is to write for twenty minutes each day for five days." She pulls a research article from the shelf. "Read the article. Leave it out for your mother to read. It can help her too. Write what triggers you, the assault, your father leaving, mother being strange. The deeper you go, the quicker you will heal," she said.

Millie looks at the wall.

"All individuals face challenges. Try not to let unpleasant experiences define who you are. Write them down. I have had unpleasant things happen to me, but I learnt to use them to grow stronger and be resilient. If I can do it, you can too," Alice said.

Millie stares unblinking at Alice.

"It's mum's fault that dad left," Millie said in a defiant tone. "She should have been nicer to dad."

Millie crunches the tissue into a ball, throws it towards the wastepaper basket, misses, watches it bounce to the floor.

"No one person is at fault when a marriage ends. People change. What we want today differs from yesterday or tomorrow. The only variable that we can count on is change."

Alice picks up the tissue, tosses it to Millie.

Millie throws the tissue ball again; this time it lands in the basket.

"The most important lesson in life is to learn to adapt to change and have a radical acceptance of life. It can be terrible or good depending on your perception," Alice pulls her chair closer.

"That's it for today. Don't forget to write in your journal." She walks Millie to the door. "In the next few weeks, we will start on Prolonged Exposure Therapy. Other girls the same age as you have achieved impressive results with relieving the symptoms of PTSD using Prolonged Exposure."

"Anyone from our support group?" said Millie.

"Can't tell you that. That would be a breach of confidentiality."

CHAPTER THIRTY-SEVEN

The sun streams through the windows. Nancy is the only client in the waiting room of the divorce solicitor's office. She never imagined she would ever be a client here. It has been over a year since Robert left; she has learnt to adapt to a world without him. She wears a plain green dress, a black belt around her thin waist, low heels and a black cropped jacket. Her auburn hair pulled back in a loose ponytail.

A pot of brilliant blue African violets enhances the receptionist's desk.

"Your African violets are lovely," Nancy said.

"It is a gift from a client." The receptionist gives Nancy a curious look.

Nancy coughs to control her nerves.

"Mr Patel won't be long," said the receptionist, returns to her typing.

Nancy knows she is in uncharted territory. As usual, she arrived early, sticks her hands in her pockets to stop them from trembling. Grabs a woman's magazine from the table, pretends to read. Replaces the magazine on the square table. Lifts her head, smells the sickly sweet smell of lemon fragrance from the commercial air freshener that sits on the window ledge. Every ten seconds, it sends a puff of pretend lemon smell into the air. It makes her sneeze. A large philodendron plant in an oversized ceramic pot sits in a corner of the room. Nancy touches the soil, is moist. The leaves shine, the solicitor must use a garden service that exchanges the plant when it becomes seedy from lack of fresh air and adequate sunshine.

She settles on one of the four blue armchairs spaced around the table. A generous sized box of tissues has pride of place in the middle of the table. She grabs two tissues and shoves them in her pockets and pretends to peer at the painting on the wall, a winery in the hills. The print reminds Nancy of a wedding at the McLaren winery years ago. They had been invited to a niece's wedding on Robert's father's side of the family. It had been a perfect sunny day, enormous bunches of fragrant honeysuckle and jasmine were tied to the entrance of the winery. The young blonde bride looked stunning in a white lace French couturier dress and veil, while the groom was dressed in a grey tailcoat suit and a matching top hat. The couple said their vows with a wedding celebrant under an arch adorned with masses of red roses in the garden. In the background were rows and rows of cultivated purple and green grapevines. The reception was held in the courtyard of the winery—cane baskets of red and blue fuchsias hung graciously from the ceiling. Huge wooden wine barrels surrounded the room. Radiant wedding couple, exotic food and endless champagne; the band thundered the latest tunes. They had joined the other guests in the dancing. Robert whirled her around and around until she became airborne.

She remembers Robert's parents sat next to each other. They played the game, for the Dunfield's sake. Maxine and Robert's father Reginald had separated, but were together and friendly for the wedding, keeping up appearances. It was always related to keeping up appearances for Maxine and Reginald. Nancy had been mindful to create a good impression, not to diminish the Dunfield family brand. She had carefully applied makeup to hide her freckles, had her hair curled and sprayed with side ringlets, wore a new crushed red velvet dress. Robert bought a new black suit; his old one did not fit him. The more successful Robert became as an accountant, he grew another size in his clothes.

Today, Nancy thought how things change, one day attending a wedding together and now at the solicitor's starting divorce proceedings. She got up and paced around the room, trying to think of something to distract her.

"Mrs Dunfield... Mrs Dunfield, come this way," said a slim man of Indian origin.

Nancy follows him into his office.

The solicitor asked questions, wrote on a large legal pad. His approach was polite yet firm. "Robert might plan to trick you out of what you're owed from the house sale." An alarmed look washed over his face. "I have had experience with men like your husband trying to defraud their ex- wives." The solicitor mentioned things she never imagined—a spouse trying to manipulate the sale of a house for their own benefit. Stealing from the ex-partner in order to spend on the new partner.

"I am glad you are on my side," she said in a small voice.

"Men change when they leave a marriage. It is as though their love for the previous partner never existed," said Mr Patel. "I will ensure your financial security."

∾

After the meeting with the solicitor, Nancy drives home. She moves through each room from the perspective of an outsider. Soon the house is to be sold and belong to someone else. She stares at the high white ceilings. In summer, the warm air rose, it was never hot in the rooms; concentrated on the ornate plasterwork around the lights in the ceiling. Nancy peers out of the bay windows in the lounge and kitchen, the light sparkles through the leadlight glass windows; she traces her fingers over the Edwardian fireplace mantel. The house contains remnants of a past happy life.

Was Robert happy here?

She moves under the timber curvatures in the hall, walks along the hall passage with the wooden floorboards and a colourful rug. Years earlier, Robert and Nancy searched for just the right runner carpet that would enhance the hall. They were ecstatic when they found it. Robert opened a bottle of champagne and toasted the rug — the *perfect rug*.

Not so perfect wife.

She touches the timberwork with symbols of fauna embedded in the wood. Millie's bedroom has its own bathroom and room for two single beds, one for Millie and one for Angie when she stays overnight. She moves to the dining room. Images of past dinner parties for ten people appear, the room filled with laughter, loud talk. She remembers waving the guests goodbye. Robert had his arms around her. They sneaked kisses as they cleared the table, packed the dishwasher, nibbled on leftover pâté and cheese. Went to bed and made eager love in the four-poster bed, woke to the soft glow of morning filtering in through the bedroom windows.

She goes outside, sits in the gazebo. The garden is a riot of colours, pink camellias, white magnolias, and red gardenias. Cacti and succulent flowers blend in with the bulbs. The jacaranda tree's purple buds are in full bloom, the peppercorn tree is green.

I will miss the garden.

Nancy catches sight of Millie's anxious face, peering out of the curtains, returns to the house.

A week later, Nancy drives to the retail hub known as Highpoint. It had been Gloria's suggestion for Nancy to meet with Robert at the Highpoint Shopping Centre in a public area, in case he tried to intimidate Nancy with his anger. Green and orange flashes reflect off the clay-coloured tiles on the floor, square tables with plastic chairs dotted around the eating area. The place was crowded with men and women and crying children. Rows of people with hungry eyes check out the food sections of Indian, Turkish, Japanese, and Lebanese food. Older men eat alone, cutting meat pies with plastic knives and forks. Nancy finds an empty table with two seats in the food hall.

Nancy glares at the entrance.

She glances up at a large man wearing a black leather jacket; he takes giant steps, cradles a black motorcycle helmet with a skull painted on the front under his arm. Nearby mismatched couples move past holding hands, a tall thin woman with a short, fat older man. Two elderly women, each with a walking frame, stand close together and gossip. Groups of teenage girls with long, straight, identical brown hair move together.

She checks the time again.

Half an hour later, Robert arrives, puffing. "Sorry I'm late." He breaks into his familiar boyish grin. He has lost weight, wears a fashionable grey jacket over black pants, it makes him look taller.

"How are you?" He stops smiling when he sees her scowling face.

"Alive," Nancy's voice blank of expression.

"I spoke to Millie earlier," his voice has an upward

tilt, runs his fingers through his hair. "She tells me she is doing well at school. Millie and Angie are still as thick as fleas...."

She goes to speak. He talks over her.

"No, you go first," he opens his hand, a sign for her to continue.

"How could you, Robert?" Her voice is thick with resentment.

"Don't make a scene." He looks around.

She clutches the handbag on her lap. "Have it your way.... I met with my solicitor."

"We agreed on no solicitor. We can work the separation details together as sane adults." He bangs the table with his fist.

"You agreed. I didn't," she said. "The solicitor said we must sell the house, as I cannot keep paying for most of the mortgage on my own." She glares at him. "You are not paying your share."

"I had every intention of sending the money for the repayments. But I have had some extra expenses." He looks away.

"I can't wait for you to decide when you will pay your share of the mortgage or not. The bank will foreclose on the house, and we will get little from the foreclosure sale." She has a burning sensation on her face. Nancy opens her bag, takes out the legal papers.

"The solicitor said I have to have your signature to sell the house." She thrusts the papers at him. "Please sign the forms."

He stares at her for a long time.

"I am to receive 70 percent of the sale, as I still have Millie to care for." She looks hard at his face, willing him to argue.

Two women at the nearby table stop talking, turn their heads, listen.

Robert's face grows dark. "It must be fifty-fifty," he said in a low tone. "I paid most of the mortgage."

"The solicitor said you might say that. Even though you paid most of the mortgage, I kept the home, enabling you to work and cared for our child."

"I will fight you in court," he slaps the table again.

"If you fight me in court, it will reduce the money we both get from the sale." She rummages in her bag for a tissue. His bullying will not work this time. "Let's make a sensible division," she stares squarely in his face. "We will be lucky to receive much between us by the time we pay the debt still owing to the house and... other costs."

He grits his teeth.

"You extended the mortgage for the renovations." Her hands shake, she grabs the edge of the table to steady herself. "I tried to talk you out of the renovations as I worried at the size of the debt if either of us became ill... but you went on with it against my wishes."

"This is so unfair. You're punishing me." Robert cradles his head in his hands.

They sit in silence. Both are afraid to speak in case they expose their vulnerabilities.

He picks up the legal papers, reads them, takes

out his fountain pen, signs his name at the attached stickers, hands the papers back to her.

"One copy is for you," she said.

Nancy puts her copy in her bag. He holds his copy.

"I never meant to hurt you. I still love you and Millie." His face has a lost boy expression.

Nancy shakes her head.

"Can't we be civil to each other?" He said.

"You ripped my life apart. I discovered the man I loved was a lying beast. While I loved you, you loved someone else. Excuse me if I am not civilised. You are a walking cliché; married man leaves wife for a younger woman." Her face blazes, she was losing control, knows the women at the next table were taking in the drama.

"I still love you," he leans forward to touch her hand.

She pulls her hand away, gives a hollow laugh. "If love is leaving me for another woman, having to sell the house, and disrupting our lives, hurting Millie... I don't want that sort of love." She coughs repeatedly.

"Thank you for signing the forms. There will be a formal letter from my solicitor to you next week." She swings the handbag over her shoulder, pushes her hands deep into the jean pockets, turns and runs for the exit, turns to glance towards Robert. He is speaking on his mobile, probably talking to Clarissa.

She finds her car, winds the car window up, pounds on the steering wheel. A wave of anger rises inside of

Nancy, burning, scalding, destroying like a bush fire that explodes in a forest, destroying all in its path.

"I hate you Robert Dunfield. You have ruined my life and Millie's," Nancy shouts in the car.

The woman in the car parked next to Nancy's gives her a strange look, starts her engine, and drives her car to another parking spot away from Nancy.

CHAPTER THIRTY-EIGHT

Tired looking doctors and nurses join visitors in the long queues at the food and beverage section of Nancy's hospital cafe, she is at a table with Gloria. It is a place of noise, clanking trays, coughing, overarching conversations, excited voices and laughter mixed with the aroma of fresh baked rolls. Friendly staff dispense food preferences to anxious patrons. They watch a man in a wheelchair, his intravenous line hanging from a metal pole. The man munches on a doughnut, a half-empty bag of doughnuts on his lap.

"It has been a dreadful day at work today," said Gloria. "Two staff off sick, two student nurses needing mentoring, a code blue in the middle of lunch. A patient transfer as we were working on the patient who had the code blue."

"Did the patient survive?"

"He did, but it was hit and miss for a while. He is in intensive care now," Gloria said.

"My day was similar, was rushed off my feet," said Nancy

Gloria takes a bite from a large berry muffin. "I never liked Robert, especially after he said that crack about Chris being a *just a fruiterer*. Robert is a stupid snob, only values those with money and power."

"I am glad you secured Robert's signature for the sale of the house... If it had been me. I might have hit him with my handbag, screamed nasty abusive words at him in public, created a stir, shamed him." Gloria punches her hand for emphasis. "Honestly, you are too nice."

Nancy camouflages her distress with a grunt.

Gloria's mobile phone rings. "Yes, I will be home soon, and I will sort it out." She hangs up, turns to Nancy. "I should go, World War three at my home. My mother-in-law is having a fit. The kids are having a Fruit Loop fight in the kitchen." She grins, stays seated.

"After he signed the house papers, I knew our marriage was totally done and dusted. Most days, I want to kick him hard," Nancy shows her teeth.

A young boy walks past, holding onto a white balloon with a small string.

"Robert refused to help me organise the furniture for storage. He's still sniffy with me because I wouldn't go fifty-fifty on the sale of the house," she said. "The solicitor your friend recommended has been brilliant. He has had lots of experience with cheating bastards like Robert." She twists her hair into a roll, pushes the hair clip to keep it in place.

Bang! The balloon bursts, the boy with the balloon cries, a woman runs over to comfort him.

"It will be a quick sale at auction. The estate

agent said he has already had several enquiries from potential buyers as soon the house was posted on the internet." Nancy looks at her nails. "By the time we pay out the mortgage and other expenses, there will be little money for either of us," she said.

"It is time to move on," said Gloria.

"Not so easy to do...," said Nancy.

"If you ask me, Robert and Clarissa deserve each other. He's an idiot. She is all phoney gloss. Chris and I were out at a restaurant when Robert and Clarissa were there. Robert was all lovey dovey with her. She seemed bored. I wanted to give both of them a piece of my mind, but Chris held me down."

Once again, Gloria answers a call from her mother-in-law. "Tell Joel and Timothy they will be in trouble when I get home." She brushes the crumbs from her scrubs uniform.

"The day I was in the city seeing the solicitor, Robert and that woman were at the traffic lights, waiting for the green light on the opposite side of the street. He bent down and kissed her on the mouth."

Gloria pats her arm.

"I forgot where I was, and how to escape, leaned against a shop window, the shop owner came out and said, 'Can I help you?' I could not speak. Sputtered that 'I saw my husband kiss another woman.'"

"She took me inside her shop, sat me on a chair."

Nancy covers her face with both hands. "I am drowning, going under for the third time."

Gloria reaches for Nancy's hand, holds it. "For men, it's fantasy sex stuff. They can be pathetic fools."

They watch a young woman wearing the blue cafe uniform remove the crockery from the next table to where they are sitting. She places them on a small trolley and wipes the table.

Nancy digs her nails into her palms. They leave a bright red mark. She closes her eyes; when she opens them, Gloria is staring at her.

"Do you need any muscle to help move your things into storage? I can arrange Chris and his brother for extra help," said Gloria.

"If you could, that would be great," said Nancy. "I've packed the smaller bits and pieces we are taking to the flat. Millie's contribution is to stand in front of me with her arms crossed and say, 'This is ridiculous.' I said to her, whatever you don't pack will go into storage. I have no energy to argue with you."

Gloria holds her phone. "I rang Chris. He will bring his brother to your house on Saturday. Between the four of us, we will finish the packing. Book the storage truck for Saturday."

Gloria stands to go. "I better rescue my mother-in-law from my kids."

"Can I leave some plants with you? The rental flat I'm considering is small, has no garden, only bleak concrete," Nancy said.

"Don't blame me if the plants die. I'm no gardener," said Gloria.

~

The following Saturday, Chris, his brother Tony, Gloria, and Nancy met at the East Brunswick house. They completed the packing just as the storage truck drove up.

Nancy had previously dug out the large monstera and other large plants and potted them into large pots. Gloria and Chris took them to their home for safekeeping until she has a home of her own again.

When they had gone, Nancy moved through the empty rooms of her home, stuffed with the ghosts of their past lives. Her footsteps echoed in the spaces where the furniture had a place, where the family lived.

She turns on the garden hose, gives the plants and trees a good soak, refills the bird feeder with seed. Cuts a twig of rosemary, smells it and places in her jeans pocket.

I hope the new owners will look after the garden.

She sits in the gazebo for the last time. Watches a blackbird run his beak along each of his feathers, he has a deep scratch and flicks his feathers back to shape. After a time, he flies away.

CHAPTER THIRTY-NINE

The East Brunswick house was sold at auction, the mortgage and other outstanding debts paid. The remaining money from the sale of the house was divided between Robert and Nancy. She has placed her share in a locked account to grow for a deposit on a small home in the future.

Nancy and Millie have adjusted to a different lifestyle and are living in a small two-bedroom flat on the first floor of a block of flats that overlooks Sydney Road Coburg. Black sprayed words and graffiti on shop windows and walls have replaced the cultivated gardens of East Brunswick. Sydney Road is a mecca for people from diverse backgrounds: Greek, Italian, Turkish, Egyptian, African. Men wear turbans, women wear head covering scarves and long concealing clothing, tattooed youth travel in groups. Bits of paper and debris float from the footpaths, sail through the air, and drift down the street. Cars are parked on the side streets and in grey concrete basements. The move has been stressful for the pair.

"The flat is temporary until I can accumulate sufficient funds for a house deposit," Nancy said.

Millie is not convinced.

"Coburg is a safe suburb. I checked with the local police," Nancy said. "The rent is affordable, and you and Angie can still go to school together as before. Angie can hop on the tram outside her home and be here in minutes. And another tram will take you both directly to the school... Think of it as an adventure," said Nancy.

~

Nancy calls Gloria. "The flat is green... I kid you not," she said. "It has an old-fashioned enamel green bath. A shower nozzle hangs over the bathtub. The bathroom basin is the same green as are the tiles and there is a green toilet."

"I am coming around to see this, sounds like it should be in a museum," said Gloria. "Does everything work?"

"The plumbing has a bit of a whine when the toilet flushes. The two bedrooms are small, only space for a bed and inbuilt cupboard. There is a modest living room with a rippled glass door as a divider from the kitchen. And a waft of garlic in the kitchen—whoever rented the flat before us enjoyed cooking with garlic. But the flat is spotless."

"Let me know if you need anything," said Gloria.

"I think we will be all right. It will take a little getting used to, but the rent is affordable. Did I mention the kitchen has an old-fashioned gas stove and oven? It takes me back to when I lived in the country. The flat comes with a laminated green and white kitchen table with matching chrome and green chairs. I forgot to mention there are two beds that came with the flat. I bought new mattresses for each of us and a divan for the living room that converts to a bed for the times when Angie stays overnight."

"You are organised," said Gloria.

"The view at the back of the flats is a cardboard factory with noisy trucks driving and reversing. The front of the flats faces Sydney Road, and a tram stop."

"What does Millie think of the flat?" said Gloria.

"She is not impressed. It was a shock to the system. She doesn't like the garlic smell," said Nancy. "I told her to think of the flat as being in an adventure, like visiting a different country. I promised her as soon as I save enough for a deposit for a house, we will move on."

"Good luck with that," said Gloria.

Two days later Gloria, Chris and their three exuberant sons check out the flat for themselves and bring a housewarming gift of a box of fruits, vegetables and yellow daisies. The yellow daisies gleam in the vase on the laminated table. The boys explore the flat, running up and down the corridor, playing hide and seek. They hide under the beds and in cupboards, shrieking with laughter, when Millie finds them. Later they explore

Sydney road, sip thick aromatic Greek coffee and delicious baklava in a local Greek restaurant.

∾

On Saturday morning, Nancy parks her car outside Woolworths supermarket on Louisa Street in Coburg. She has a grim look on her face, hates supermarket shopping at the best of times, dislikes it even more on a Saturday when mothers and fathers rush in packs to the supermarket, frantically buying groceries before taking their children to various sporting activities; she was one of those mothers in the past. Nancy is in the fruit section choosing potatoes when a woman bangs her trolley into Nancy.

"My fault, sorry," said the elegant woman. She has an irritated expression on her face. "Nancy...." the woman calls out, recognising her. "How are you and Robert going?" The woman was the marriage guidance therapist Robert and Nancy had seen previously. Nancy remembers the counsellor had suggested that Nancy had been paranoid to think that Robert may have had a lover and had ignored Nancy's concerns and taken Robert's side.

"Robert left me for the woman he was having an affair with during our marriage," Nancy's face dead pan.

The counsellor's face reddens. "I'm sorry. Robert seemed committed to you."

"He convinced everyone," said Nancy.

~

It is night at the Coburg flat. Nancy's brain bounces from anger to acceptance. The furious momentum that drove the sale of the East Brunswick house and move to the Coburg flat has evaporated. She is now unsure how to proceed—which way to go. Nancy stares out of the window at the night sky. The streetlights illuminate the road below, trams and cars roar past, shadows of people move in the street below. The street occasionally echoes with the voice of a drunk staggering out of the corner hotel.

It feels like I am in a foreign country and have not learned the language.

She checks on Millie, who is sound asleep. Watches the second-hand slip around the old-fashioned wall clock—time measured from one moment to another. Nancy has a peacefulness inside her, a burst of strength. "I can do this," she tells herself. "It is not so hard. People move all the time." But knows she is in uncharted waters.

CHAPTER FORTY

Each afternoon after school, Millie and Angie go home together. Angie walks with Millie to the front of the Coburg flats. Angie then catches another tram home. Some days, Angie's mother drives them. Millie does not use the elevator in case there is a strange man in the lift. Instead, she runs up the one flight of stairs, two steps at a time. She locks the flat door as soon as she gets in and secures the safety chain on the door, then leans against the door.

"Made it," she said.

Her sense of safety is paramount, is always alert for anything that might imply danger. Is super vigilant, perceives the newness of the area as a hostile place. Millie hates surprises, has to know what is happening ahead of time. She sits on her bed, swings her legs back and forth. The bed differs from her old bed, the new mattress is hard and uncomfortable, her old mattress had just the right amount of sag. Her old bed from the Brunswick house was too wide to fit through the door of the flat. All their furniture is in storage. She wonders if she will ever see her comfortable old bed again.

Millie warms up a piece of homemade apple pie in the microwave, scoops two big measures of ice cream on top. Takes the dish to the living room, turns on the television.

Did I lock the door?

She goes back to the door and checks the lock. Listens to the noises from the other flats. A television murmurs next door; somewhere, a door slams, the sound of footsteps in the hall.

The doorbell rings, it startles Millie.

Who is at the door?

She shudders, her face breaks out in a sweat.

The doorbell rings again.

Millie stands immobile. Her phone rings.

"It is mum, please open the door. My hands are full, and I can't reach my keys," said Nancy.

Relief slides over Millie. She unlocks the door to Nancy, who stands at the doorway holding two shopping bags. Millie takes a shopping bag from her mother. "Sorry, I didn't know it was you," she said in a small voice.

Nancy sees Millie's pale face and wide eyes. "I should have called you before I came to our door," she holds her daughter tight. "It will get better, I promise you."

Nancy places the bananas, peaches and potatoes and the cooked chicken on the table. She knows the move to the flat and unfamiliar neighbourhood has been traumatic for Millie. She can't afford to be angry at Robert because it could harm her daughter's delicate emotional state. Millie's moods are still up and down.

There are many advantages to living in the Coburg area. Nancy and Millie have explored the restaurants up and down Sydney road. Turkish food is their favourite, especially donor kebab, and they enjoy Meze salads, roasted vegetables and skewers of meat. The Savers charity shop is like a cave of treasures, cheap and exotic, and is a favourite with them both.

Millie has periodic repetitive nightmares of being chased and dragged into bushes. She sits up, switches on the bedside light, gets out of bed, checks the room, her heart pounding. Once she is assured she is safe, goes back to bed with the light on. Now and then, the nightmares terrify her, and she slips into her mother's bed. But this does not happen as often.

Alice continues working with Millie to gain control of her fears.

CHAPTER FORTY-ONE

A beggar sits on flattened cardboard in the street, squats on the footpath near Clarissa's Northcote apartment. The man wears a ragged, dirty t-shirt and pants. He holds a brown cardboard sign with scribbled words stating his homeless state. A bored dog of an unknown breed sits on the stained blanket at the man's naked feet.

"Have you any spare coins?" said the destitute man.

Robert usually ignores the beggars. But today rummages through his pockets, places three gold coins in the man's hat. Walks away, returns, pulls out his wallet, drops a $20 note into the man's hat.

The beggar grabs the money, stuffs it in his pants pocket, leaving the gold coins in the hat. "Bless you," he said.

Robert presses the lift button to Clarissa's apartment, dings the doorbell. As soon as the door opens, he pushes a large box of chocolates in Clarissa's hands. "Hello, darling," he says as he kisses her passionately.

～

Last Sunday, Robert organised a picnic for the two of them at the Botanical Gardens. It had been a brilliant sunny day; a slight breeze played with Clarissa's hair. She wore a tight sleeveless red dress that highlighted her curves. He carried the picnic basket and rug to a sunny spot near the lake. Spread the black and red checked rug on the lush grass. They drank champagne from plastic cups, ate the small savoury tarts that Robert had bought from the continental baker. They lay on the rug and spoke of their future.

"I want to travel to USA and visit Hollywood," she said.

"My choice is the Grand Canyon," he said.

"Let's make a plan to go to America next year," she said.

He thinks of the cost. Robert hands Clarissa a card decorated with corny hearts and flowers. Inside, there is a love note that reveals his love and joy to be with her.

"How sweet," said Clarissa, peeked inside the envelope.

He chastised himself; he should have added a gift.

They returned home in the evening, slept together, and woke up to eat at a nearby Indian restaurant.

I am a lucky man.

He misses Millie and has pangs of guilt leaving her. Tells himself she has to accept that he has a life as well.

CHAPTER FORTY-TWO

Nancy shivers as she drags the faded cotton curtain across the window of the Coburg flat. The old gas wall heater rattles and makes strange noises, it sounds like a jet engine but does not give off much heat.

Millie is in her room, attempting to finish her assignment on *The World Health Organisation.* She opens her textbook, takes notes, Googles the internet for further information. Googles for a pair of red zipped boots, finds they are available locally, plans to buy them, will use her birthday money from Maxine. She is easily distracted. Alice has taught her strategies to stay focussed, but it is difficult.

"I don't have any energy to cook tonight," said Nancy. She had once been known for her elegant dinner parties, spending hours preparing the best cuts of meat and vegetables and delicious sweets. In those days, being married to Robert meant enjoying an extensive food budget. Now it is different. Meals are based on what is in the fridge.

"What to make that is quick and easy?" She rummages through the almost empty fridge—six eggs, a small lump of cheese, half a loaf of wholemeal bread, and a carton of milk. Opens the pantry cupboard - two tins of tomatoes and dried pasta. "My pay is not until the end of the week. This will have to do." She opens the packet of pasta, throws it into the boiling water to cook, heats the tomato, grates the cheese.

"Dinner," she shouts down the hall.

Millie pulls her seat to the table. "Pasta again," she pulls a face.

Nancy's face reddens. "When my pay comes in, we can lash out at the supermarket."

"It smells nice," said Millie. She finishes the pasta, reaches for the lone banana in the fruit bowl.

"How was work?"

"A day filled with chaos and madness," Nancy said. "The patients and their relatives have become demanding these days. No one wants to wait; they want attention immediately. And if they don't get seen quickly, they take it out on the staff. We had another code grey today, potential violence. A patient's son threatened the treating doctor. Luckily, the doctor ducked as the man swung a fist at him. Code grey is called most days." She places her fork on the table. "The best part of the day is coming home and seeing you."

Millie grins.

"What about your day?" said Nancy.

"We had a new maths teacher, cute, just out of Uni. Angie said he was a hunk and kept sneaking looks at him. She could not concentrate on her maths. He asked her a question. But she had zoned out and did not know what he said. I whispered to her what he said. And gave her the answer."

Millie touches her nose- an auspicious sign.

Nancy noticed the gesture. It has been a long time since Millie has touched her nose when happy.

They clear the table and place the plates and cutlery in the hot soapy water in the sink. They work as a team these days, sharing the household tasks, pulling together in the same direction. Nancy leaves the dishes to dry on the drainer.

Millie returns to her bedroom and the internet.

Later in the evening, Nancy is at the kitchen table, surrounded by bank statements to her left. There is a pad on her right with a handwritten list of the due bills: rent, food, electricity, gas, school expenses, fuel, insurance, credit card, psychologist's fee. One column for her fortnightly pay and the money that Robert provides for Millie. She adds them up again. The outgoing expenses are more than the money coming in. Nancy has been managing the imbalance by paying the most important bills with her credit card. She can only pay the minimum payment on the credit card each month and is slipping further into debt. She remembers the empty printer cartridge she took to Cartridge World to be refilled.

"Ready for you on Monday," the Cartridge woman said.

Nancy adds *the printer cartridge* to the list of bills to be paid.

There is always one more thing.

For the first time in her life, she is overdrawn at the bank and her credit card has almost reached its limit.

I could work an extra shift at a nursing agency on my days off.

But is worried if she does the extra shift, it might have a negative effect on Millie and her mental state, which swings from good to fear and anxiety. Nancy jumps when the gas heater makes another *whoomph* sound.

When Robert lived with them, their joint wages were enough for an indulgent life. Robert managed the money, and he paid the bills. "Perhaps I should use some of the money that is locked away for a future home deposit," she shakes her head. "Now I am talking to myself," she said aloud.

A tram outside is dinging, with each ding growing louder and more impatient. Nancy pulls back the curtains. Two men push a car that has broken down on the tram tracks. Eventually, they push it to the side of the road and the tram passes. The street is well lit. She sniffs Indian food from the flat above, footsteps running up the stairs.

She knocks on Millie's bedroom door. "How's the homework going?"

"I will do it after I finish talking to Angie."

Nancy drags herself into the shower, sighs with relief when she slips into bed. Despite her weariness, sleep does not come, lies awake, going over the details of the day.

Earlier, she had rung Robert, "Can you please increase the parent's allowance for Millie?"

"I can't do that. I have too many expenses myself," Robert said.

She turns on the lamp, pulls out the book she bought for $2 from the charity shop—Cormac McCarthy's *The Road*. It is a bleak dystopian novel. Stares at the pages but cannot absorb the words on the page. She places the book on the floor. Night-time is the worst time for her, has not been sleeping well, limps to work flush with caffeine. It is easy to keep busy during the day. However, at night, the demons of self-doubt and anxiety dance in her mind. Robert's leaving has triggered a lack of confidence, something that had been dormant, the orphan girl brought up by aunts. Her outer guard ripped off, she is exposed, is again the vulnerable motherless child.

I wish my mother was alive to advise me what to do.

She is ashamed to ask for medical help for her growing depression, tries to hide it. Does not want to take antidepressants, she must stay alert for Millie's sake. Has read the article that Alice gave Millie, is writing in an old exercise book but is no better.

CHAPTER FORTY-THREE

At four-thirty on a warm afternoon, Tessa, Angie's mother, parks her black Audi in the No Standing area in Sydney Road in front of Millie's flat.

Millie grabs her backpack and jumps out of the car onto the pavement. "Goodbye, thanks for giving me a ride."

"See you tomorrow," said Angie, waves goodbye.

The car zooms off.

Millie scans the entrance to the flats, glances up and down the street. There are the usual trams, cars, Sydney Road people, no lurking strangers. A woman pushes a yelling baby in a pram on the footpath. Two elderly women pass in the opposite direction. One wears a black headscarf, the other has no headscarf, her short, grey hair is on display. Millie opens the front entrance of the flats and sprints up the flight of stairs to the first floor. She holds the door key in her hand, quickly unlocks the door, slams the door behind her. Leans against the door, sighs in relief.

She jumps when she hears a curtain flapping in an open window in the kitchen, closes the window with a bang. Drags the backpack to her bedroom, empties the bag onto the bed, searches for the half-eaten sandwich in her lunchbox, eats it. Connects the school laptop into the house charging plug. The room is much smaller than her previous bedroom at East Brunswick. This room has only space for a bed, a small table and a cupboard for clothes. Under the bed are schoolbooks and shoes. The small table next to her bed has a smiling picture of Millie and her father taken outside the East Brunswick house years ago. Tacked on her wall with blue tack are posters of her favourite bands. There is a large green stuffed Kermit the frog; he has pride of place on the black and red rug, which covers the doona on her bed. Millie takes her school blazer off, throws it on the bed, takes off her shoes and socks, pads into the kitchen. Opens the fridge, takes the last slice of homemade lasagne, heats it in the microwave. Leans back in the chair, hands clasped behind her head. The microwave makes a beeping sound. She notices a message propped against a vase of yellow freesias on the kitchen table.

I should be home by 6:00 p.m. love mum xx.

Millie checks her phone, scrolls through Snapchat, Tic Tök, YouTube. Spots a pigeon walking back and forth on the windowsill outside the window, gets up to have a closer look. The bird sees her and flies away. She peers at the road below. Trams thunder past, their bells ringing to warn pedestrians and cars. Across the street, a group of schoolchildren wait for a bus.

Her mobile phone rings, "hi, dad." Millie breaks into a smile at his voice. "How's it going?"

"Good, life is great." He has a lightness to his voice.

"Can I spend Christmas with you and Clarissa?"

He seems surprised by the question. "Mmm," he said. "We ... plan... to have Christmas with Clarissa's family."

"I could come too," she twists a lock of her dark hair.

"Princess, it's not a suitable time now."

"You could have Christmas with mum and me," her voice grows louder.

Robert clears his throat. "That won't work either."

"It's not fair. I want to spend Christmas with you," her voice is a shout.

He can hear her distress. "Look," he said. "You will see me on Christmas Eve when I bring your presents."

"I don't want presents. I want to spend Christmas with you." She hangs up the phone.

Millie holds her head in her arms, trying not to cry.

The door unlocks. Nancy is home. She sees Millie's downcast face.

"Dad doesn't want to spend Christmas with me," said Millie.

Nancy wraps her arms around Millie, holds her for a long time. "Robert's life is complex just now. Give him time."

She loathes the shared parenting. Yesterday, in frustration, Nancy smashed two plates, threw them to the floor; pieces splintered and rolled into corners of the kitchen.

Millie had called out, "Psycho" from her bedroom. She had to vacuum the tiny pieces. There were three minor marks on the floor where she broke the plates. She hopes they will not lose the bond money over it.

∼

Last Wednesday at Alice's office, Alice and Millie had agreed to start on Prolonged Exposure therapy. One step involves discussing Millie's assault several times to reduce the assault's emotional impact. Alice tapes these sessions, encourages Millie to listen to the tapes at home, which Millie does. She is determined to overcome PTSD. Is diligent in attending the support group with the other girls. Writes her journal as instructed by Alice.

I cried today. Dad prefers to spend Christmas with Clarissa and her family than mum and me.

∼

Nancy and Gloria walk next to the Maribyrnong river, close to Gloria's home. The path by the river is crowded with joggers, brisk walkers, mothers with prams.

"I struggle with my insecurity. My emotions echo Millie's moods. If Millie is happy, I am happy."

"Are you writing as Alice suggested?" Said Gloria.

"I have a notebook for the purpose."

Last night she wrote, *I am powerless to stop my daughter's pain. When Millie cries, it reinforces what a failure I am as a parent.*

"I am dreading Christmas. It will be the first Christmas without Robert," Nancy said. She moved off the path to let two joggers run past.

"Millie asked Robert if she could spend Christmas Day with him and Clarissa, but he refused."

Gloria shakes her head. "I cannot understand Robert."

They both move to one side of the path, this time to allow three cyclists to zoom past.

Nancy said, "My Christmas will be quiet, a simple luncheon at the flat with Millie and Aunt Stella." She cocks her ear to a magpie singing. "I could invite Maxine, but I know she's going to a friend's gala event. Can you imagine Maxine sitting on the chrome chairs at the green flat?"

"I would swap your quiet Christmas for the chaos at my home on Christmas Day. The kids running riot, my mother-in-law clapping her hands, trying to get us to play some silly game, the bickering in the background. Chris guarding the barbecue, not allowing anyone to infringe on his domain. Just to think of Christmas day makes me exhausted." She turns to Nancy. "Why don't you join us in the bedlam?"

"Thanks for the offer, but we will be fine," said Nancy.

∼

Yesterday, while Nancy and Millie were having dinner

at the flat, Millie expressed her desire to be friends with Clarissa. "If dad likes her, I will too."

Nancy's mouth became taut. She could not believe her daughter wants to befriend the person who destroyed her marriage. "Ask your father," Nancy said through clenched teeth.

Millie rang Robert. "Dad, I want to be friends with Clarissa."

The silence was long and uncomfortable. "Maybe later," his words, controlled.

He intends to keep the two sections of his life separate.

~

Millie was in the kitchen packing her backpack for school. "Are you doing anything special on your day off today?"

"It is my catch-up day. I will take the washing to the laundromat, do the food shopping, pay some bills," said Nancy.

"Why don't you buy a treat for yourself," Millie said.

"I might," said Nancy.

After she finished her errands, Nancy goes into the Flame dress shop, notices a rack of simple dresses reduced by fifty percent. Takes a blue shift dress from the rack. Pulls off her old jeans and black T-shirt, tries the dress on. It fits perfectly.

It would look great with my black jacket. But Christmas is coming. I should think of Christmas gifts.

She replaces the dress on the rack.

~

Nancy catches the tram to Bourke Street Mall. The city is crowded with desperate shoppers rushing in and out of nearby shops, men and women lugging parcels. Loud hailers play Christmas carols and entice shoppers to special buys. Young children excitedly wait in line outside the department store to see the decorated Myer window displays. There is a Disneyland theme this year with Mickey and Minnie Mouse, Donald Duck and Goofy characters moving in circles and ablaze with lights and music. Children stand transfixed against the windows.

Nancy sees her friend Janey walking towards her. Janey has her arm around her latest boyfriend. She looks luminous, long black hair cascading over her shoulders, wears a bright blue dress, woodsy perfume forms an arc around her body.

"Meet Charlie," Janey puts her hands out as a contestant in a television show.

"Nice to meet you," Charlie said, shaking Nancy's hand.

He is a dark-haired Italian man with a thick black moustache. He reminds Nancy of an actor whose name she forgot.

"We should make a foursome for dinner with you and Robert," said Janey.

Nancy shakes her head.

"Oh, sorry, I forgot." A blush rises on Janey's face.

Nancy makes a slight grin to show she does not care.

The world revolves around pairs; it makes sense unless you are single. Nancy thinks she should join a Singles group. What if the men are weird and potential rapists? What if the women are young and glamorous? How could she compete?

~

That night Gloria rang Nancy to persuade her to join her book club meeting. "The group meets once a month at the Pizza and Spaghetti restaurant on Lygon Street Carlton. It's a friendly club and will be good for you to get out," she bats off Nancy's objections. "I will pick you up at seven, and even if you hate it, the Italian food is first class."

"I am not ready to socialise."

"No excuses, it's time to move on," said Gloria. "I know you have read the book for discussion."

The book club meeting is a noisy affair. Twenty people sit around a large table in an Italian restaurant. The group consists of older professional men and women. They discuss Hilary Mantel's *The Mirror and the Light*. Nancy has read the three books in the trilogy related to the Tudor times and Thomas Cromwell and King Henry.

When it was her turn to speak, Nancy said, "I found the book absorbing as a reflection of the psychology of

Thomas Cromwell. The power struggles between the characters could apply to issues of today."

Gloria smiles encouragement.

After the meeting, the group enjoys creamy pasta and baskets of garlic bread washed down with red wine. A divorced man sits next to Nancy. He refills her wine glass, pulls her into the conversation. He tells her he is a dentist and asks if they can meet again.

"I'm still sorting myself after a separation," said Nancy.

"I guarantee you will date within the year." He has deep brown eyes and a similar stocky build as Robert. He prints his name and phone number in large letters on a paper serviette and hands it to her.

"Ring me when you are ready. I hope to see you at the next book club meeting." He pats her hand. "We're discussing Gabor Mate's book, *In the Realm of Hungry Ghosts.*"

"I loved that book," Nancy said.

"We have similar tastes."

On the drive home, Gloria relays gossip about the members. "George, the chap you were talking to has a reputation as a ladies' man, flits from woman to woman, breaks lots of hearts."

Nancy stares straight ahead.

Later, when she is back at the green flat, she screws George's serviette in a ball, throws it in the bin.

Once to have your heart broken is too much. Twice is just careless.

CHAPTER FORTY-FOUR

It's morning at the green flat. Millie is on the move. The kitchen door opens, slams shut. Cupboards open and bang, light switches click on and off. The fridge door opens and shuts, a chair scrapes on the floor. The TV is turned on, followed by muffled voices and music.

"Where's my backpack?" Millie sounds annoyed, as though someone had stolen it overnight.

"Look under your bed," said Nancy. "You often leave it there."

"Found it," Millie said. It's as if she is welcoming an old friend.

Eventually Millie is ready. "Bye mum, Angie is at the door. Can you pick me up after school? I need to go to the library to finish my family history project." Millie swings her backpack to her shoulders.

"Love you, take care," said Nancy, kiss goodbye.

"Bye mum," Millie is upbeat, cheerful.

Nancy exhales. She sinks into the still warm bed, has a pile of notes spread over the bedcovers, is reviewing the notes from the last lecture at the university. It seems a long time ago. Has a large pad where she scribbles notes of things to do.

~

Millie and Angie exit the crowded tram onto Sydney Road after school. Millie eyes a man sitting on a bench who resembles her assailant. "It's him." Millie said, pointing to the bent scruffy man on the opposite side of the road.

Angie puts her arm on Millie's shoulder. "It's not him; someone who looks a little like him." She has become accustomed to Millie's outbursts. By the time they arrive at the flats, panic has overwhelmed Millie.

She races up the stairs, opens the door, bangs the door to her bedroom so hard that the windows rattle.

"What is it, Millie? Let me help." Nancy said.

"Go away, leave me alone," Millie's distress reverberates behind the closed door.

Nancy feels helpless, her own panic rising, develops a tightness at the back of her throat.

She phones Gloria, "I can't do it anymore." Her head falls forward, heart hammers in her chest. Her daughter is hurting, and she cannot help.

Twenty minutes later, Gloria arrives. "We are going to Williamstown Beach, ice cream and the beach now," she said. "No arguments allowed."

Gloria and Nancy share a large rock at the edge of the sea as they lick their ice creams. They watch the tide come in; small boats bob on the horizon. Seaweed is tossed onto rocks, creating a green slime. The seagulls are watching, hopeful for food scraps. The ocean roars as it rolls to the shore.

"Millie doesn't mean the words she says. You need to pretend to function as though you are confident. Don't let her see you crack, or she will crack too." Gloria licks the dripping ice cream off the cone edge. She turns to face Nancy. "Show some spirit. If you have a breakdown, I will inherit Millie and—God forbid—Maxine and Robert by default."

Nancy looks out to the sea. "The bank manager rang. He refused to extend my overdraft. I must take out a bank loan. He treated me like an idiot, gave me a lecture about remembering to have the repayment money in my account so they can deduct it each month." She screws her face. "His damn condescending attitude made me furious, bad enough not having money without treating me with contempt. I wanted to snap back at him, but I bit my tongue." She ran her fingers through the sand. "Anyway, the loan is good. I can pay some of the school expenses and the car insurance... the other bills will have to wait until the next payday."

"It's tough," said Gloria, cleaning her glasses with a tissue where chocolate ice cream had smeared. "Money issues are the hardest. We struggle financially and there are two of us working. It must be harder for you," said Gloria.

"Millie grumbles, as we must cut back on spending. That's the problem with sending a child to a private school. She mixes with rich kids and thinks I am mean when she can't have what her friends have," said Nancy.

"What if you took Millie out of the private school

and enrolled her in a local government secondary college?" said Gloria.

"I am afraid the profound change in school and friendships might be detrimental to Millie's mental health. Hard enough now, changing schools might make things worse."

"Have you asked Robert for help?" Gloria said.

"I have pleaded with him.... I asked him to pay an instalment on Millie's orthodontist costs. Robert sent a cheque, and it bounced."

Gloria groans.

"The orthodontist rang apologetically. I promised to pay her next pay. I rang Robert. 'What's going on? Your cheque bounced. How could you do this to me, to your daughter?'"

'I don't know what you are talking about,' Robert pretended innocence."

"Each week, I make a list of the most pressing bills. My pay does not cover the costs. Robert's contribution is a bounced cheque."

"What a monstrous creature... I can lend you some money if things are desperate."

"No, I need your friendship. I would hate to avoid you if I couldn't pay you back." She looks out at the sea. "Robert used to do all the finances, but I am learning fast."

"Promise me, no nervous breakdowns on my watch. Stop caring so much, wanting to make everything nice for Millie. It is not possible. Life is a pain. And you must accept it. Sometimes not so bad."

Gloria throws a pebble into the sea. "Grab what you can that makes you happy, turn your head from the rest. Millie has to build up her resilience, learn to deal with the crap in life." She shoves her bare toes into the warm sand. "Millie is dumping on you because she's secure in your love. You must set boundaries. Don't take the rudeness." She picks up a handful of sand, watches it flow from her fingers. "When the tide goes out, the sand is clean. Be as the sea, let it ebb away," Gloria said. "I should write a book about sea metaphors. One of those new age books," she laughs.

Later that evening, Nancy hears the cars roaring near the cardboard factory. She is aware of the coming and goings of the different shifts at the drab factory. The morning shift starts at 7:00 a.m., the next 3:00 p.m., and the night shift starts at 11:00 p.m., similar to nursing shifts. She watches the cars come into the factory grounds as others glide away. They are an alarm clock, of sorts. She ponders what kind of cardboard containers they make. If people need the money, they will work at any mind-numbing job.

She peers at the old house nearby from her window; it has dry unkept lawn. Often, she has walked by the dilapidated house with knee-high dry grass in the front, scattered old newspapers, lowered canvas blinds. She has seen a glow inside. Someone lives there. The backyard is sparse, nothing except four big black plastic bags of rubbish which have split open revealing: old newspapers, empty tins, take-away food containers, and old clothes.

She has seen noone coming or going from the house. Perhaps an old man or woman lives there, too frail to leave the home. She wants to knock on the door and make a welcome noise.

I must stop being a country girl with country hospitality. The occupant may be involved in something illegal, a meth lab or a home for criminals.

Outside, a bitter, howling wind begins. It blows at the eaves, creating women with demented hair and messy skirts—the wind whooshes obscenities through cracks in windows and doors. The rain smashes on the window, cars drive through tidal waves on the roads. There is little heating in the flat, the gas heater is unreliable. Nancy wears a thick jumper and her puffer jacket. Tonight, Millie is staying at Angie's. They are working on something for Christmas. Angie has been a tolerant friend, accepting Millie's dark mood swings and periods of wanting to be alone.

I miss the old garden. I wonder how the blue wrens are going.

Robert had rung earlier, wanting to speak to Millie. Once again, Nancy sought his financial help with the increasing bills.

He told Nancy to improve her budgeting.

CHAPTER FORTY-FIVE

Outside the Coburg flat, there is the usual noise of Sydney road traffic with honking cars and clanking trams.

"I am different from you. If people don't like me, that's their bad luck." Gloria throws her arms up in the air to make a point, knocks the plate of oatmeal biscuits to the floor of the green flat. She bends to retrieve the biscuits. "Personally, I don't waste my time on people who aren't good for me. My perspective is that we are born alone and will die by ourselves in the end. My priority is for me." Gloria said. "Of course, Chris and the kids are high on my list." She dunks her biscuit in her drink.

"I hated that my marriage ended," Nancy said. "I thought having a husband and family would compensate for not having a mother or father. That might sound silly." She picks up another biscuit. "I want what you and Chris have... a love that is deep."

Gloria snorts, "You see what you want to see. It is an illusion, dear friend. Chris and I argue a lot about the kids, his mother, what to eat."

"But you respect each other. Your love for Chris shows by action and deed," Nancy said. "All my life, I worked hard to improve myself. I could have had ten degrees, been born beautiful and still would not have been acceptable to Robert." She makes a sad face.

"You married a fool. Next time it will be different," said Gloria.

"Never. I will never get close to another man."

Gloria raises her eyebrows. "Let's see what the future holds. To change the topic, your geranium cuttings are doing well," Gloria points to the trim pots on the kitchen windowsill, eight small pots of red and pink geraniums. "I almost forgot. We're having a small party for Chris's mother on Saturday. Why don't you and Millie join us?"

"It sounds tempting, but I should work on my thesis. My supervisor is angry at me, as I have not completed the analysis," said Nancy.

Gloria and Nancy's friendship has survived through good and troubled times. During Gloria's third pregnancy, the doctor ordered total bed rest for Gloria, in danger of a miscarriage and losing her baby. Nancy would arrive at Gloria's house in the morning, after dropping Millie off at school. Chris and Nancy became a relay team. Chris would leave for the fruit shop. Nancy stayed with Gloria, and her boys, Timothy and Joel, who called Nancy 'Mummy two.' When Chris came home from work, Nancy returned to her own home. On the days Nancy worked at the hospital, Chris's mother cared for Gloria and the boys. Gloria had a complex birth, requiring an emergency caesarean. The third baby, another boy, Alexander, was born a healthy baby.

Robert made known his displeasure with Nancy for spending so much time at Gloria's house, cooking, cleaning and looking after the two boys.

∾

Later in the day at the Coburg flat Toni Childs's *Don't walk away* is playing in the background. Nancy wraps a towel around her wet hair.

Robert rings, "I've found some money for Millie's dental work."

"When can I expect the money?" Nancy looks at her short nails.

When was the last time I wore nail polish?

"By the end of the week," he said. "I'm sorry for the delay...I... I have had unexpected expenses," he does not explain.

She does not ask.

Will the money arrive as promised?

∾

Tuesday, the Coburg flat, Nancy wears a white shirt and black trousers and jacket- her academic clothes, she calls them. The red curly hair hangs over her shoulders. She had requested the day off from work to attend a workshop at her university on how to use the latest computer packages for the data analysis of Grounded Theory. She is currently working on the thesis part of her master's course, has already passed the core subjects with High Distinction, and has completed the interviews of the caregivers and their experiences in the emergency department. Some of the carers' comments have resonated with her own experience when Millie was a patient.

The Grounded Theory Workshop takes place at the leafy green university in Carlton. Twenty students sit at individual computer terminals, following the instructions on coding and developing a credible Grounded theory. The workshop instructor, a male academic, shares his experiences of using this research method. Nancy takes copious notes, is inspired to use this method of analysis for her interview data. At the end of the workshop, each student is given a software package to practice at home.

Nancy walks to the university library and borrows three books on grounded theory coding. She sits on a wooden bench outside the library, breathing in the peaceful atmosphere of the trees and green plants, is nostalgic about her old garden, wonders how the blue wrens are going.

One day I will have my garden again.

≈

Back at the green flat, she hangs ten large sheets of butcher's paper, blue-tacked to the wall in the corridor. She rereads her interview notes over and over, writes any emerging codes or categories, scribbles them on the butcher's paper. Steps back, compares the notes. She moves from chart to chart, sometimes on her knees, writing on a lower sheet, other times on a step stool scribbling on the top page. Pulls back, reading, thinking, engrossed, giving birth to something unique. This is something she has never done before. Her study investigated the lived experiences and perceptions of mothers waiting in the emergency department with an injured child. The mother's comments included *victimisation, mothers being excluded from decision-making processes by the medical staff, feelings of powerlessness, fear, and hunger.* Nancy thought hunger had been a strange comment as volunteers provide food and drink and there was the hospital cafe nearby. However, the mothers said they did not want to eat in front of their children, who were fasting for procedures. They were reluctant to leave the wounded children even for a few minutes for a meal at the cafe.

"You look funny climbing up and down," Millie said when she returned from school. She crunched on an apple, head to one side. But read the coding words with interest.

Nancy worked on the analysis over the weekend, going over and over the transcripts until the coding came out right.

~

A week later, Nancy arrives at the university again for her scheduled appointment with her thesis supervisor, Professor Lancaster. His office is orderly, four colour coded manila folders stacked neatly on his desk. The books on his bookshelf are alphabetically sorted. His cup sits on a coaster with the university logo. The Professor is a short, older man, grey hair slicked back, wears a brown corduroy jacket and a black shirt and trousers. He has a critical attitude towards the nursing students in his research subjects but tolerates them as they bring funding for the university. He peers over his glasses at Nancy, who is wearing her academic black suit and white shirt for confidence.

"I am sorry for the delay in bringing these.... I ...life has been complex," Nancy said. She hands him her work, bites her lip as he scrutinises the coding on the butcher papers unfurled on his desk.

After what seemed like forever, he looks up at Nancy, as if he's seeing her for the first time.

"You have fresh ideas here." Professor Lancaster pushes his glasses back on his face. "Nancy, splendid work. You could extend this into a PhD at a later time." He rolled the papers and handed them back to her. "Now is the hard part. Write down your ideas and formulate a theory."

"My goodness, thank you." Nancy blushes, luxuriates in the comment, is shocked by the sheer unexpectedness of his positive remarks. She replays his words in her mind.

Splendid work; could expand to a PhD.

"Keep working. You are on the right track. I want to see your grounded theory fully developed when I see you next week," he said.

She closes the door and does a little dance outside his office.

When she returns to the flat, rings Gloria and shares the news.

"Well done," Gloria said. "It looks like I will have to buy a new outfit for your graduation."

I have to finish this degree. It will enable me to have a better-paying position and a better future for Millie and me.

CHAPTER FORTY-SIX

"I want to stay at the Casino complex this weekend," Clarissa said. They are eating meatballs and spaghetti with spicy tomato sauce at the local Northcote Italian restaurant. "You owe me, as you are staying rent free in my apartment," she said, the look on her face accusatory.

Her comment came as a thunderbolt to Robert.

I am paying for all the expenses, food, electricity, gas. I never see Clarissa paying the rent. Not even sure what the rent is or who is the estate agent.

"Now is not the right time to splurge on an expensive hotel," he said. "Do you know how much a room costs at the casino tower?"

Clarissa has a bored face.

"I believe the rooms start at $450 a night," he said. "It is not a suitable time to splurge. I have Millie's orthodontic bills to pay, child support, and other bills." He sounds nervous, looks around as though he half expecting Nancy to be nearby and could hear him.

Clarissa ignores his words. "Don't be stingy. Let's stay at the casino this weekend." She presses up close to him and kisses him on the lips.

"Next month would be better," he said.

She caresses his face and head. "This weekend would suit me better."

"All right," he said. His voice carried a note of resignation, he has difficulty in denying Clarissa when she turns on the charm. She changes moods in seconds. He does not recognise her when she lets down her guard; the sweet, girlish Clarissa underneath is pure steel. One moment loving, the next demanding and determined, used to having her own way. Another thing he has learned is the amount of money Clarissa spends on herself, makeup, beauty products, gym membership. Her lush blonde hair requires an extensive cash flow to hairdresser for colour touch-ups. She has to have weekly massages, nails to be done, clothes, always clothes and spa retreats.

∾

Robert booked a suite at the Crown Towers in the heart of Southbank, close to the Casino Entertainment Complex. Their suite had a panoramic view of the city centre, the room luxurious with gold silk curtains, antique furniture, and plush carpet. The bathroom had a deep bath with ornate trimmings. The outsized bed was outfitted with a pure-white thick doona and six pillows.

"This is my kind of world." Clarissa throws herself on the massive double bed.

They decide to explore Southbank and walk along the Yarra River. The Crown Casino and Entertainment complex has eight gas towers that shoot spheres of fire in the air at hourly intervals in the evening. The swish of the Casino flares lights up the sky and illuminates the passing traffic of people. They enter the gambling section of the casino, watch serious gamblers play blackjack and roulette. The electronic gaming machine area is a dark windowless cavern, the bright coloured lights of the machines create a mystical glow. Mainly older men and women sit as if hypnotised in front of the machines, endlessly pressing buttons on the machines. Few converse with their neighbours, as they are too intent on the spinning reels and promise of a jackpot. Or hope for a chance to break even with a win that matches their losses.

Clarissa puts $50 into an electronic gaming machine, pushes buttons, as if on cue, her machine bursts into music. "I have won $800," she claps her hands, presses the 'collect' button. A card shoots out with the amount she has won. She joins the queue at the machine that converts the card to cash, collects the money, folds it securely into her purse.

An angry woman with grey, stringy hair walks up to Clarissa. "I played on that machine for an hour and a half and lost $500. You came along and won my money. That is not fair," she said.

"That's luck for you," Clarissa said.

The woman glares at Clarissa. "The $500 was my pension money and now it is gone. How am I going to eat?"

Clarissa ignores the woman, grabs Robert's arm

and drags him away. "I'm tired of the gambling venue. Let's check the designer dress shops. You can choose something nice for me."

Robert knows *the something nice* would be expensive.

The designer boutiques are name brands, elegant, classy. The merchandise does not have price tags. Clarissa talks to a reed thin silver haired woman dressed in black and wears a gold name badge which stated her name is *Josephine*.

"I want a formal dress similar to what Julia Roberts wore in the movie Pretty Woman," said Clarissa.

The shop assistant bows, disappears behind a curtain and brings three elegant gowns in assorted colours over her arm.

Clarissa's eyes shine. She caresses the fabric of the deep purple velvet dress. "I must try this on." She disappears into the red wallpapered change rooms.

Robert cools his heels on the sumptuous blue settee of the designer shop, surrounded by two other men who tap their feet nervously.

Minutes later, Clarissa reappears wearing the purple dress. "What do you think?" she said. "Do I look like a blonde Julia Roberts?"

"Better than her," he said and gave a wolf whistle.

Clarissa repeats the dress presentation with the two other dresses. Finally, she chooses a tight fitting long green velvet dress with cleavage that enhances her breasts.

Robert grits his teeth when he sees the price for the

dress, he pays with his credit card. Clarissa demands green satin high-heeled shoes to match the dress. He paid for these. But refused to pay for the $4,000 Prada bag.

"No," he said.

"Please...."

"Another time," he said and replaces his credit card in his wallet.

Robert gently steers Clarissa away from the boutiques.

They return to their suite.

Later that night, Clarissa wears the new dress for dinner at the Rockpool Bar and Grill, an upmarket restaurant. When she enters the exclusive restaurant, all eyes are rivetted on her. "I was born to live like this," said Clarissa, excited as a child.

Robert is anxious. How can he tell Nancy that he cannot pay the instalment on Millie's orthodontic bill, as he promised?

CHAPTER FORTY-SEVEN

Nancy's mobile rings, she is in the kitchen of the Coburg flat.

"Happy birthday, Nancy," Robert's voice is subdued.

She pulls a face when she hears his voice.

"I can't pay Millie's bill at the moment. Some unexpected expenses have come up." He sounds like a small boy wanting comfort, wanting to dump his problems on her, as he did when they were together.

She stares at the ceiling, notices the cobwebs, wants to scream at him but cannot... Millie is sitting next to her.

Nancy passes the phone to Millie. "It's your father," Nancy's face is granite-like.

~

Millie crafted a funny birthday card for Nancy and brought a box of her favourite chocolates. Aunt Stella sent a flowery card with warm words. Gloria, Janey, and Maxine sent cards.

Gloria paid for them both to have a flotation session. "You will love it. It is a deep relaxation session. You lie in a bath of warm liquid suspended in a warm solution of Epsom salts and listen to piped music in the dark." She giggles. "The Dead Sea meets New Age."

The flotation session did nothing for Nancy. During her time in the capsule, her mind was on the unpaid bills clipped to the bulldog clip. Her brain found it hard to let go. In addition, her car had developed an oil leak that needed attention.

How much will it cost to fix?

Her anxiety increased the longer she stayed in the tank.

They met after the float. "Did you like it? I found it relaxing. I almost fell asleep," Gloria said.

"Mmm...," said Nancy. "Not that way for me."

CHAPTER FORTY-EIGHT

Nancy and Millie live in a part of Coburg where the leaves on the plane trees cling to branches, afraid to let go. Power lines are draped over concrete poles. The road chocked with unforgiving cars that control the motorways and hunt in packs. Concrete edges the nature strips, refusing to let the grass grow wild. Uneven concrete footpaths create a danger to joggers and weakened men and women with walking frames. Fences patrol closed gardens. Rose bushes are pulled tight against rods to keep them straight.

Nancy is at the green flat. She holds an oval silver picture frame of a smiling man and woman—her parents. She loves this photo. It is tangible evidence that she once had living parents. Her parents' heads touch, both wear contented looks. Her father had red hair and freckles over his nose. The mother's brown hair hangs around her soft, radiant face. Nancy has no memories of her mother, only what Aunt stella has told her. But imagines her mother was a gentle, caring person. Nancy touches the gold chain around her neck, the one Aunt Stella gave her.

"Mother, I wish you were alive and could guide

me on how to deal with the problems I am having with Millie and Robert."

She goes to Millie's bedroom, who is lying on her bed, reading. "Hey," Nancy said. "What are you doing?"

Millie looks up. "Alice lent me a book on PTSD." Hands it to Nancy. "You might find it interesting," Millie said.

"I miss our old home. The way life used to be with dad there..." said Millie.

"Being a family is what I miss, and my garden...." Nancy said. "Not the house as much."

In the corner of Millie's room is the easel, a sheet of paper covering *the eyes.*

CHAPTER FORTY-NINE

The Coburg flat is hot, the windows are open, a fan blows warm air over Nancy's face.

Dianne, her childhood friend, rings

After normal pleasantries, Dianne blurts out. "Nancy, I have terrible news,"

"Oh my God, what has happened?" said Nancy. She puts her hand on her chest, steeling herself for the news.

"I have been diagnosed with inoperable breast cancer...." Dianne's voice breaks, stops talking to regain her composure.

The words echo in Nancy's ears, tries to make sense of them. "That's dreadful. Have you had a second opinion?" She feels guilty that she has not contacted Dianne for a while since Robert left to live with Clarissa. Nancy rubs her eyes. What can she say?

"The oncology specialist explained it. Palliative care and pain relief are the only treatment available for me." Dianne's voice grows faint on the phone.

Nancy remembers Dianne telling her about the curious lump in her armpit. Dianne had dismissed it as a reaction to a new underarm deodorant. "So, the lump in your armpit wasn't a deodorant reaction?" Nancy said.

"I should have dealt with it sooner. But work has been hectic at school. I had to work late because several teachers were off sick, and I had to cover their classes. You told me to see a doctor, I put it off. When the lump got bigger, the local doctor referred me to a specialist. They found the primary in the breast. It had spread to the liver and lungs, and you know what that means."

"How can I help?" said Nancy.

"Stay in touch. Say a prayer for me. I am sorting my personal papers ... and the funeral. At some stage, I will be admitted to palliative care in Melbourne, so it is easier for my sister to visit me." She said. "I feel bad for not disclosing this to you earlier. You were under the pump with Robert leaving and having to shift."

"You know I would have dropped everything for you," said Nancy.

"Yes, you would have .... That's why I didn't tell you sooner. The reality is you couldn't have done anything...." she said.

When the call ends, Nancy places her head on the table.

Joe dies and now this....

Millie turns to look at Nancy as she opens the refrigerator door. "Mum, are you all right?"

Nancy can barely say the words. "Dianne has inoperable cancer."

"Oh no," Millie puts her arms around Nancy.

CHAPTER FIFTY

Nancy is chopping vegetables for a roast dinner in the kitchen of the green flat. The chopped parsnips and pumpkin pieces are arranged neatly in the baking tray on the bench. The chicken is cooking in the hot oven. Nancy peels the potatoes carefully, puts the knife down.

"Damn," she cries.

Blood trickles down her finger, she has cut herself again. The small knife has a power of its own. She washes the wound, places a band-aid over the cut. continues peeling.

Once when she cut pumpkin for soup, she sliced the top of her thumb and had sutures for the cut.

I wonder where this strange fear of knives originated.

CHAPTER FIFTY-ONE

The storm that the weather reporter had predicted never arrived. It is night, a car door bangs in the street, a car speeds off, a dog barks in defiance. The bedside lamp shines in the bedroom of Clarissa's apartment. She scratches furiously over her arms and legs. Red marks appear where she has scratched.

"Stop scratching," said Robert.

"I can't help it," Clarissa whines child-like.

Her childlike attitude was appealing once. "Do something. Apply ointment. It's annoying." Robert sits up in bed.

"I must be allergic to something," said Clarissa.

"Stop." Robert places his large hand over Clarissa's smaller hand to stop her scratching. She continues to move her hand under his.

Clarissa ceases scratching for a second, but the uncomfortable sensation returns, and she scratches again.

"I'll never sleep at this rate." Robert grabs his pillow, storms into the lounge room, tries to stretch out on the couch, is uncomfortable, is too tall for the small couch, his feet stick out at the end. Gets up, thumps the pillow into shape, his leg cramps, rubs his leg. He can hear her scratching, making up for a lost time, soothing herself.

"I might be allergic to the new strawberry-scented soap," she said from the bedroom.

Robert does not answer.

If it was not the scratching, it was her sniffing.

"Sniff, sniff."

"Use a tissue," he said.

"Can't help it."

She damaged his car. "Not my fault," she said.

Forgets important things related to him. "I forgot. I can't help it."

Clarissa remembers work commitments, hairdressing and beauty appointments, never late for her gym sessions.

Robert thinks living with Clarissa is like being with a ten-year-old spoilt child. He left Nancy in the first wave of passion. Sometimes he regrets it.

CHAPTER FIFTY-TWO

It is six pm. Robert gazes out of the window of his work office. The sun sets behind the skyscrapers in the distance, a warm orange glow spreads over the sky. He returns to his desk, swivels back and forth on his office chair. Checks his mobile for messages, opens the door, looks down the narrow corridor.

I hate waiting for late clients.

Checks his watch.

Clarissa should be at the apartment by now.

Something happened today that set him thinking. His watch band broke, he took it to the jeweller's shop to be fixed. Robert saw the engraving on the underside of the watch.

I will always love you.

It had been a wedding present from Nancy fifteen years ago.

The watch has lasted longer than my marriage.

Robert is unsettled. He misses Nancy and Millie, their shared friends, even Aunt Stella—tough as boot leather. He wants to ring to see what they are doing, misses being part of their routine.

"When can I stay with you and Clarissa?" said Millie the last time they met. "Angie stays with her mother during the week and her father at the weekends. We could do this," Millie had said.

"Now is not a good time," he said.

"You always say that. When will it be a good time?"

≈

Robert and Dean are at the local hotel. Thirsty men elbow each other for space and down their drinks in quick succession.

"There is no way I can cope with two children in the same apartment," Robert said. "Clarissa requires constant attention. Millie becomes emotional if anything upsets her. Both of them drain me. I love them both, but together under the one roof would spell disaster." He takes a sip of his beer.

"It is difficult to juggle my current life between Clarissa and Millie. When I speak with Nancy or Millie, I have a knot in my gut. I know what I have lost. It is hard to break the connection to them." He looks away. "It is stupid to want both women, Clarissa for her sexy independence and Nancy for her reliability. I always trusted Nancy."

"I have told you before, and I say it again, you were a stupid idiot leaving Nancy," said Dean.

Robert ignores the remark, sips his beer. "Nancy did not adapt to my professional position, and she stayed friends with Gloria and Chris- the fruitier. I move in different circles now. Clarissa fits in better with them. She knows how to dress, to impress, to make small talk. With Clarissa on my arm, I am invincible."

Dean shakes his head and snorts.

'Did you bring me any treats?' "Clarissa says when I have been shopping. The diamond tennis bracelet was a big hit." Robert stopped talking and checked his phone. "I have spent more money on elaborate gifts and expensive perfumes for Clarissa in the time we have been together than in the fifteen years with Nancy."

Dean rolls his eyes and shakes his head again.

"Not that I am complaining. Gorgeous girls should have pleasant things. And her pleasure becomes my sexual pleasure."

"It is always about sex with you," said Dean.

"I wish she might cook a proper meal now and then. I have been doing most of the cooking and we eat out. But her other qualities make up for this."

"You made your bed, you need to lie in it," said Dean.

"You are not being helpful," said Robert.

Robert takes a long gulp of beer from his glass and wipes his mouth. "Since living with Clarissa in her apartment, I have morphed into someone I do not recognise. Another thing disturbs me—Clarissa's friends. I am in a twilight world with them and do not fit in with their wild drinking and drugging." He drinks again from his glass. "Clarissa's father is a braggart, a pompous fool, gives unwanted advice."

"You are full of complaints today. I thought you

said you were happy," said Dean. He goes to the bar to order another jug of beer, remembers to bend his head under the overhead beam near the bar. It nearly hit him on the head last time. Sometimes he forgets how tall he is. Robert used to call him *weed*. Dean returns to the table with the beer and several packets of nuts, throws one to Robert. He opens his packet, places a handful of peanuts in his mouth.

Robert picks at his packet of nuts. "Clarissa's cousin Sophie said, 'Ring me when you tire of Clarissa.'" He pauses. "I told her I would never tire of Clarissa."

'You will.' Sophie said and gave me a sly smirk as she walked away.

"At work, they know I am living with Clarissa. A colleague made a crack related to being knackered. The other accountants give me a sneaky look. 'Way to go, man,' said one. I hate being the butt of office gossip."

Dean does not reply.

"Clarissa has been nagging me to start formal divorce proceedings. She wants to get married and have a baby. Yesterday she showed me a picture of the wedding dress she wants, $6,000. To wear for one day, I said."

'Wedding dresses cost that much now. We can have a honeymoon in America.' she said.

"Your life sounds like a soap opera, and just as superficial," said Dean, refilling their glasses.

"Last week Clarissa dragged me to view a house, an elaborate mansion, in Balwyn. It has a pool and a special room for movies. I am not as rich as you think," I said.

'You can afford it. Your old house in East Brunswick was expensive,' she said.

"I tried to tell her we had extensively renovated the house. It was not as flashy as when we bought it."

Robert pauses.

"I will not go through the marriage and baby routine again," Robert said.

"My bet is on Clarissa," Dean drains his glass.

CHAPTER FIFTY-THREE

Robert is sitting at his desk at the Masters and Smith office, he has been thinking of Millie and her issues. Robert wants to involve Millie more in his life with Clarissa, but it may be premature. He jumps when his work phone rings.

"Robert, can you come down to my office now?" Said Nick, his voice sharp.

"Sure, is something wrong?" said Robert, a tightening in his throat.

"I will fill you in when you get here," Nick said.

Robert closes the door to his office, walks down the hall to the elevator. He wishes he had a crystal ball. So many things once were perfect and ended up badly. His marriage to Nancy started off in the heat of passion but ended up bland.

Robert taps on Nick's office door.

"Come in," said Nick. "Sit, sit," he gestures to Robert.

The multiple plants in Nick's office always catch Robert's eye. The soft green effect in the office is in contrast to Nick, who is a hard and unemotional boss. His boss could be fifty-five, hair thinning on top and turning grey, a florid face.

"I will get to the point," said Nick. He leans back in his chair. "I had to sack Edwards today," he sighs as if he is sad, but his eyes and manner are steely and hard. "I am in a pickle and need someone to take over his clients immediately. You could carry Edward's portfolio at short notice. Of course, it will be a promotion of sorts and an increase in pay. But you will have to work hard." He fingers the leaf of his spider plant on his desk. "I don't want the fact that I sacked Edwards to get out. I will say he resigned and left."

"What did Edwards do?" said Robert. Bit his tongue as soon as he said it.

Nick stares at him. "Edwards was not loyal to the company. He was getting paid by me and asking for *special favours* from the clients." He said *favours* with emphasis. "I will not be cheated out of my business." He punches some numbers on the phone.

A fragrant, smiling Clarissa appears.

"I want you to organise a small function at the Hilton hotel to acquaint Robert with his new clients."

"When," she said.

"As soon as possible, if you can secure a booking for next week." He waves her out.

After she left, Nick gave Robert a hard look. "I know you left your wife and hitched up with Clarissa. What a stupid thing to do." He got up and sat on the edge of his desk, closer to Robert. "I am warning you once, your relationship must not affect your work here or you will be out."

Robert blinks.

"I am unhappy about any personal relationships between my staff. It never turns out well for the company. Never." He glares at Robert.

"I hope you are the exception."

~

The small function at the Hilton hotel to introduce Robert to his new clients is a subdued affair. Drinks and savouries are provided. Clarissa wears a red dress, blonde hair wound goddess-like on her head. Robert is proud to have Clarissa hanging off his arm as they walk into the dining room of the Hilton hotel.

I am a lucky man, promotion, increase in pay, and the love of an extraordinarily beautiful woman.

CHAPTER FIFTY-FOUR

Millie returned from an afternoon with her father. She has an angry look on her face, slumps in a chair in the kitchen of the green flat.

"Dad ignored me. I may as well not have given up my Saturday to be with him. He spent most of the time talking on his mobile to Clarissa."

Nancy grits her teeth.

"Clarissa rang all the time, wanting to speak to dad. It was supposed to be *my* time with him. To top it off, dad asked me to help him choose a 'just because' gift for Clarissa," she said. "We trekked around Myer and David Jones looking for something special for her. He ended up buying her expensive perfume." Millie wipes her nose with a tissue. "It was my time with dad."

"Your father is going through a strange period," her words sound robotic.

A few hours later, Robert calls Nancy to tell his side of the story from the afternoon.

"I was trying to cheer Clarissa by buying a gift. I thought Millie's feminine touch would help."

"That's not the way it works. You have no brains at all," Nancy said, her anger rising. "It was Millie's time with you. Not for you to be distracted by your lover's needs."

"You have become bitter and hard," he said.

She hung up on him.

To appease her anger, Nancy fiddles with her plants, removes dead leaves, waters them. Repots two. She sorts drawers and cupboards in the small kitchen, rearranges the cups and saucers. Takes a load of washing to the nearby laundromat.

CHAPTER FIFTY-FIVE

The palliative care ward is quieter than a regular ward. It seems as if the nurses float while they perform their duties. Light streams through large windows that overlook a garden of green lawn, eucalyptus trees bordered by masses of pink and blue hydrangeas. The reception area is filled with the gentle aroma of daphne flowers wafting through.

Nancy has spent the last two days next to Dianne's bed in the ward. Millie is staying with Angie. Nancy holds a bunch of crumpled, soggy tissues in her hand. It has been six months since she had been told of Dianne's diagnosis; she has deteriorated, is close to death, slipping in and out of a morphine fog. Pictures of Joe, family and friends peer at her from the corkboard next to the bed. Nancy's hand covers Dianne's.

"Do you remember when we played truant from high school to see our favourite pop group in Melbourne?" She pulls the chair closer to the bed. "We sneaked off from school, caught the train to Melbourne and joined thousands of screaming fans at the Southern Cross hotel." She searches for a clean tissue in her bag. "All we could see were the top of the group's heads." Nancy looks out of the window. Dark clouds are gathering in the sky. "When we returned home, we were the envy of our class. Aunt Stella was not pleased—she grounded me for a week."

Dianne flickers a smile.

She can hear me.

"Do you remember Bruce?" She glances at Dianne's thin body shape under the blankets. "Bruce was in the waiting room at the hospital last week. He has become fat.... Remember how he used to bully me and called me terrible names? I was so scared of him."

There was no response from Dianne this time.

Nancy paused, feeling uncertain about whether she should proceed. "You were my protector. One day you punched him hard on the nose .... remember he ran howling to the teacher...." Nancy spoke in a quiet voice. "I recognised him straight away. 'Hello Bruce,' I said. I used to be Nancy Richardson. We attended the same primary school." He stared at me blankly and walked away.

Dianne moans.

Nancy presses the nurse's call button. A nurse materialises with morphine. Dianne is quieter after the drug is administered.

∾

Nancy is aware death hovers around crisis admissions in the emergency department. The staff do what they can to save lives; they learn to be resilient.

"Harden up or you will go under," a senior nurse

told Nancy when she had been a new nurse graduate. She couldn't harden. Each patient's death affected her. An elderly male patient hit by a car while crossing the street stayed in her memory. The man sustained multiple injuries and clung to Nancy's hand whilst the doctors worked on his wounds.

"Am I hurting you?" he said.

"No," Nancy lied.

"Don't be sad," the old man said. "I will be fine." He died soon after.

Nancy had to shake off the sadness of his death before she finished the shift and returned home.

She recalls former patients who had been resuscitated and spoke of their near-death experiences. Nancy had shared information with a nursing colleague related to a conference she had attended related to death and dying. The principal speaker had been Dr. Kubler Ross, who had been a forerunner in the growing evidence related to death, dying, and near-death experiences.

"I wish I had attended the conference," said the nurse colleague. "It might have answered some questions for me." She lowered her voice. "I have told no one what I am about to tell you." She turned her head to see if they could be overheard. "When I was a patient in the intensive care ward, after an allergic reaction to a medication, I died." She paused. "I floated out of my body and could see the medical staff trying to resuscitate me," the nurse said. "When I left my body, Bill, my darling husband, who had died earlier, opened his arms and held me tight." She stopped. "Then they resuscitated me back to life, and I was back in my body in the ward with tubes, couldn't speak." The nurse wiped her forehead. "I was not grateful to be resuscitated and brought back. The team expected me to be thankful for saving my life. I wasn't." She turned away. "One good thing. I don't have any fear of death anymore."

~

In the palliative ward, day becomes night, and Dianne dies peacefully. Nancy stays next to Dianne's bed for a long time after her death, remembering their shared experiences, grateful for their friendship.

Later, Nancy walks to her car. The sky opens with torrential rain, thunder, and lightning. She counts the time between the flashes of lightning and the thunder, just like she did as a child. The shorter the count and the closer the thunder, until it thundered and cracked. She was never sure how correct it was predicting the thunder. Rain poured, drenching, cleansing, refreshing, creating newness.

"I hear you, Dianne," Nancy shouts at the sky. "Goodbye, my beloved friend. Say hello to Joe for me."

CHAPTER FIFTY-SIX

Clarissa runs her manicured fingers through her blonde hair, swivels on her seat at her desk, which is in front of Nick's office. Her desk is like Clarissa: immaculate, organised. The computer screen shows a sea scene. A small vase of red roses sits to the left.

A tall thin male client hovers in front of Clarissa's face, his narrow face accentuated by a dark-haired ponytail; he wears an expensive grey tailored suit. The man smells strongly of expensive aftershave. He is a valued client of Nick's. The wealthy client owns a racetrack and three apartment complexes.

"Are you married?" said the man

"Nope." Clarissa flicks her blonde hair behind her ears.

He edges closer. "Neither am I. My new car is outside. Would you like a spin in my red Porsche?"

Clarissa touches his sleeve. "That sounds like fun."

At that moment, Nick opens his office door and beckons the client into his room.

Across the room, Robert has been watching the flirtatious interaction between the client and Clarissa. He marches over to Clarissa and hisses in her ear.

"What is going on with you and the man with the Porsche?"

"What do you mean?" Clarissa said.

"That client of Nick's."

"I'm paid to be friendly." She fiddles with Robert's tie.

Robert realises the others in the open-plan office are staring at them. He bends closer to Clarissa. "I left a wife and child for you. You owe me."

"We're not married. I don't owe you a thing." She turns her back to him and studies the screen on the computer.

Robert stares up at the ceiling, annoyed with himself for becoming angry. He knows Clarissa is a flirt. They are a couple now. She should change.

∼

The next day at the Masters and Smith office, clients come and go, phones ring, conversations rise and fall. Most of the staff in the front office have heads bowed over computer screens.

The pony-tailed man appears again and hovers around Clarissa's desk.

"Can I help you?" Robert again materialises from nowhere.

"Waiting for Nick." He smiles at Clarissa.

Robert glares at Clarissa. She avoids his gaze.

There is a standoff with the client talking to Clarissa and Robert interrupting. Eventually, Nick calls the client into his office. He sees Robert. "Have you finished the Thomas account?"

"Working on it..." Robert said.

The man winks at Clarissa as he goes in.

Robert seethes with unresolved anger.

∾

Later that night at Simpson Street Northcote, at Clarissa's luxury apartment. Clarissa pours a glass of icy water from the dispenser on the fridge door, sips it slowly. She keeps one eye on Robert, who is padding back and forth on the polished wooden floor in his bare feet.

"It upsets me to see you flirting," his loud voice vibrates through the room.

"I wasn't flirting, just being friendly. Stop being such a prude." She takes another sip from her glass.

"You were giving him the come on." He is measured in his speech, trying to hold back his anger.

"Stop being insecure. I hope you have calmed down by the time I return from the gym." Clarissa picks up her gym bag and walks to the door.

Robert opens the sliding door to the balcony with the panoramic views of the city and the Dandenong ranges. He watches her car come out of the parking area under the apartments. She gives him a small wave and drives off. He goes back inside, pours a strong whisky and soda. He rifles through the fridge for something to eat. Finds a slice of yesterday's takeaway pizza, he heats it in the microwave.

The final divorce papers have been signed by Nancy and Robert and are lying in his briefcase. He has not told Clarissa.

CHAPTER FIFTY-SEVEN

The Accident and Emergency Department has a sign at the Nurse's station 'staff only beyond this point.' Rushed footsteps on the polished lino floors, staff of various ages and uniforms go in and out of the nurses station. An Italian interpreter waits next to a patient on a trolley.

An invisible voice broadcasts that there is a "Code Blue in the emergency department, cubicle two." Trolleys and staff rush towards the cubicle. "Call X-ray. I think we have a pulmonary embolism," said the first doctor to arrive. The medical staff perform their emergency procedures, while a young man yells at the nurses in the next cubicle.

"I am warning you. The aliens are listening through your mobile phones. They intend to destroy earth in ten minutes." The young man pulls at the cubicle curtains, tries to grab a nurse as she walks past. She attempts to pacify him. The young man is in psychosis, waiting for the psychiatrist. His shouts become louder and more incoherent. He rants about aliens infiltrating earth.

"Switch off your mobile phones." His voice rises to a scream. "The aliens are transmitting through them.

Switch off your phones if you want to live," he yells. His voice, filled with desperation, echoes in the ward. "They are coming."

The invisible voice says, "Code Grey in cubicle three."

Dr Ferris and four black-shirted security men appear at the young man's cubicle. The doctor carries a kidney dish which holds a filled syringe.

"Watch out! The aliens are here." The hysterical patient cowers in the cubicle's corner, covering his face with his hands. "Don't let them near me." His cries become increasingly frantic. Then he is quiet. Dr. Ferris and the security team leaves. A nurse stays with the now sedated patient.

Nancy is in the next cubicle treating a plump woman with wiry black hair who murmurs in an unknown language. The woman points to her bloodied foot and pulls a face. Nancy gestures for her to climb onto the trolley. The woman shakes her head. She points to her foot. Once again, Nancy motions for her to get on the trolley. The woman shakes her head harder. Nancy attempts to remove the tea towel wrapped around the woman's foot. Suddenly, blood gushes out. She reapplies the cloth, applying pressure. The material is soggy with bright blood.

"Need help," Nancy presses a red buzzer on the wall. Two porters arrive, part the curtains. They lift the protesting woman onto the cubicle bed.

Dr Tom Ferris runs in, pushing a trolley. Nancy explains the situation to him.

"What language do you speak?" He said.

The woman shakes her head.

"We need an interpreter," Dr Ferris said.

In another cubicle, a man of seventy-six has fallen from a ladder while clearing leaves from the guttering. The man is unconscious, not responding to verbal commands. His wife is distraught. "I forbade him to climb the ladder. He didn't listen to me, lost his balance and fell backwards onto the concrete paving, smashed his skull. I told him not to go up the ladder," she said for the fourth time. "I told him that Brendon, our son, was going to clear the guttering next week. Stubborn fool," she whispers, kisses his forehead.

Another ambulance brings a young woman who is unresponsive. She swallowed a bottle of sleeping medication when her boyfriend left her. There are four road accidents, two severe asthma attacks, heart emergencies, and people with elevated temperatures and youths who are affected by methamphetamine and heroin. Nurses and doctors rush from patient to patient, their stethoscopes swinging from their necks. Orderlies wheel patients to undergo diagnostic tests. Radiologists bring portable machines to provide X-rays to patients in cubicles who cannot be moved.

"Stand back," the radiologist said to a nurse going past. "You don't want to be zapped."

A youth, his arm in a white cotton sling, strides to the nurse's desk. "How long do I have to wait to have the plaster applied to my broken arm?"

"Please be patient. We know you are here," said the ward clerk.

The youth mumbles something incoherent and moves back to his cubicle.

At the end of the shift, Nancy provides the handover of her patients to the night staff. She locates her car in the car park and heads home.

∾

When she returns to the flat, Millie is watching television.

"Were you busy tonight?" Millie holds a half- eaten chocolate bar.

"Very busy. I am making a vegemite sandwich. Do you want one?" Nancy has her head in the fridge.

Millie munches on the chocolate bar. "Did dad leave because I have been difficult since the assault?"

"It had nothing do with you. We had marital problems for a long time." She bites into the sandwich. "To tell you the truth, I was never sure why your father married me. I think just to annoy his mother. But I was besotted with him." She wipes the crumbs from her lips.

"We were mismatched from the start.... I was such an airhead." She places the plate in the sink. "When things started breaking up for us, I went into panic mode and dragged Robert to marriage guidance. In the end, I had to accept he did not want to be married to me." She ran detergent and hot water over the dishes.

"You can't hold a person if they are desperate to leave you."

"Are you bitter that dad left?" said Millie.

"Not so much now."

"I used to hear you arguing. You were mean to dad," said Millie.

Nancy stares straight ahead, regains her composure. "I wanted the marriage more than he did." She places the dishes in the draining rack.

"What are you watching?"

"*Casablanca,*" said Millie.

"That was a favourite of mine," said Nancy.

She sits next to Millie, wraps Aunt Stella's knitted rug around both their legs. The peacefulness of home is an antidote to the madness at work.

CHAPTER FIFTY-EIGHT

The Healthy Choice Fruit Shop is on busy Sydney Road Coburg. The shop has a front with concertina windows that open out to highlight the fruit and vegetables. Gloria and Chris are sorting the produce for the front display. Two shop assistants are off sick. It is Thursday; a steady stream of fastidious customers arrive, predominantly from Greek, Italian, Lebanese and Arabic countries.

"I never liked Robert," said Chris Vella. "Robert seemed to look down on us because we ran a fruit shop." He lifts a box of oranges onto a trolley, moves it to the front near the avocados.

"I appreciate you helping me on your day off," he leans over and kisses Gloria on the cheek. She kisses him back.

"I am happy to help. I'll have to collect the kids from school at three. They love to come to the shop to assist."

"To eat, you mean, the kids are always hungry," he said.

They continue sorting and stacking the fruit and vegetables into the designated areas.

"Robert has been a jerk to Nancy. Do you know

she had to get a bank loan just to manage the bills? Her beautiful home sold, and lives mucked up because of Robert." Gloria shows her teeth. She picks up the avocado box and places the avocados one by one onto the display, removes the damaged ones.

"Nancy was an innocent girl, married to the first man who asked her. I tried to warn her that Robert was phoney. Nancy was too good for Robert and his stuck-up mother... Fancy wanting to be called Maxine and not Grandma." She wipes her hands on her apron. Places plump tomatoes in place, carefully checking for blemished or spotted ones. She finishes the tomato stand, organises the white onions into kilo mesh bags.

"Good morning, Mrs Galotti," said Chris to a customer hovering nearby. "Do you need any help?"

"I'm only getting a few things today." The woman takes six apples, two cucumbers, lettuce, weighs one kilo of tomatoes in her basket. She takes the produce to the counter; Chris follows her to the register.

"You go for your break. I can manage the register," said Gloria.

"Will do." He disappears to the back of the shop.

Gloria knows the regular customers, asks about their families. They know she is a nurse and often ask for advice on health issues.

A woman drags a bag of books to the counter. "These are for your boys. My children have outgrown the books. Now they spend too much time on their screens," she said.

"My boys will love them. We try to control screen

time, but it is hard. Chris only allows them to use their tablets on weekends," Gloria said.

CHAPTER FIFTY-NINE

It is early afternoon when Robert returns to the apartment building where he lives with Clarissa. The first thing he notices is the red Porsche parked in the street. His eyes narrow, and a red poker of anger bursts into his chest. He runs up the stairs to their apartment, pulls open the door. The Porsche owner and Clarissa are sitting close together. The client sees Robert's face and scrambles out of the room. After a few minutes, the Porsche speeds down the road.

"You told me you were going to the hairdresser," Robert said.

"It's my life," Clarissa said.

"I don't get you."

"You should talk. It suited you to come here before you left your wife." Clarissa pokes a finger at his chest.

"You make me sick." He goes to the fridge and pulls out a beer. As he pours the beer, she slips out to the bedroom, closes the door, straightens the messed sheets. She looks around the room for any telltale signs.

They do not speak for two days. After work, Robert buys a bunch of roses. "Let's forget the whole thing happened." Robert hands the flowers to Clarissa.

Clarissa throws the flowers on the table. "If you love me, start divorce proceedings with Nancy now." She crosses her arms. "Until then, consider me a free agent."

"We don't have to marry to be together," Robert said, trying to make her see sense. He is unsure who this Clarissa is, certainly not his laughing sweetheart.

"I do." She does not look at him.

"You should leave right now." She points to the door. Her face could not be read.

"You don't mean that," he said in a soft voice.

"If you don't go now, I will call the police." Clarissa picks up her phone, starts pressing the buttons.

He stares at her for a moment, hoping she will change her mind. When he realises she will not go back on her words, he gets his suitcases and packs his things.

Clarissa has her back to him the whole time.

∼

Robert calls Dean. "Can you put me up for a few days? Clarissa and I had a misunderstanding. We need some time away to sort things out."

"You can stay for one week, no longer. My girlfriend is coming back from overseas, and I don't want you here when she gets back," said Dean.

Robert calls Clarissa many times. She does not respond to his voice messages.

The next few days are miserable for him, has a burning in his gut. Rejection tastes bitter. The spark has gone out of his life, he cannot sleep. Is not focusing on work, is late for clients' appointments.

He calls Nancy. "I made a terrible mistake leaving you and Millie," he said. "Can I stay with you?"

"No. Never," Nancy said.

He considered staying with his mother but could not cope with her criticism. He books a hotel. At night he parks his car outside Clarissa's apartment, watches her come and go, hoping to speak with her.

A police officer taps on the driver's window. "Sir, we have received a complaint that you are stalking a lady in the apartments. If I see you here again, I will arrest you. Do you understand?"

Robert drives away.

He texts Clarissa. She does not reply.

CHAPTER SIXTY

Nick, his round face flushed, marches unannounced into Robert's office. He hasn't knocked. Robert stands up as soon as he sees him.

"Nick...?" Robert said.

"I warned you about Clarissa." Nick gestures for Robert to sit. "Your work is suffering," he pokes at a folder opened on Robert's desk. "The clients are complaining." His face is bricklike.

"I have put time and money cultivating these clients to the point they are loyal to my company." He leans into Robert's face. "I will not see you destroy my hard work. For God's sake, snap out of it. You are better than this. Clarissa is what she is," Nick said. "Get back with your wife, create stability in your life. Forget about Clarissa."

Robert stares at him.

"The last thing this firm needs is a distracted accountant. There are millions of dollars on the line." Nick pokes him in the chest. "Straighten up and focus on your work. Alternatively, you can leave. I cannot afford to carry deadwood in my business."

"This is the first and last notice. Shape up now."

Nick storms out of the office, slams the door behind him.

Later, Robert tries to speak to Clarissa. "I miss you," he whispers.

"Start divorce proceedings, and we can be together."

When Robert returns to his office, a client is impatiently waiting outside.

"My time is money." A furious look on the client's face.

Robert scribbles notes to show he is paying attention.

CHAPTER SIXTY-ONE

It is eight pm when Clarissa pulls on her gym leggings and sports bra. Her hair tied back in a ponytail, white sneakers on her feet. She plans on thirty minutes of focused exercises, does this three times a week. Clarissa has done the research on sports medicine and heads for the twenty-four-hour gym near her apartment. She has been a regular at this gym for three years.

"Hi Clarissa," said the man with glasses at the reception desk. "You're looking good." He gives a wide smile. "Do you want to have a drink with me after work tomorrow?"

Clarissa said, "I will let you know."

He makes the same comment to her each time he sees her. He is not her type. She plans to end up with someone growing in his career and wants all the good things which wealth and position bring. Robert meets her criteria; but he tells her he is still married. She does not want to be involved in another messy relationship with a married man and have him return to his wife and family. Clarissa has a strategy, a rational plan to meet her goals; plans to be tough with Robert until he gives in to her requests for a divorce.

As she walks into the gym rooms, the overpowering odour of sweating bodies hits her nostrils.

"How are things?" Said a man in his forties. He wears a red bandana on his head, a drenched t-shirt, has been beating his fists into a punching bag, his face drips with sweat. He dries his face on a towel.

"Doing fine," Clarissa said.

She does not want to chitchat, has work to do, plays heavy metal music through her earbuds to hype herself. She begins her workout with stretches, then moves to weight training and adds weights to her dumbbells. Wipes her face with the towel she carries. Does a series of squats, lunges and crunches. She checks the heart monitor on her phone.

She texts Robert. "How are the divorce papers going?"

Robert responds immediately, begging to see her.

'Not until you sign the papers,' she texts.

Clarissa joins her friend Gemma in the treadmill room.

"How is it going with Robert? Has he caved in yet?" said Gemma.

"It's proving harder than I thought." Clarissa increases the speed on the treadmill.

CHAPTER SIXTY-TWO

Robert presses the front doorbell of Nancy's flat. She peers through the security hole, makes an audible groan when she sees it is Robert at the door.

"Can I come in?" Robert said.

"What do you want?" An exasperated tone in Nancy's voice.

"Please let me come and live with you and Millie."

"No, I already told you that the marriage is over," she said.

"Can I come in?" He said again.

Nancy unlocks the screen door.

He bursts in, nearly knocking her over. Has lost his swagger, appears lost, his size diminished.

"I want to come back because I miss you and Millie. Leaving was a dreadful mistake... I had midlife issues." He flops on a chair at the kitchen table, places his hands on his head, is wearing his work suit.

"Millie wants me back," he looks around the room. "I will help with the rent ... and help with the other bills." He looks up at her. "I know you are struggling financially. With the two of us sharing the expenses, like old times, it will be easier."

Nancy exhales. "Our lives are not swinging doors

for you to come in and out as you choose." She places her hands on her hips.

"I have changed." His voice sounds weary.

"Not that I can see."

The front door opens, Millie bounces in from school. When she sees Robert, she runs towards him. "Dad, you came to see me." Millie gives him a hug, her face shines with pleasure.

"Yes," he mumbles. "I came to see you."

Millie senses the coldness in the room, turns to Nancy.

"Have you two been fighting again?" Millie looks from Robert and Nancy and back to Robert. "You two are just like children, always bickering. Can't you learn to be friends?"

She grabs Robert's arm. "Come on, dad, let's go for a milkshake."

"Will you join us?" Robert looks hopefully at Nancy.

"No thanks, I have work to do." Her face is like thunder. She hears them pound down the stairs.

As soon as Clarissa snaps her fingers, he will go back to her.

Millie returns alone. She glares at Nancy. "Why can't Dad live with us? You should give him a second chance."

"When it is over, it is over," she said. "He still loves

Clarissa and only wants to live here because Clarissa has thrown him out and he hates living by himself."

"You could try. You may hit it off again and we can be a family again. Like we were."

"No, this will never happen."

Millie flounces off to her room. Bangs the door.

Robert has been working on her again. There are only two bedrooms, and I am not sharing my bed with Robert.

Two hours later, Robert called. "You make me so angry."

"What, my fault again?"

"I told Millie we could be a family again. She wants that. Change your mind for Millie's sake. I can pack and be at your flat in 30 minutes."

She shakes her head. He refuses to hear her words. His pleading irritates her. "It will never work. I have no trust nor respect for you," she said.

"Look…" I admit I had a stupid midlife crisis going off with Clarissa. "But she is not important to me anymore," he lied.

Nancy is unmoved. He is looking for a simple solution to his accommodation issues.

The marriage is dead, beyond resuscitation.

CHAPTER SIXTY-THREE

It is late afternoon when Nancy drives her blue Yaris to the local park. She stops near the children's playground, undoes her seat belt and slips out of the car.

Children are swinging on monkey bars, sliding down slides. She enjoys coming to this small park on the outskirts of Coburg, far from the noise and bustle of the trams and cars on Sydney Road. She meanders down a winding path. Small yellow flowers are sprouting from the bushes. Nancy reaches into her pocket and bites on an apple. The juice runs down her chin, wipes it with the back of her hand. She is trying to centre herself amongst the plants and trees. Usually, nature works its magic, but not today.

Robert wants to return to the family.

Millie has been pouting and sulking all week since Robert asked to come back. Anger rises inside of Nancy and cannot contain its energy.

Does he think we are doormats, that he can wipe his feet on us whenever it suits him?

She moves to the abandoned church on the edge of the park. It is a place for homeless men and women to shelter from the dark. It is a square wooden room, dark. Tiny shafts of sunlight break through the darkness, illuminating the wooden slats on the walls. The old church is bare of furniture and has little resemblance to its former glory. There are only floorboards and a strong, irritating smell of ammonia. Flies buzz mournfully in tight circles, resembling circling aeroplanes in the room's corners. The wind blows, making the building shake—the roof flaps in unison. The floor is uneven, the wooden planks sway.

Someone must check on the homeless.

Later, Nancy sits on a concrete bench.

Robert tried to make out he was homeless.

She watches three boys kick a football to each other. They run and jump in the air, catching the ball. The sun slips away and with it the warmth of the day. A nearby garden is graced by the overhanging branches of an old avocado tree, creating a canopy of coolness and a peaceful environment. Birds call out to each other, one bird answers, a song of hello. Insects chirp and complain. The park is wet; it had rained earlier. A collection of various succulent plants bunch up against each other, egging each other to keep growing, grow taller and flower. Butterflies and dragonflies flutter by. The trees move in time with the soft wind, this way and that. The park's centrepiece is a flowing fountain with drenching water, two statues of children at the base. Ceramic frogs with staring eyes are lined along the edge of the fountain. She notices a part of the park roped off with yellow tape. Someone has dug a hole to remove a dead plant and fill it with something new.

I need to plant something new in my life.

CHAPTER SIXTY-FOUR

Robert and Dean are at a restaurant near St Kilda beach on a cold, foggy morning. They had planned a walk along the beach, but the chilly weather slowed them down.

"You are a fool," said Dean.

Robert looks straight ahead, ignoring Dean's gaze. "I have no idea how I got into this mess. I have always been level-headed."

Dean scoffs, "You're kidding yourself. You have never been level-headed."

"To tell you the truth, I have difficulty recognising who I am. My employment at the firm is in jeopardy. My boss has threatened to sack me." He bites into a pastry. "I have worked my butt to get where I am, and it is about to go pear-shaped because of Clarissa." He takes another bite. "I caught her flirting with another man, and she threw me out because I objected."

"I can't determine if it's your ego or you're just plain stupid, but either way, you certainly messed up your life. Clarissa is a good-time girl. Your hormones hampered your brain. Now you have to suffer the consequences," said Dean.

"Clarissa won't see me until I file the divorce

papers." He stares at Dean. I am unsure of what I am achieving by not informing Clarissa the divorce is completed.

"Crash." Broken cups and hot coffee litter the floor.

Dean immediately jumps up. "Here, let me help you," he said to the server.

"My first day on the job," said the young woman, "Probably my last."

"We all make mistakes," said Dean. He collects the broken cups and places them on the tray. "Get a cloth so no one slips."

Dean returns to their table.

"Nancy won't take me back. But Millie wants me back." Robert brushes the crumbs off his shirt. "I hate the nomad life, loathe the hotel I am in. The only good thing is that it is close to work. The fellow next door at the hotel has his television on so loud that I cannot hear myself think. Mercifully, he goes to bed early. There is a guy on the other side of my room who blasts heavy metal music at night."

"So let me get this straight. You're considering returning to Clarissa, but she won't agree unless you sign the divorce papers, and you haven't mentioned that the divorce is completed. In the meantime, you are interested in returning to live with Nancy and Millie." Dean shakes his head. "I cannot believe it."

"Clarissa wants marriage and babies. I will not be manipulated into marriage," said Robert.

"You can't have both women, a foot in both camps. Somewhere you have to choose." Dean looks up as the young server comes to the table with a fresh cup of coffee.

"This is on me. Thanks for helping me," she said.

"No problems," Dean said.

Dean turns to Robert. "Maxine always said you were the smart one, but she was wrong. You are like her, clueless as to what is important."

"Are you sure I can't come and live with you?" said Robert.

"Are you hard-of-hearing? I told you before. Jenny is back from overseas," he said. "The last thing I need is you hanging around my space when my girlfriend is there."

He stands up and pays the bill. "Come on, let's go for the walk along the beach. The sun is out. The sunshine may bring you to your senses."

CHAPTER SIXTY-FIVE

The Racecourse Complex is famous for The Melbourne Cup horse race, but today is hosting a conference on mental health. Amongst the myriad of rooms and levels is the conference room, microphone wires taped to the carpet in a snake-like pattern that goes from the back power outlet to the podium at the front, white walls, grey carpet, poor lighting.

Nancy joins the queue to register for the Mental Health Conference, wears her good suit, the black pantsuit with a white cotton shirt, carries a black briefcase. She is attending the conference to listen to a world-renowned expert on PTSD. Collects the freebies: pens, scribble pads, stickers, a carry bag labelled with Zyprexa in large letters, which forces the participant to be a walking advertisement for the company.

She finds her seat, looks around to see if she knows anyone. Conferences are a way to keep up with seldom seen colleagues. Nancy casts her eyes on the woman seated in front of her. The woman plays incessantly with her long, dark hair, combs her fingers through the hair over and over. A tactic that soothes.

"Hello," said a familiar voice. "Can I sit here?"

Nancy shuffles up to make space for Dr Tom Ferris from the emergency department. He is a tall, thin man with a receding hairline, older than the other registrars at the hospital. His voice has a humorous quality.

"I didn't know you were coming to this conference," she said.

"Earning educational credits." His voice sounds sheepish, like a child caught in a naughty act. "Have I missed anything?"

"They haven't started yet."

Tom goes through his bag of freebies.

A woman in a grey suit, red scarf folded carefully around her neck, comes to the podium. "We are ready to start. Can you hear me?" Taps the microphone. She fiddles with the computer, places a USB stick into the computer, starts the PowerPoint. Taps the microphone again.

The late arrivals shuffle in.

The first speaker is a robust man of fifty, wears an old-fashioned checked jacket, white shirt and striped tie, with black trousers. He takes his glasses off, peers at the audience. The speaker speaks without looking at his notes, shows his confidence with public speaking. He keeps one hand in his pocket, the other on the pointer, which he uses on the PowerPoint screen. The man is a high-powered CEO, oversees The North-Western Mental Health group. He places his glasses on his head, peers at the graphs, his voice takes on an impatient edge.

Nancy thinks the organisers had pressured him to

speak to this conference. The tone of his presentation does not fit the conference. It appears rehashed from another presentation. It is a statistics driven account of the number of patients admitted into mental care establishments over the last few years. He elaborates on the excessive costs of mental health for each state government. The audience shuffles, and a few individuals pull out their phones. More graphs follow, then pie charts.

"In conclusion," he said and keeps talking. He speaks for ten more minutes before finishing. "Sorry, I don't have time for questions. I have an important meeting with the Premier." Jams his papers in a folder and briskly leaves. Four of the audience leave when he leaves.

"That was boring," said Tom. "I hope they are not all graphs and pie charts."

"Me too."

The next speaker is a blonde-haired woman wearing tight jeans and a navy jacket and high black spiked boots. Reads her notes as if reading a term paper, head kept down, lifting her head up only to click to the next slide. She avoids locking eyes with the audience, uses Snoopy cartoons in her PowerPoint. The speaker discusses her research on Thought Field Therapy, calls patients, clients. "Problems arise in the unconscious, while solutions lie within the unconscious," she said. The woman lifts her head and at last faces the audience, waves her hands around, her voice going faster and becoming louder. "Forgiveness has to be on a subconscious level."

She stops abruptly and walks away.

Tom nudges Nancy and rolls his eyes.

The woman behind Nancy keeps coughing and coughing. Nancy brings her a glass of water.

"Thank you, my dear," she said. "Smoker's cough."

At the end of the morning session, Nancy and Tom line up with the others for tea and sweet biscuits. They move outside with the smokers.

"Strange place for a conference," said Tom.

A woman who appears to be about 26 years old lights up a cigarette. "My sister attended The Melbourne Cup two years ago. A horse stumbled and fell. The stewards erected a screen around the fallen horse." She sucked hard on the cigarette. "They shot the horse in front of my sister; she heard the horse jump as the bullet fired. When she next came to the races, all she could think of was the poor horse's death."

"That's horrible," said her friend.

Tom raises his eyebrows, looks at Nancy.

"Is this how you spend your days off?" said Nancy.

"I need to get away from the blood and gore," Tom said. "I used to be an art teacher before I was a doctor. Teaching was challenging enough, but this doctoring business is a whole new level of complexity." He dunks his biscuit in the teacup and eats it. "Most of the time, I am like Sherlock Holmes, trying to work out the diagnosis of the patient."

A call on the loudspeaker invites the participants to return to the conference.

"Come on, Sherlock, time to return," she said.

They return to their seats.

"How is the conference so far for you?" Nancy moves closer to Tom.

"I came to listen to the grief counsellor, but I'm afraid it might be a statistics-driven presentation," he said.

The speaker Nancy came to hear is the next presenter, a psychologist and an energetic woman. She provides further insights into her research on PTSD. The woman elaborates on the patient's experience of hypervigilance, flashbacks, and mood changes. "Those with PTSD who are lucky enough to receive effective treatment for their symptoms early do better than those who do not. People recover and can have a healthy life. It takes time. It is a zigzag track, back and forth, a minor improvement and then backwards and a little healing and back." The speaker is enthusiastic about her topic.

Nancy sits on the edge of her seat, listens intently.

The psychologist mentions different treatment modalities. "Mindfulness increases the connectivity between the amygdala, making it less active. Eye movement desensitization and reprocessing therapy may help. Exposure therapy is important. And, of course, there are medications and age-appropriate support groups." She surveys the audience. "PTSD is a deep-seated stress disorder based on trauma. People will go along well, and then a trigger can set off another PTSD attack and seriously impair that person's life. I researched various treatment categories, such as talking therapies, medication, exercise, mindfulness, and self-help. My research has identified that a combination of all works best," she said.

Nancy scribbles notes.

Tom looks at Nancy.

"My child has PTSD, and I want to be up to date with the latest information," Nancy said.

A ten-minute break before the next speaker.

A man taps on Tom's shoulder. "Hi Tom."

Tom introduces the man as a colleague. Health professionals make up most of the audience. The buzz of the chatter rises during the break.

"Quiet, please, be seated for the next speaker," said the woman with the red scarf.

The following speaker is the grief counsellor, a stout man wearing a pinstriped suit with an open-necked white shirt. He is a psychologist employed in a large non-profit organisation—his research is based on the emotional needs of long- term grieving patients. "The needs of grieving people are complex. They require unconditional support, someone to talk to and hold on to who shares their grief process. Memory work and support groups are crucial in assisting them in moving on and developing closure. Some never recover from their grieving and maintain the pain of loss," he said.

Tom gapes at the podium as though caught in a trap.

Nancy watches as the colour drains from Tom's face.

The speaker finishes with great applause. Tom claps loudly.

"Let's sneak out. I think we both need a strong coffee," Nancy said.

Tom follows.

CHAPTER SIXTY-SIX

It is 7 p.m. at the Sydney Road flat. The wind blows against the windowpanes, causing the small geranium pots on the window ledge to shiver in their pots. Millie and Nancy have finished dinner.

"I have my illusions," said Millie. "And I want us to be a family again." She puts her fork on the table, stares hard at her mother.

"Robert doesn't want to return to us because he misses us, but because his romance with Clarissa is not working out. I don't want my heart broken again," said Nancy.

"What about what I want?" Millie said, her voice rising. "Don't I have a say in the issue? Don't I matter? I want my father to live with us. I don't care for how long he stays or if he goes back to Clarissa." She has pleading eyes. "Just for a while, it would be fantastic to be a family again. Who knows, he may stay."

"Millie, you are too young to understand," Nancy said.

"You are so mean. I want dad back with us."

"I am trying to protect you from disappointment," Nancy said.

Millie pushes her chair back and runs to her bedroom.

Nancy collects the plates and runs the hot water. She can hear Millie talking loudly on the phone with Angie.

"I hate my mother," said Millie.

Nancy calls Gloria. "Robert says he loves Millie but does not willingly support her financially. Now he wants to come back, raising Millie's hopes. How can he do this to his daughter?" She holds the phone close to her mouth.

The wind has dropped outside.

"Lust blinds men's eyes," said Gloria.

"I don't care what the excuse is—Robert must learn to deal with the consequences of his actions. He has always been a selfish, self-absorbed man, uses people, then neglects them. If Robert returns, the next time someone else catches his eye, he would be off. I'm sorry for ranting. He infuriates me."

"I want to give him a hard slap," Gloria said.

"You will need to wait in line for that," Nancy said.

CHAPTER SIXTY-SEVEN

Robert and Millie spent the afternoon playing ten-pin bowling. They return to the flat at dinner time.

"Can dad stay for dinner?" Millie said.

"It is nothing exciting, just a lamb casserole."

"That sounds great. You were always a fantastic cook." He pulls a chair and sits.

Millie and Robert exchange sly looks. Millie sets a round of cutlery for him.

Nancy and Robert are learning to be pleasant with each other for Millie's sake and are no longer in a dance of watching for signs of weakness, ready to pounce.

"How are things with you and Clarissa?" Nancy said.

"Clarissa refuses to see me until I sign the divorce papers." His voice fades.

"We have signed the damn papers," her face reddens, her voice rises.

"I haven't told her yet," he said. "Because Clarissa wants to get married and have kids, and I don't."

Nancy stares at him. "Why is it always related to you and what you want? You are a selfish, horrible man."

"I told you I do not want to get married again and

have kids," he is shouting now, bangs his fist on the table, making the dishes wobble.

"No. No, leave him alone. Mum, stop it. Don't yell at dad." Millie covers her ears, hyperventilates. "I can't bear it when you both fight." Tears stream down Millie's face. "Stop it, both of you. You are killing me...."

Nancy brings her a glass of water.

Robert is shocked, stares at Millie.

"Inaction is as bad as doing the wrong thing," Nancy said.

CHAPTER SIXTY-EIGHT

It is midday at the emergency department, white walls, white cubicles, equipment on wheels. Rows of blue gloves of assorted sizes are hanging on the cubicle wall. A trolley clatters past with trays of meals for the patients who are not fasting and able to eat.

The porter wheels a dishevelled man in a wheelchair. He wears layers of grubby jumpers and torn, dark blue pants. His face is stained with dirt and grime, his brown eyes shine, looks older than his years. The doctor has examined him; he tells his story of trauma to the engrossed medical students.

"I was at the tram stop, and a fat woman fell on top of me. She had a stroke or something. She squashed me flat on my back and I landed on the tram tracks. My lucky day, as no trams ran over me, although my back hurts." He rubs his back.

The medical students take notes, ask if they can examine him, question him about pain and whether he lost consciousness. They take his blood pressure, examine his heart and lungs and reflexes.

Dr Tom Ferris is in the background overseeing the students.

Nancy hears the man's loud voice, pulls back the

curtains of the cubicle. "Frank, what are you telling these students?" She beckon's the students outside, places her pen in the pocket of her scrubs. Tells them to follow her a little away from the cubicle so the patient cannot hear what she has to say.

"Frank likes to tell a good story. He tells a similar tale each time he comes here. The sad reality is Frank is homeless and uses medical issues to access care when it's too cold outside," she said. "What Frank needs right now is food and a hot drink, a shower and a safe place to stay. He is a nice man. I usually provide sandwiches and a hot drink and organise a carer from St Vincent's homeless program to provide a bed for him."

"So, he is faking his injuries," said one medical student.

"Not faking but compensating for the lack of services. His mother died of a heroin overdose when he was young, later his father disappeared. Frank has had to fend for himself since he was fourteen, has no living relatives, and has been homeless ever since."

Dr Ferris comes out of Frank's cubicle. "I've checked Frank. He's fine. He said he is ready for a nice hot cup of white tea, two sugars and a round of sandwiches."

Tom notes Nancy's kindness to the homeless man.

CHAPTER SIXTY-NINE

Nancy edges down the aisle of the Virgin Airlines plane; men and women block the passageway as they search for their seats. Nancy finds her seat and edges into the small space by the window. Her heart pounds with excitement. It is the first time she has been on a plane in years and wants to discover who she was before Robert lost his mind over Clarissa. The flight attendants wear bright red pullovers and beige slim trousers. Those with long hair have it tied neatly back in ponytails, the look young and energetic; they walk down the aisles making sure the passengers have fastened their seatbelts.

A scholarly looking grey-haired man in the seat next to her said, "Are you staying in Canberra long?"

"Just for the day," she said. "I am going to Canberra to visit my friend Suzanne, who sustained two leg fractures falling from a cliff while abseiling."

"Oh, dear, that must have hurt," he said.

"We have been friends since our university days," she said.

He goes back to his book.

Nancy buckles her seat belt tight and peers out of the window. Sunshine is filtering through the clouds in Melbourne. The weather report suggested a sunny day in Canberra. Nancy has bought a gift for Suzanne, a recent release from one of Suzanne's favourite authors-David Baldacci.

The plane taxis on the runway and lifts effortlessly into the sky. Nancy glances at the man next to her. He is pale, grips his seat, looks as though he was going to be sick.

"Can I help you?" Nancy said.

He shakes his head. "I am terrified when the plane takes off and lands."

Nancy speaks softly, "I'm a registered nurse, so you will be safe with me. I will talk to you until the plane is stable. You can hold my hand if it helps."

The man grips her hand tightly. He relaxes his grip when the plane stabilises. The colour returns to his face. "Sorry."

"It's not a problem," Nancy said. "They will pass hot drinks soon. I can see the trolley."

She remembers the last time she visited Suzanne. They were living in East Brunswick, still a family. Robert had gotten into the habit of working long hours, coming home late, exhausted.

"I am drained," Robert had said, throwing his briefcase on the floor as soon as he walked through the door. "What is there to eat?"

"I worry you will have a heart attack. You are working too hard," she said as she heated his meal.

She remembers there were strange things. Robert avoided looking at her directly, started going to the gym twice a week, which was out of character for him.

"On a health kick," he had said, patting his gut. He started buying new clothes for himself, a blue shirt and fancy socks.

"Where did you get these?" She held up the socks covered in Donald Duck figures.

"The secretary at work bought the socks for her boyfriend, but they were too large. She gave them to me. I bought the shirt on a whim." He did not look at her face. He was always too tired for sex. She had convinced herself that everything was fine. He was working hard for them.

Today, towards the end of the flight, the male passenger next to Nancy stiffens as soon as it was announced the plane was about to descend. She put her hand out for him to grasp. Again, he breaks out in a sweat, keeps his eyes tightly shut, clings onto her hand. They land safely and the man opens his eyes and sighs with relief. "I should have therapy to overcome this stupid fear." He hands his card. "If ever you need a lawyer, I can repay your kindness." The card read *Michael Kent, head solicitor for Grace and Miles*.

"I will keep you in mind," she said.

When Nancy enters the arrivals lounge in Canberra, she is met by a loud scream.

"Nancy... Nancy over here." Suzanne almost tumbles out of her wheelchair. Her husband, Shane, holds the wheelchair to stop it toppling over.

"Hello, my poor darling." Suzanne gives Nancy a long hug. "That brute Robert. Fancy him leaving you after all that nasty stuff with Millie's attack." Suzanne is a loud brunette, wears a white loose caftan which semi covers the extended plasters on both her legs.

They have been friends for years since meeting at university during their nursing degree. Gloria, Suzanne and Nancy were known as *The Three Musketeers.* They were always together, studied, socialised, and quizzed each other on exam questions. It was Suzanne who initially introduced Nancy to Robert.

Today, the three decide to go to Floriade, a renowned Canberra spring garden event. The sunny day has brought dense crowds. The loudspeaker blasts the song, *Where have all the flowers gone?* The heady scent of roses, hyacinths fills the air. Thousands of multicoloured flowers are set out in artful clusters. The red and yellow tulips are a favourite with Suzanne and Nancy.

Shane manages Suzanne's wheelchair as they meander through the banks of swirling colourful flowers. Nancy and Suzanne talk excitedly like children at a birthday party. They lick ice creams from cones and retell stories from their past. Shane drives them to the Red Hill Restaurant at the top of a mountain that overlooks Canberra. The view of the valley below takes in the buildings around Parliament House. The conversation between the women becomes expansive with each glass of white wine.

Around four in the afternoon, Suzanne becomes fatigued. "My legs hurt. I need to go home and rest."

～

Suzanne and Shane's home is an open planned design with walls of glass and metal that opens to a considerable cactus garden. Highly polished wooden floors are dotted with thick white rugs. The focus is modern with soft comfortable white leather armchairs. Angled mirrors on the walls reflect the light from outside. Suzanne stretches on a leather couch. Shane orders Indian curries for takeaway. The women never stop talking and laughing.

At nine pm, Nancy looks at her watch. "If I want to catch my plane to Melbourne, I should make a move to go."

Suzanne pulls a face, "I want you to stay longer."

Nancy promises, "Next time, I will."

Shane drives Nancy to the airport, Suzanne stays behind.

"Thank you for coming. You have been wonderful medicine for Suzanne. This is the first time I've seen Suzanne laugh since the accident," said Shane. "Please let me pay for your flight. I know finances have been tough for you since Robert left." He reaches for his wallet.

"No, certainly not. You have already paid for lunch and dinner. I should pay you," she said.

At the departure lounge, she checks to see if the nervous passenger on the previous flight was waiting. He wasn't.

It is after 11pm when Nancy returns to the flat. Millie and Robert are watching a movie.

"Thank you for looking after Millie. Good night." Nancy hands Robert his jacket.

"It is late. I might stay here tonight. I can sleep on the couch," Robert said.

Nancy's face is stone like.

"Come on, mum, let him stay," Millie said.

"It is over, you know it, and I know it."

"Mum ..." shouts Millie.

"Good night," Nancy holds the door open.

"Sort out your life. Both Clarissa and I want that."

He opens his mouth to argue, closes it, takes his jacket and walks out.

CHAPTER SEVENTY

A large green hedge hides the wooden cottage from the street. Sandra and Tom Ferris bought the Richmond cottage when Sandra his wife was alive. The simple house once belonged to a Greek man and his family. When he died, the house was listed as *a renovator's delight*. They spent months renovating the wooden house. Tom paints the exterior every two years, does the repairs. It is eight in the evening when Tom unlatches the gate to his home.

It has been a long and complicated day at work. He is still wearing the white doctor's coat over his black slacks and blue shirt. The coat has small spatters of blood and dirt near the pockets. His mind hovers over the sick patient in the trauma unit. Has he forgotten anything? He retraces the details of his shift and the treatment of the unknown man with multiple fractures and head injuries. The man had been standing at the traffic lights waiting for the lights to turn green when two drivers racing each other mounted the footpath, striking the man. The drivers fled the scene on foot after the accident.

Tom unlocks the front door, drops his backpack, he steps inside. Has to stop himself, saying, "Sandra,

276

I'm home." She has been dead for five years, and a part of him still expects her to come and greet him wearing the apron she always wore when cooking. He switches the lights on. The house is as Sandra had decorated it. Nothing has changed. In the living room, the comfortable dark blue lounge chairs are in the same place. The blue carpet matches the drapes. The polished pine floorboards in the kitchen blend with the pine cupboards and table. A brown terracotta paved garden surrounded by purple lavender plants is visible from the kitchen.

Tom's phone vibrates. "Hello, Tom speaking." The call is from the relieving doctor at the hospital requesting more information related to the unknown patient.

"Do you want me to come back to the hospital? Ring me if you get into any trouble."

The other doctor said he would ring if he wanted more information.

He fills the kettle with cold water, switches it on, sets out one cup, one English breakfast tea bag. Turns the radio on to Radio National. The warm voice of the radio presenter is a familiar guest in the empty spaces of his home. He opens the fridge door and takes out two eggs. Finds the frying pan, switches the hotplate on. While the eggs are cooking, he opens a tin of baked beans, adds it to the pan. He reads the mail—two bills. Sandra was the one who dealt with their finances. He tells himself he should organise direct debit, but he never gets around to it. Tom goes to the white walled bathroom to change his clothes and wash, catches sight of himself in the mirror—always a shock. He is getting bald on top, looks more like his father.

God, I look old.

Goes back to the kitchen, sits down to eat, washes the dishes and puts them away. Sits at the table, unsure what to do next. It is dark outside, sees his reflection in the glass window.

The phone vibrates again. The previous doctor rings to inform him they solved the patient's problem. "Relax and enjoy your evening."

Tom studies the painting easel in the kitchen's corner. He frequently paints after work to relax.

CHAPTER SEVENTY-ONE

Nancy visits Aunt Stella in her retirement home. She was in her flannel nightgown and pink dressing gown. Aunt Stella grimaces as if in pain.

"I'm going to bed early," said Aunt Stella and pats her swollen abdomen.

"Have you spoken to the doctor?" said Nancy.

"The doctor ordered a scan."

"Oh, I nearly forgot. I bought you a dress. Can I see if it fits?" said Nancy, opening the shopping bag.

Aunt Stella removes her nightgown, tries on the pink and green cotton paisley dress. "I love it. Where did you find it?" said Aunt Stella, her eyes sparkle.

"The dress found me. I was at the florist shop; it was in the window of the shop next door. It is a gift, so don't go on about paying me," said Nancy.

"Are you sure?" Said Aunt Stella.

"I am very sure," Nancy said.

"Hold on while I pin the hem. It's too long for you." Nancy adjusts the length. "I'll take the dress home tonight and alter it. You can wear it when we have lunch next week if you like."

Aunt Stella embraces Nancy. "You are a dear, always looking out for me."

It seems like yesterday that Aunt Stella adjusted the hems of my school dresses.

≈

Disco music vibrates from the hotel down the road from the green flat. Saturday night's loud music plays until midnight. When the music stops is followed by a heightened racket of loud voices and slamming car doors and cars racing away into the night.

Millie is asleep in her room. Nancy snuggles under the warm doona on her bed. The electric blanket is switched on, a warm rug wrapped around her shoulders. Nancy has a textbook on her lap. She looks up as a quick burst of rain pelts on the windows, making a strange twang sound.

Outside, a woman screams and screams.

Nancy grabs her dressing gown, rushes to the street to see if she can help. Three men from the flats are already on the footpath. They are arguing with a large, heavily tattooed man, who appears drunk and ready for a fight. The male has been trying to drag the young, terrified woman into his car.

"Let her go, mate," said an onlooker. He has already phoned the police.

"Get in the car, slut," the man said to the cowering woman. "Or I'll beat your brains out." The man staggers towards the woman, his fist outstretched.

Just at that moment, a police van with flashing lights arrives. A huge, thickset police officer, not in the mood for pleasantries, steps out of the car with his hand on the gun in his holster.

"Stop right there," said the police officer to the tattooed man.

Another police officer materialises. They attempt to frog march the man towards the police van.

"I will get you for this." The tattooed man raises his fists at the woman. "I will find where you live, and you will be dead. You're a bitch leading me on and then knocking me back." He tries to break free from the police, but they have twisted his arms behind his back and placed handcuffs on his wrists.

"Come on, you're in enough trouble for one night," said the officer. They bundle the protesting male into the van.

The young woman is around 18 years, with long straight black hair, wears a short-flowered dress and black boots. She sits on the wet kerb, crying.

The older police officer touches the young woman's shoulder. "Did he hurt you? Do you want to press assault charges against him?" He squats next to her.

The crowd forms a circle around the police officer and the woman.

"He threatened to hit me," she sobs. "I was afraid he would."

The police officer said, "Lady, we can order a taxi for you. I will wait with you until it comes."

He waves to the crowd from the flats. "Show's over. Go home." The crowd slowly disperses.

"Fancy hooking up with such a creep," said one man from the flats.

Nancy wanted to ask if the girl was OK, but the police officer was adamant they should leave.

Back at the flat, Nancy finds Millie, rolled into a ball, rocking back and forth on her bed. The drunk man's shouts had triggered the remembrance of her assault. Nancy holds Millie until she is calm. "Just a stupid drunk man causing problems. The police straightened him out.... you are safe."

They decide to watch a movie as a distraction until Millie calms down and falls asleep.

The green flat creaks as it moves in the cold. Nancy hears something move behind the plaster wall, a rat or possum scurrying in the wall spaces. The sound reminds her of her childhood home in the country. Timber the dog would strain at his chain at night, barking at passing kangaroos or possums.

CHAPTER SEVENTY-TWO

It is evening at the green Coburg flat. Cars and trams rush outside, creating a familiar cacophony of noise. Nancy has a watering can in her hand as she tends to her plants. The flat has slowly developed into a miniature botanical garden. The window ledge has a row of miniature plants—red fuchsia, small bright yellow daisies, tiny Daphne plants. She trims the wandering Jude creeper, which cascades carelessly from the bathroom and toilet window ledges. Two small palms vie for space in the lounge room. Millie's bedroom window ledge is home for a long green ivy. Nancy's bedroom windowsill has six miniature cactus plants. Most of the plants are neglected plants from the nearby plant nursery bought cheap. Nancy calls them her "rescue plants." They line up like soldiers, in same-sized pots. She has been fortunate to have generous neighbours and friends that share cuttings with her. She has a bag of potting mix in the laundry cupboard, old newspapers, and a trowel. The plastic pots are from the Reject shop and recycle depots. She uses flat plastic tops from take-away containers to place under the plants to stop spillage when watering. A good day for Nancy is to visit the local plant nursery, walk up and down the aisles admiring the colours and types of plants.

"When we have our own home, I will have a greenhouse and propagate masses of herbs and vegetables," she told Millie.

"When will you know when you have enough plants?" said Millie.

"I don't think I will ever have enough," Nancy said.

When the plants grow too large for the windowsills, she gives them to others in the flats. Nancy gifted a white geranium plant to a neighbour, an Ethiopian lady. The neighbour shared a pot of a spicy rice dish with Nancy, she is aware the woman is lonely and makes a point of chatting with her when she meets her on the stairs.

"The plant you gave me has many flowers," the woman said.

"How are your boys doing at school?" Said Nancy.

"They are struggling with their English and schoolwork. The school is providing some tutoring. Hopefully, they will work hard and catch up with their lessons," she said.

CHAPTER SEVENTY-THREE

Nancy hammers away on the laptop, working on her thesis on her days off. Now and then takes a break and swims in the local Leisure Centre. Inside the Centre, another world, a time warp, a time when nothing matters but the water and having fun. It is a place for families, a row of prams line one side of the pool near the entrance. Women carry babies with slicked back wet hair, eyes luminous with wetness draped in pink towelling tops with hoods. A tiny girl of about four walks past. She has a thin brown ponytail, wears a bright pink T-shirt and denim skirt, holds a phone to her ear. A man, possibly her father, walks beside her as she speaks on the phone. He carries a backpack, his hairy legs and multiple tattoos on his arms and legs belie his tender caring of the little girl.

The Centre has been renovated; the pool and dressing rooms are now blue, the light flooding in from the large windows gives it a Greek island look. There are new open spaces for eating and meeting with friends. Nearby a free book exchange in a side room, Nancy is a frequent user, exchanges books on a weekly basis.

An elderly woman passes wearing a long black skirt

that reaches her ankles. She shuffles with a wooden walking stick, hobbles painfully towards the heated pool and nearly topples over. A group of gossiping women stroll past, wrapped in sodden towels after aqua aerobics. The energetic ones pound on exercise machines, eyes glued to the television screens. Five men are lifting weights. The local pool is a community of people coming together.

Swimming lessons are in progress in the children's pool. A disabled boy perfects his kick in the water. Squeals of joyful children's voices ricochet off walls as they splash in the pool. Cries of "Watch me, mum."

A girl in a yellow frilly swimsuit jumps in the toddler's shallow pool and drenches her mother with water.

Nancy remembers when they were a family, Millie played with the other children at this pool. Robert used to make a great show, diving into the adult pool, throwing up sheets of water, followed by quick, fast strokes. He swam like a champion at first, arm over arm, kicking, then slowed down and stopped. Nancy started slowly, managed more laps.

Today, Nancy slips into the pool, swims ten laps to the end and back without stopping. The water is exhilarating. Later she attends a yoga class, the yoga instructor said, "Tell yourself I am enough." She had been laid off by her company when they restructured, lost her job as a program developer, but reinvented herself as a full-time yoga instructor with a strong spiritual connection.

I need to reinvent myself.

CHAPTER SEVENTY-FOUR

Nancy wakes with a sense of dread. The wind has banged and thrashed, overturned rubbish bins and smashed twigs against the windows. Wild winds are a reminder of her powerlessness. She showers, dresses in white cotton slacks and a black T-shirt. Nancy wakes Millie and drives her to school.

She goes to *Mininios* opposite the tram depot on Sydney road. It is a bustling cosmopolitan cafe with a strong influence of Muslim culture. Men with black beards and white tunics read newspapers, women with bright eyes and heads covered in colourful scarves, sit in groups. Young girls sip drinks, eyes glued on mobile phones. Outside, the traffic rolls like a river, trams rabble past, trucks and cars compete for space on the narrow road. There are elaborate shops with Arabic writing, mannequins dressed in gold dresses suitable for a queen. The jewellery shop windows are full of gold bracelets, chains, and earrings. Nearby are Halal butchers.

Nancy checks her watch, finishes her Turkish coffee. She drives to Gloria's house in Moonee Ponds. The house is an old-fashioned triple fronted brick house, a mowed front lawn and no-nonsense green shrubs in the garden.

She knocks on the door.

"Come in," said Gloria, wears old faded blue jeans and a green t-shirt and a weary expression.

"I warn you. I am on the warpath today." Gloria glances around the room. "Excuse the mess." The room is littered with Lego blocks, small fire engines, books and toys that belong to her three young sons. "The boys are at school. I know the place looks like a bomb exploded in here. I should tidy it up. But as soon as I do, the boys will be home and mess it up again."

"I can help you," said Nancy, getting up.

"Don't worry, I will clean up after. I would rather talk to you. How are you?"

"Still trying to find my way in life. When are you working at the hospital next?" said Nancy.

"I have the next three days off." Gloria moves a half-eaten piece of toast to the end of the table.

"I have to take my mother-in-law to the doctor's one day. She needs to go to the dentist the next, and on the third day I must take her to the podiatrist." Gloria said. "I shouldn't grumble. She loves the boys and looks after them whenever I ask."

"You look miserable," Nancy said. "What's up?"

"Janey is driving me nuts," Gloria pushes a strand of hair from her glasses. "Since Janey has come into money, she feels justified to point out my issues. She who has never had kids and tells me how to bring up my children."

"You and Janey have been great friends for years," Nancy has a worried look on her face.

"That's what you think." Gloria blows the fringe from her face. "Get your head out of the clouds and see the world as it is. Stop deluding yourself."

"I hate it when you and Janey fight. Can't you make peace again? Allow her another chance?"

"Never. I don't need Janey in my life."

"We all have a different drum beating inside of them, telling a unique story," said Nancy.

"My drum is out of sync with Janey's drum," Gloria said.

"Why don't you show your vulnerability? Friendship is too precious to leave to ill-conceived words," said Nancy.

Gloria groans. "Nancy girl, you are living in la-la land. No way."

They do not speak for five minutes.

Nancy hated the breakdown of her marriage and the slow destruction of friendships. If Gloria and Janey are fighting, she will have to take sides. It will be a loss for her.

"How are my plants doing?" Nancy said, changing the topic.

"They are alive, if that is what you are asking," said Gloria.

They go outside and inspect Nancy's large pots from the East Brunswick home.

"You are developing green fingers. I do like the

tinsel around each of the plants; very Christmas," said Nancy.

"The boys decorated them," laughs Gloria.

"What would I do without you, dear Gloria?" said Nancy.

CHAPTER SEVENTY-FIVE

Tuesday morning at nine, at the neat green flat. Millie is at school; Nancy has finished her chores. The flat smells of lavender floor cleaner.

Nancy rings Gloria, "Today is an anniversary of sorts, it is two years since Robert left."

"Good riddance to bad rubbish. Apart from the financial side of things, you are better off without him." Gloria glances at the stack of dirty dishes in her sink. "I should get into the dishes before my mother-in-law comes to look after the kids whilst I am at work." She hangs up.

~

Once again, it's another Christmas. Nancy makes a half-hearted effort at a list of presents to buy. She plans to buy a small Christmas tree and decorate it with baubles from the charity shop and purchase a few gifts for close friends and family.

The last thing she wants to think about is gift buying but catches the tram to the city and walks to the Bourke street Mall. It is crowded with ill-tempered shoppers scurrying in and out of shops. Nancy enters

Myer, a large Melbourne shopping emporium, the place overflowing with frantic shoppers with glazed looks in their eyes. In the background, *Jingle Bells* plays over and over on loudspeakers. She moves through the aisles of perfume counters, sprays a little French perfume *Joy from Jean Patou perfumery* on her wrists, checks the price, $400 for a small bottle. She shakes her head in disbelief at the price. Years before they separated, Robert had bought her a bottle of Joy duty-free from one of his trips overseas. It was a magnificent indulgence. The perfume lingered on her mind, today the aroma of the perfume brought back a happier time in her life. After applying a small amount of the tester to her scarf, she takes a whiff of its fragrance and then puts the tester back on the counter.

She takes the escalator to the Christmas specialty section; takes a moment to pause and absorb the masses of red festive decorations and Father Christmas figures. *Silent Night* is played over the loudspeaker on this level of the store. Strangers push and prod at trinkets to give as gifts.

Nancy notices a magnificent red music box on the counter. Opens the lid. A dainty ballet dancer in a pink tutu swirls in time with the music. This jolts her, memories of other Christmas appear. The music box and dancer remind her of one such machine when she worked as a junior nurse in a children's ward many years ago. She recalls caring for a young girl in a coma from an undiagnosed illness. The young girl had an angelic face, a blonde sleeping beauty. It appeared as if she could wake from the coma at any moment. The parents were barely out of their teens, eyes hollowed out with distress and pain.

The girl's mother had said to Nancy. "We always play the music box. It is Belinda's favourite thing on earth." The young mother ran her hands gently through the unconscious girl's hair. Bent over and kissed her on the forehead, telling her words of love. When the red music box lid opened, a tiny ballet dancer dressed in a pink tutu whirled around to the music, something from Mozart. The mother wound the music box, and it played over and over. "Please play the music box when we leave and talk to Belinda as though she can hear you. Tell her what you are doing so she knows," she said. "We will be back early tomorrow morning. Tell her that," she stops, overcome with emotion. Her husband put his arms around her shoulders and gently led her away.

After they left, Nancy rewound the music box over and over and spoke to the girl as though she could hear her. 'Belinda, I plan to turn you over, so you don't get pressure sores.... Belinda, I intend to freshen you up with a sponge bath.' The girl appeared lighter, seemed to emerge from the coma.

When Nancy arrived for her shift the next afternoon, she discovered that Belinda's bed was unoccupied. Belinda had died overnight.

She thought of the young parents and their love for their cherished daughter.

❧

Today Nancy thinks Christmas shopping is futile. Millie has reverted to experiencing flashbacks of the attack. At least once a week, Millie sees someone who reminds her of the assailant. Nancy is again walking on eggshells, afraid to say anything that will set Millie off on an emotional tirade.

What is Christmas when Millie is so damaged?

She goes home empty-handed.

CHAPTER SEVENTY-SIX

Nancy shivers, pulls the navy-blue dressing gown closer to her. It is six a.m., the flat is freezing. She glances at the calendar pinned on the corkboard on the kitchen wall. It is August the 25th, the date of her wedding anniversary. Even with Robert gone from the marriage, he has left a trail of shared memories that burn as they come up to her mind.

The monster that is Sydney road is waking up, trams clang and snake down the street.

Five years ago, Robert had organised a weekend at the Grand Chancellor Hotel for their anniversary. Their hotel room overlooked the Melbourne city centre. They had eaten an extensive meal that included prawns and crayfish, drank a bottle of French champagne.

Robert had tipped his glass to her. "To my beautiful wife that I will always love and adore."

"To my husband...," Nancy raised her glass. She wore the white pearls he had given her as an anniversary gift. They clinked champagne glasses.

This is what she had always wanted, a family of her own, devoted husband, beautiful daughter. Life had been perfect, one moment surrounded by a husband's love and security. Then life went in another direction.

Today she pulls the dressing gown cord tighter.

CHAPTER SEVENTY-SEVEN

Robert left the office, slipped into his car, and drove toward the hotel. He switched on the radio; an old song played-*Puff the Magic Dragon*. An image came to mind of Nancy and Millie singing the song. They were in the kitchen of the East Brunswick house; Nancy was cooking a lamb roast. Millie was ten, hair in pigtails. They were singing along to the song on the radio. He had been working at home and came down to inquire about the noise. "Keep the noise down. I'm trying to work."

Puff the magic dragon... Millie and Nancy kept singing on top of their lungs.

He had rolled his eyes and said, "Oh my God." But he secretly loved to hear them singing. This was before Millie's assault. Today when he listened to the words. They cut deep.

The attack on Millie changed the dynamics of all in the family, his marriage, even his image of Millie as his daughter and Nancy as his wife. Nancy stayed focussed on Millie and her concerns. He did not know how to fix Millie. Falling in love with Clarissa had been a miracle. Now that was gone as well. He flicks the radio off and drives to the hotel underground park.

Robert feels he is surrounded by grey: grey concrete, grey posts, grey spaces without end. He presses the lift button, exits on the third floor and strolls to his hotel room.

I need someone to come home to each day

.

CHAPTER SEVENTY-EIGHT

The phone rings after midnight. Clarissa had been asleep in her apartment. She checks the caller ID before answering.

"Hello," she said.

"Clarissa," said her father. "I have bad news for you."

Any phone call from her father no matter what the time always spelt trouble. She sits up in bed, wraps the sheets around her body, switches the lamp on next to her bed. "Do you know what the time is?" She yawns.

"I know it's late, but I need to give you a heads-up. Charlie Spangle, the real estate agent from Hooker, is coming to your apartment early tomorrow. He is going to give me a quote. I need to sell the apartment now," he breaks out into a coughing fit.

"Are you still smoking? You told me you were going to stop," Clarissa said in an annoyed voice.

"I will... I promise... I'm in a bit of a jam at the moment ... yes, financial ... I know what you are going to say."

Clarissa purses her lips.

"I need cash in a hurry and must sell the apartment now." He coughs again. "The agent will tell me what

its current worth is... I will list it for sale immediately."
His voice sounds strained.

"But.." she starts.

"I won't kick you out on the street. You can come
back home and stay with mother and me. Besides, you
earn enough to rent something yourself," he said. "You
will have a few weeks before you have to move out."

"This is terrible. I love living here."

"I know you do, but I need the money in a hurry.
Sorry, sweetheart, life is a tad awkward at the moment.
Got to go, bye," he hangs up.

Clarissa swears and throws her pillow to the floor,
goes to the balcony. The clear night exposes the city
lights in the distance. She could never afford to rent a
luxurious apartment like the one she was in. Her father
will make a quick sale, for $4 million plus. Clarissa goes
inside, rummages for a pen and paper, starts a list. The
furniture and white goods belong to her father. Her
clothes and personal things are the only things she
needs to pack. They will fit into three suitcases.

I am so sick of this moving around.

When Clarissa was younger, the family moved in
with her father's German mother for a year. Again,
it was another episode of her father's financial
unravelling, and he could not afford the rent on their
home. They shifted in with grandmother in her two-
bedroom housing commission flat. In one bedroom
were father, mother, brother Jed, Clarissa, and their
two cats. Two inflatable mattresses on the floor for the
children. Mother and father slept in the double bed with

the cats. Grandmother in the other bedroom. The cats hated each other, snarled and hissed as grandmother's cat vied for supremacy. Her grandmother spoke a little English and treated Clarissa as a princess.

To live with her parents was not an option. Her father's chaotic lifestyle of highs and lows unnerved her sense of order. She checks her bank balance, not enough for a rental bond and month's rent in advance.

I should not have had the weekend pampering spa.

Robert could provide a stable, comfortable future, but he was still married, and she would not compromise.

Robert has to divorce his wife.

CHAPTER SEVENTY-NINE

Nancy seems to run into Dr Tom Ferris everywhere at work. They are often on similar shifts at the emergency department. She enjoys working with him, respects the way he treats the patients. But is curious about his grief issues, he appeared in deep distress when the grief presenter spoke at the Mental Health Conference. She plans to ask Tom on hints how to improve Millie's art therapy since he was once an art teacher.

"Hello to my favourite nurse," Tom said, a wide, toothy grin on his face. "Have I told you that those blue scrubs you are wearing are bewitching?" He raises his eyebrows.

"The white doctor's coat looks fetching on you," Nancy said in a playful voice.

~

It is warm today, the sun shines encouragement through the windows. It is one p.m. in the crowded hospital staff lunchroom. This is a safe space for the medical staff to interact with each other. The urgency of bleeding patients and gunshot wounds are absent. There are no overdoses. No desperate relatives clinging to the staff, and those in need. The staff periodically check their mobiles to see how much time they have left before they return to the ward. Vibrant conversations and laughter fill the room. The microwave is in continual use. The buzzer goes off as the next staff member heats their meal. Personal mobile phones ring loud. The table is littered with paper bags, disposable containers of half-eaten food and paper cups.

Nancy and Tom are squashed next to each other at the long table with the other staff. His plain cheese sandwich is homemade.

"Do you often make your own lunch?" she said. "The doctors usually buy their meals."

"I usually make my lunch. Not exciting, but cheap and healthy," he said.

She bites her lip, looks around, lowers her voice. "I wonder if you could give me any tips on how to help my daughter with her art. Two years ago, a stranger badly assaulted Millie, and she is still having issues. She sees an excellent counsellor who encouraged her to paint her problems on canvas." Nancy hesitates, has said too much. Her face reddens. "Millie keeps painting these terrible wild eyes over and over." She takes a deep breath. "How can I help her expand her art beyond the scary eyes?"

"I can come around and examine her work," Tom takes a bite of his sandwich. "When I was a teacher I worked with problem students. Art therapy, they call it now."

"That would be wonderful." The noisy lunchroom is music to her ears. "Thank you," she smiles. "I appreciate it." Writes her address and phone number on a piece of paper and hands it to him. He puts it in his pocket.

"I will ring you when I am free," he said, gives Nancy a troubled look, did not know her background.

A week later, Tom arrives at the green flat. It has been a chilly, windy day. He wears a black beanie over his thinning hair, blue jeans and a thick black puffer jacket; he carries a small portfolio of his own art.

Nancy wears two jumpers layered over each other and fleecy navy tracksuit pants. "Did you have trouble finding parking? It is always difficult around here."

"I took the tram," he said.

She ushers Tom into the kitchen.

Millie is at the table talking on the phone to Angie.

Nancy closes the laptop and moves her notes to the sink bench.

Tom sits next to Millie. "Hello Millie, my name is Tom. I hear you are a budding artist."

Millie looks up from her phone. "Talk to you later, Angie. We have a visitor." She looks at her mother and then Tom.

"I am not an artist. All I do is dab paint on paper," said Millie.

They discuss his role at the hospital and how he

knows Nancy. Millie is curious. He is a friendly man, and she sees her mother is relaxed around him.

"Let me show you my paintings," Tom opens his portfolio, spreads out the paintings on the small space on the kitchen table.

Millie studies his work intently. "Your paintings remind me of the universe and the milky way in the sky."

"It's supposed to be something esoteric. But the milky way will do," he said. "Painting is a visual language. There is nothing original there. I am quoting art experts here. Art should have elements of line, colour, shape, form, and space and meaning on a canvas." He points out aspects in his painting.

"I would love to see your art. Your mother tells me you are painting expressive eyes. And bring paint and brushes so we can practice."

Millie finds her most recent painting, collects paints and brushes, returns to the kitchen. She shows Tom her painting of grotesque bloodshot eyes on a black background.

Tom's eyes flicker when he sees the painting, gives Nancy a quick glance. "Your work has the things I just said. Here are examples of line, colour, shape, form, and space." He points to the various aspects of the eyes of the attacker that Millie had captured.

Millie looks intently at her painting.

"You have explored the tactile experience related to the emotional and symbolic significance of your pain."

Millie has a quizzical look on her face.

"That's art teacher talk. It means you got it."

Millie tilts her head with interest. "I always considered my art as fury a type of graffiti."

"It is more than that. Art expresses our inner workings, a type of shorthand that defines who we are."

Nancy stays in the background. She is heartened by Tom's ability to connect with Millie.

"Colour exists in relation to other colours and will be a different shade depending on the sunlight or shade, in artificial light. Let's look at the black in your background and see if we can improve on it." He explains how he makes the dark colours clearer by adding other colours to the mix. Tom mixes the paints to achieve a dreamy texture.

"You have raw talent." Tom wipes the brush on an oil rag. "Your heart shows your hand how to proceed. That is real flair." He replaces his paintings in the portfolio. Places the brush and paints back in Millie's box. "If you work on your technique, you could be a talented artist. I suggest you have formal art lessons."

"I did not know," Millie said.

"Now you know." Tom has a hard look at the room.

"Whoever painted this flat liked the colour green."

Millie giggles, "Mum calls it the green flat."

He glances at the rows of small plants lined like soldiers on the window ledge.

"Someone has green fingers."

"That's mum. She can make a stick grow."

"I would like to take you and your mother to a good art gallery and show you genius art. That is how I learnt what was good and what was mediocre."

"I would like that," Millie said.

～

The following Saturday, Tom, Millie, and Nancy met at the National Gallery of Victoria. Tom spoke of Vincent van Gogh's painting, *The Empty Chair* at the Impressionists section. "The painting symbolised the artist's loneliness and disengagement from the world. See the sunlight yellow of the chair. Look at the colours of the tiled floor. You can understand how he is by from the bleakness of the contents. Vincent was a master at the use of colour," he said. "Like you Millie, he painted from the heart. Just looking at the *Empty Chair,* you experience his sadness and mental health issues. Vincent used his art to heal."

He turns to Millie and says in a faint voice. "I used art to deal with my grief when my wife died." Nancy and Millie look at each other. This tall, assertive man has exposed his vulnerability.

"Is that why you became a doctor?" Millie said.

"Yes, I think so." Tom looks away. "At the time of my wife's illness, there was little treatment available for her type of cancer. There is more available now." He pretends to look closely at a painting on the wall.

Millie and Nancy wait.

"After a while, the doctors said there was nothing

more they could do for Sandra. So, I brought her home...." He looks directly at Nancy.

"Watching her die slowly and in misery nearly killed me." His voice is breaking.

"Sorry," he blinks. "I'm letting my tongue get away with me. Truth is, I painted my way out of deep depression when she died." He kept his gaze on Nancy. "Even now, when I cannot sleep, I take out my brushes and paint."

"I sometimes paint when I am triggered... It's better than taking it out on mum," said Millie.

Afterwards, they go their separate ways. Tom goes to the hospital. He is the registrar on duty for the late shift.

Millie and Nancy check out the gift shop.

CHAPTER EIGHTY

Robert has his elbows on the chrome table in the flat on Sydney Road. Nancy stands with her arms folded.

"I will cover the cost of Millie's art lessons if you let me move in with you," said Robert.

"No bribery," Nancy said. It was ludicrous that he was still angling to shift in with them. "I told you before and I am telling you again, there is no room for you," she said.

"I could share your bed," he said in a small voice.

"You have to be kidding." A part of her was enjoying seeing Robert humbled but distrusted his portrayal of a desperate man. It would not work on her anymore.

The noise from the street echoed in the background.

"I could sleep in Millie's room, and she could sleep with you."

"Not going to happen."

"I could sleep on the sofa." he stared straight at her. "We could rent a bigger flat with a third bedroom. I could pay half the rent and expenses." He was getting flustered, hates to lose an argument.

"As soon as Clarissa rings, you will be off, and it

would leave me with the larger rent. This place is all I can afford at the moment." She stares into his face.

"Are you going to pay for the art lessons for Millie? This is not a bargaining trip for you."

"You have become hard. It is not a good look for you," he said.

"When you left me, I had to become strong." Her voice softens.

"I will make you a hot drink and we can discuss how much the art lessons will cost you."

She takes out two plain white mugs from the cupboard and sets them on the table, opens the glass jar with the last of the Anzac biscuits she baked at the weekend, places them on a plate in front of Robert.

Finally, Robert relents and pays for the art lessons for Millie at the Council of Adult Education.

On the floor in Millie's bedroom in the green flat and under her bed are art books from a charity shop: *How to paint and draw techniques* by Brian Liddle, *Van Gogh* by M. E. Tralbaut. She has set the easel in the corner of her small bedroom near the window in an endeavour to catch the afternoon light. The small table holds brushes, paints, and paint rags. Old sheets are spread are on the floor for protection. Millie wears an old shirt of Nancy's as an art smock. It hangs on a hook on the door when not in use. She paints scenes of trees and flowers these days and often has paint on her fingers, although she still bites the nails to the nail bed.

~

When his shift allows, Tom has become an addition to Gloria and Nancy's debriefing sessions at the cafe at the hospital.

"Do you think that you and Chris could join Nancy and me for a fancy art event?" Tom said.

"You could bring Chris," he reddens. "We can go as a foursome, sort of double date with friends."

"I should have asked you first," he said, looking at Nancy.

"I'll ask Chris," said Gloria, dialling his number.

"An artist friend told me about this art event, and it was a spur-of-the-moment idea," he said.

"Chris said he would like to join us," said Gloria, clicking off on her phone. Nancy's face is red, flushed.

He said double date.

The conversation returns to the water pipe that broke in Gloria's ward and created a minor flood. The hospital staff moved the patients to the corridor of another ward until they fixed the problem.

~

A week later, the four dress the part of art connoisseurs. Tom wears a black suit, white shirt, and black bow tie. Chris wears a black and white checked sport jacket, black T-shirt, and trousers. Gloria wears a vivid blue dress and a matching blue and red shawl. Nancy dug out her black cocktail dress and the gold chain Aunt Stella had given her. She fingers the chain around her neck.

They pile into Chris's Toyota people mover. Chris's mother agreed to babysit the three boys.

The upmarket art gallery in South Yarra has overhanging trees that create a moving pattern over a freshly clipped garden. The artist's home is the art gallery. He is renowned for his huge paintings of red poppies. Original paintings cost $150,000 or more, while signed limited-edition copies cost $1,000. The artist's wife, a leggy brunette, carries a sleeping baby while mingling with the guests. Servers fill champagne glasses and pass delicate pies filled with salmon and chives.

Tom, Chris, Gloria and Nancy make a production of peering at the paintings. Tom explains the art techniques. They pretend to be wealthy buyers, debating where the paintings would sit best in their houses.

"This one would be wonderful above our bed," said Chris.

"No, I think it would look best in the bathroom," said Gloria, and laughed.

∽

They return to the flat for refreshments, Angie and Millie join them. When Gloria and Chris leave, Nancy walks Tom to his car, which is parked in the hotel car park a block away.

"I had a wonderful time." Nancy was timid, unsure of what to say.

"Me too," he said.

He kisses her softly on the lips. "Nancy, you are an incredible woman."

CHAPTER EIGHTY-ONE

Maxine's dining room is awash with the music from *The Marriage of Figaro*.

"Robert told me if you had not been so determined to do your Masters, he would not have become involved with Clarissa," Maxine frowns.

Nancy does not reply. She places a small pot of red geraniums in Maxine's hands. "These are for you. Since my close friend Dianne died, I do not want to waste time. Life is over so soon." She looks for a visual clue to continue. It's impossible for her to decipher Maxine's facial expression. They have never been close.

Nancy's face reddens as she says, "I was hoping we could put our differences aside. I hope the geraniums make you happy. I want us to be friends, for Millie's sake." She watches her mother-in-law with interest.

"They are nice." Maxine holds the plant for a long time.

The grandfather clock chimes the hour.

"Thank you," Maxine's voice was husky, is unsure what to say. She stares at Nancy intently, thinks that perhaps she had been wrong. It was Robert who was out of his class. He left a wife and child with special needs to go off with a foolish young woman.

Maxine places the pot on the table, walks to Nancy, puts her arms on her shoulders. "We have not always agreed. But we both loved Millie and Robert. I know your studying has nothing to do with Robert leaving. He always used excuses to escape responsibility."

"Robert could not come to terms with Millie's assault. Sadly, he left, and you had to manage." Maxine tilts her head, listening to the music.

"He's not emotionally strong like we are," Maxine said. "We both had to struggle in our youth. Robert never had to. It was my fault. I created an easy life for him. The boys had what I never had, spoilt them with excesses that gave them a sense of entitlement."

"Maybe one day I will be as strong as you," said Nancy.

Maxine snorts, "Strong is not a word I use for myself. I prefer devious... cunning...." The light from the open window shines on her face.

"Next time you speak with Millie, ask her about her art lessons. Her work is good," said Nancy.

"Have you seen Robert recently?" Maxine said.

"Robert has been a thorn in my life since Clarissa kicked him out of her apartment. He has been angling to stay with Millie and me. He rings most days; makes any excuse to come around to the flat, usually at dinnertime." Nancy pulls a face. "What can I do? Millie adores Robert. I cannot rock the boat, or it will upset her. Any sort of conflict causes Millie to have a panic attack. Robert remains stubbornly on the edge of our lives. One moment pushing to come back, pleading midlife syndrome for his leaving. Is contrite and wants another chance. Later, blaming me for things that did not go according to plan. This is the worst kind of gaslighting."

Maxine's face shows no emotion.

"Sorry, I shouldn't rant. Robert is your son," said Nancy.

Maxine expressed her astonishment at the man Robert has turned into.

"I have more gifts... this is an orange cake I made as a peace offering. For the sake of Millie, I wish for us to be closer." Nancy reaches into the carry bag at her feet, places an oval orange cake on the table.

Maxine is silent for a long while. Goes to the kitchen and brings back two plates, forks and a knife.

"Make a wish for the future," said Maxine, handing her the knife.

"My wish is for Millie to be happy." Nancy's voice breaks.

"That's my wish too," said Maxine.

CHAPTER EIGHTY-TWO

The Hyatt hotel is Nick's latest choice for a cocktail party to impress notable clients and their partners. Opulent art décor decorates the hotel. The environment is upmarket, elegant. Nick again instructed the senior accountants they had to attend and mingle with the clients. Servers dressed in black supplied crab and lobster treats and two choices of red and white wine.

Nick drones on while thanking the clients for their patronage and support.

Robert detects a scent of Chanel No. 5 perfume from across the room. Clarissa is standing by herself. He finishes the discussion with a client, crosses the room.

"How are you?" Robert speaks carefully, half expecting to be rebuffed.

"Fine," Clarissa looks bored.

"Nice turnout for Nick's function. No matter how rich they are, a free meal is a free meal," he lowers his voice, leans towards her.

"The divorce papers have been signed by both of us... You are looking at a divorced man."

Clarissa stares unblinking at Robert.

"I'm having a terrible time at my hotel. The people upstairs have drunken parties, stomp around at all hours. Another man keeps his television on loud, driving me nuts." He looks at Clarissa. She has not walked away as he half expected her to do so.

"I am looking to rent something more appropriate," Robert said.

"Perhaps we can rent a place together," she said.

Robert almost drops his wine glass.

"Father has to sell the apartment. He needs the money. Pity as it suited me."

Robert puts down his drink.

"Do you want to go somewhere quieter so we can talk?"

Clarissa places her glass on the table. They leave together.

PART 3

Later

CHAPTER EIGHTY-THREE

The sun flashes through the lace curtains of Aunt Stella's yellow and white kitchen. She has been telling Nancy about her bus trip to Sovereign Hill with her Elderly Citizens' Club. In the background the television news channel ABC 24 states that a bush fire is burning out of control in Victoria, and a strange new illness affecting parts of China.

"We had the best day," said Aunt Stella, her face beams. "The club bus drove us to Ballarat. We sang the old songs on the bus, had a marvellous morning tea with scones and strawberry jam when we arrived."

She pours the hot tea from the brown teapot with the knitted blue and red tea pot cover. "I had a go at gold diggings and panned for gold." Aunt Stella wears her favourite hand knitted green cardigan over the striped shirt and pleated maroon and red Fletcher Jones kilt that has seen decades of wear. "I didn't find any gold, but there was gold in the day. We oldies had a wonderful day." She moves the neat slices of Madeira cake closer to Nancy for her to take a slice. "I even had a bumpy ride on an old stagecoach," she said. "That was a bad idea. I had to hang on tight and had to sit for a while to get my breath back."

Aunt Stella rubs her chest.

Nancy takes a second piece of cake.

"At my age, I don't want to miss a thing. I may not have a second chance," said Aunt Stella.

"This cake is delicious," said Nancy.

"I baked the cake as soon as you told me you were visiting."

"I tried to ring you Wednesday. Were you out?" Nancy said.

"Wednesdays, I usually do my messages." Aunt Stella stares out of the window, a frown forms on her face.

Nancy notices the apprehensive look spreading over Aunt Stella's face. "Did you go to the doctors? I am thinking you may be sick and not want to worry me."

"I did not go to the doctor," Aunt Stella wipes her mouth with a linen serviette.

"A secret lover," Nancy grins.

"No secret lovers around this retirement village."

Nancy has a pang of concern that Aunt Stella is hiding something but decides not to explore it further.

The conversation turns to rose propagation and the best way to remove aphids from roses. "I squeeze the aphids," said Nancy.

"I can't do that." Aunt Stella shakes her head. "I mix soapy water, add peppermint oil and throw the lot over the aphids. They drop to the ground smelling of peppermint."

Nancy places her hand over Aunt Stella's soft,

wrinkled hand. "When will you tell me where my parents are buried? I have a sentimental idea of placing flowers on their grave and say a prayer. Since Robert left, the connection to my parents has become important, even at a burial site," Nancy said. "I was not interested before, but now I am." She looks deep into Aunt Stella's face. "I don't mind if their graves don't have a plaque."

Aunt Stella rubs her chest again, a pained expression on her face, coughs three times, has a look of fear on her face.

Nancy fetches a glass of water, takes Aunt Stella's pulse.

"Please don't ask me. I can't tell you now," Aunt Stella speaks in a whisper, "What I can tell you..." She inhales. "You were a much-loved child. Both your parents adored you." Her face hardens. "They loved you as much as you love Millie. At the proper time, I will tell you."

It annoys Nancy; she is not asking for much, an opportunity to honour her parents. Perhaps Aunt Stella is ashamed to reveal her parents are buried in a pauper's or communal grave.

"Do you have any wedding pictures of my parents? I only have one photo and wonder if there are more." Nancy speaks in a measured tone, watching the reaction from the woman who has been like a mother to her.

Aunt Stella gives an exasperated sigh. "Elizabeth and Sandy didn't have the money for formal wedding photographs." She said this in a loud voice, looks around, says in a quieter tone. "Money was tight. They organised their marriage on a shoestring." She looks away.

"But there are wedding photos of Ruth and Jack." Nancy knows she sounds harsh.

"Jack's father was a photographer. He didn't charge for them." She stops to regain her composure. "I promise you will know all at the *proper time*." She holds a cotton handkerchief to her eyes.

Nancy is confused. Each time she broaches the subject of her parents' grave, she is met with a strange reaction from Aunt Stella.

CHAPTER EIGHTY-FOUR

Nancy, Tom and Millie are lunching at a Japanese restaurant in the centre of Melbourne. Outside, metal and noise control the streets, trams go by, bells clatter and clang. The lucky tram passengers in the crowded trams will find seats. Those standing lurch back and forth with the tram's rhythm, stopping and starting. It has been raining outside but is dry in the inexpensive Japanese restaurant. Inside are pictures of meal choices which fill a large screen behind the counter. Men and women in waterproof jackets and closed dripping umbrellas wait in line to be served. Chairs scrape against the floor, doors open, slam shut, footsteps trudge up and down the stairs. Two Asian girls on the table next to them eat sushi with chopsticks, their expressionless faces stare at mobile phones.

A fan whirls above Nancy's head; she looks up. The throbbing motor makes a *swish, swish* sound, cool air blasts over her face. Despite the wet weather, they are going to an art gallery where Tom's friend Mark is holding his first art exhibition.

Millie and Nancy have ordered a vegetarian bento box with an assortment of tempura eggplant, sweet potato, rice, and pumpkin. Tom relishes Gyoza dumplings and shares Nancy's rice. They sip miso soup between mouthfuls of food.

Nancy attempted to look the part of an art lover; wears a black cocktail dress, low heels, hair in an up style with gold hoop earrings that match the gold chain around her neck. Her sodden trench coat is dripping on a peg on the wall nearby.

"Do you enjoy working in the emergency ward?" Millie said.

Tom has a quizzical face. "Why do you want to know?"

"Just curious, going from art teacher to a doctor in emergency must have been spectacular," said Millie.

"I do like the work. Most of the time, I am at my wits' end, trying not to miss anything major when I assess a patient." He glances at Nancy. "I usually rely on the nurses to clue me in what is going on with a patient when they take preliminary observations. When I enter a patient's cubicle, it is as though I am stepping into the middle of a chapter of their life story."

A metal tray clanged to the floor nearby. Tom turns toward the sound. The rain sheets against the windows almost drowning out his deep voice. "A person's life journey can be affected, and their future can change because of an illness or injury that brings them to the emergency department." He speaks in a soft voice. "For example, a stroke may permanently disable a person. Or if they cut their foot while gardening wearing flimsy shoes like thongs and if the wound becomes infected, the person could suffer from severe sepsis and potentially die." He eats another spoonful of rice. "The treatment that I administer will have future consequences for the patient and their family." He rubs his eyes. "If I miss anything in my assessment, the wrong treatment may make the patient sicker and even die."

Millie has her hands on her chin, taking in the conversation. She has had a growth spurt recently and is now taller than her mother. She is awkward and has not adjusted to her new height, wears a large shapeless windcheater and matching jeans, clothes to hide in. Her brown curly hair falls to her shoulders. She has become a striking young woman but cannot see that in herself.

"I like that. You walk into a person's reality and are respectful. You change from focusing only on the medical stuff to what is important for the patient."

Outside, a fire engine blares for traffic to move out of the way to let it pass, followed by a screeching ambulance and police car. Nancy turns to the window. "I wonder if they are going to our hospital."

Tom tilts his head in reaction to the noise coming from outside. "I always remind myself that an emergency department is a terrifying place for the average person. Waiting for hours in the waiting room before being seen by a doctor. Or travelling a long way by ambulance or helicopter. Patients come into emergency overwhelmed, powerless and afraid," he said. "I want to be the type of doctor who never forgets a patient is a person, not just a medical condition." He wipes his mouth with the paper napkin.

"I'd like you to be my doctor," said Millie.

"I hope you never need to have me as your doctor," he sips the last of the miso soup.

Nancy has a surge of affection for both of them. Tom wise, Millie intrigued. Nancy recognises a remnant of the girl Millie was, the curious Millie who always asked questions.

"You will appreciate Mark's unique painting style," Tom said, changing the subject. "Mark has dyslexia. He found school challenging, but his art tells a magnificent story of his struggles."

"How do you know Mark?"

"He was a student of mine years back when I was teaching. Even then, he had remarkable artistic talent. I encouraged him to keep working on his unique style. I was pleased when he invited me to his first exhibition," Tom said.

"How did Mark manage with his schoolwork? My best friend Angie has dyslexia, and she struggles with schoolwork."

"Mark's parents learnt what they could about dyslexia to help their son. They bought a *Reading Pen* that can run over printed text and voices the text, mastered speech recognition software, which turns text to speech." He turns his head as another ambulance races past. "His mother read chapters aloud from Mark's textbooks into a tape recorder. Mark listened to them, scribbled notes, memorised what he could.

He taped the school lectures that were important for exams. But he shone at art, was a natural, understood the effect of light and dark better than I did. Having a problem in one area in your life can strengthen you in another. This was true of Mark."

Tom uses his chopsticks to play a tune on his plate. "I'm talking too much, boring you." He looks sheepish.

"I will tell Angie what you said." Millie watches a man try to push his way to the front of the queue at the counter, only to be pushed back by a Japanese woman brandishing an umbrella. The man strides to the end of the line, holding his head up high.

"Did you know that the famous artists Leonardo da Vinci and Pablo Picasso both had dyslexia?" Tom said. "A dyslexic person often has strong visual skills, powerful imagination and above-average intelligence. Recent research shows that the right side of the brain is stronger than the left in individuals with dyslexia." Tom finishes the miso soup. "A person who has dyslexia could have an added advantage in understanding two- and three-dimensional concepts. So, having dyslexia as an artist can be a good thing." He leans back, crosses his arms.

"I didn't know that," said Millie. "I'll let Angie know she should pursue art. I have never been interested in art before. Now, I want to learn more." She fiddles with her chopsticks. "I like what you said, art healing the mind and compensating for lack—these are new ideas for me."

"Do you know *Pop Art*?" said Tom.

She shakes her head.

"In the 1950s, artists started incorporating ordinary objects like tins of soup or advertisements into their art. Popular culture inspired it." Tom tilts his head. "Art can be anything. It is good to use alternative mediums, such as crayon, etching, computer imaging, collage, sculpture. The list is endless. Once you view art as a medium of expression, you will see it around you." He draws circles on a paper serviette. "We can incorporate these circles into ideas that can become art."

"I like the idea of using my hands with clay to make art," said Millie.

"Great idea. I don't have a kiln anymore, but you can take a course that will allow you access to a kiln."

The trio arrive at the converted gallery, which was once a small church, now renovated, the wide sweeping walls covered in large paintings. A sizeable crowd of friends and onlookers are gathered there. Mark is a tall, youthful, energetic man with long, flowing brown hair, is dressed all in black. His enormous paintings of abstract figures capture the bright surrounding light and echo the darkness from the walls. The figures appear to climb from the walls to mingle with the crowd below. When Mark spots Tom, he runs to embrace him, calls to his parents, who were helping at the exhibition.

"Mum, dad; look who is here, my favourite teacher on this earth."

Tom, so glad you could make it." Mark's father energetically shakes Tom's hand.

Mark leaps onto a chair. "This is Tom Ferris who showed me how to locate my inner artist."

The crowd claps.

Tom makes an embarrassed face.

≈

Two days later, Nancy introduces Tom to Aunt Stella, who is up to her arms in flour and butter, making date scones. She dusts the flour from her hands on her checked apron, insists they stay; goes to a cupboard, opens the special cake tin for honoured guests, cuts a generous slice of fruitcake for them both.

"Best fruitcake I have ever tasted. Is it possible to have another slice, please?" Tom licks his fingers.

Aunt Stella cuts him a thick slice.

He devours the cake, brushing the crumbs onto his plate. "Nancy told me you are the best cook in the world. I agree with her," he said.

Aunt Stella cuts two more pieces and places them in a plastic take-away container for Tom to take home.

Tom asks questions related to Aunt Stella's life in Moama. "My uncle Gordon lived near Moama. My brother and I used to spend Christmas holidays with his family." Tom mentions the uncle's name; Aunt Stella said she knew of him.

That evening, Aunt Stella calls Nancy. "Tom is a vast improvement on Robert."

CHAPTER EIGHTY-FIVE

It is midnight. Robert wakes in Clarissa's luxury apartment. The panoramic floor to ceiling windows show Melbourne city in the background. He pulls on his dressing gown and opens the sliding glass doors to the private balcony. Looks out at the landscaped gardens and outdoor spaces below, breathes in the night air. Earlier, he had woken to Clarissa's legs intertwined with his during the night. He listened to her muffled noises when she turned over, dragging the doona to her side. His toothbrush and toiletries are again in the bathroom next to Clarissa's. The speed they reconnected surprised him. One moment, they were talking at Nick's cocktail party, drinking at a local hotel, afterwards had sex in Clarissa's apartment.

He has been cautious, afraid to let his guard down, fearful Clarissa might take him for a fool, still has misgiving of the marriage, baby juggernaut. In the meantime, they are creating a life together and attending auctions, looking for a suitable apartment. Robert feels he has run a marathon and won, he is back with the woman who inspires him; is ready to do whatever Clarissa wants.

Clarissa's father was delighted with the apartment

sale. He doubled his investment and improved his finances.

Robert's boss, Nick, cannot fathom any man who allows a woman to rule his emotions, a sign of weakness in his eyes. Nick would never leave Denise for another woman; he relies on her to care for his son and maintain his home life, so he can focus on other aspects of his life.

CHAPTER EIGHTY-SIX

Millie and Nancy are in Alice's Parkville office. Alice speaks in a measured tone as she moves around her office searching for the Exposure Therapy articles, finds them in her office cupboard and hands them to Nancy. Millie is wearing her usual black over-large windcheater and ripped blue jeans. Nancy's face is blank, a nervous twitch forms near her lips.

"Read the articles, they explain everything. When we meet again, we can discuss them further," Alice said. "Exposure Therapy is evidenced-based. The research shows it has a positive effect on long-term PTSD."

Nancy reads aloud, 'To regain control over a stressful event, you need to return to the event.' "I am not sure what that means." The nervous tick becomes pronounced.

Alice flicks the hair from her face. "For the last few weeks Millie and I have been working together on her *emotional* response to the assault," she lets the information sink in. "The last step is to do In Vivo—return to where the assault occurred."

Millie pulls the hoodie further over her head, looks at her feet.

"It is like a spider phobia," the psychologist said. "People can be desensitised from the fear of spiders. You start with small steps and support. With time, people can overcome their fear of spiders. It is the same desensitisation with PTSD. The body and brain learn that past events cannot harm again."

Alice opens her appointments diary.

"We still have to enlarge on relaxation and visualisation techniques." Alice looked directly at Millie, who shifts in her chair. "We have discussed this already. I want to emphasise that in my professional experience, desensitisation techniques work with PTSD."

Millie's face crumples into a frown, closes her eyes.

"We have been preparing for Exposure Therapy, meeting once a week for several weeks," Alice softens her voice. "We have gone over the events of your trauma, and you have written about your experiences. From the retelling of your trauma, the negative aspects have decreased." She looks at Millie. "I know you have played the tapes of our sessions at home." Alice clears her throat. "When the time is right, we will undertake In Vivo Exposure. This involves real-life interaction with the fear that is crippling your life." Alice tilts her head to one side and adjusts the collar of her jacket.

Millie stares at Alice, "I am terrified ... of parks. I cannot go near them." Her voice is a whisper. "Do I have to return to the place where that evil man hurt me?"

Nancy glances at Alice first and then at Millie. "My daughter is upset. Do you know what you are asking her to do?"

"Your concern is valid, but you must trust me. I have had satisfactory results with other girls in similar situations to Millie," she said. "This is necessary to ensure that Millie's life is not restricted, so we must try it." She lets the words sink in, removes her glasses. "By the time we return to the place of the trauma, Millie will have acquired mastery over the event." She glances at Nancy. "I have been teaching Millie coping mechanisms. After the In vivo session she will see the assault as it was—a random event that should not colour her future life. It must not..."

Nancy coughs to hide her anxiety.

Alice bends to the same height as Millie, takes her hands in hers. "Your fear of the park and being near large clumps of bushes is something I understand. You are always on alert, ready to flee," said Alice in a gentle voice.

"I will be with you each step of the way and will make sure you are safe. And your mother will be there."

Millie looks at her mother. "Can Tom come with us? I want him there."

"I'll ask him," she said.

∼

It has taken weeks of patient work with Alice for Millie to even contemplate returning to the park where the horrific assault took place. Alice, Millie, Nancy, and Tom drive to the park on the appointed day. It started as a sunny day, bright with promise. Later, the sun hides behind dark clouds when they reach the park.

Millie wears the same windcheater and ripped blue jeans.

Alice and Millie have rehearsed what emotions and reactions might come up and the best ways to deal with them. They move towards the path in the park Millie had trodden two years earlier. Millie shivers, small beads of perspiration shine on her face. The others walk behind at a distance.

The park is peaceful. Eucalyptus trees face skyward, creating shelter and shade under their branches. The green surroundings have always been perfect for weddings and commitment ceremonies. A woman pushes a small girl on a swing, sings *Old MacDonald had a farm* and makes a loud "Oink here, oink there."

"Higher mum," said the girl.

The mother makes the swing go higher.

Alice and Millie stop. "We are now at the point when the stranger asked you to help him find his dog." Alice casts a glance at Millie. "Look around you. What do you see?" Her voice is reassuring.

"A playground, swings and slides," Millie's words come out as a whimper. Her eyes are wide.

"What else?"

"A mother is pushing a girl on a swing." Her eyes

dart around the park. She wants to run away, hide, escape.

"Stay with the moment. Take in the details," Alice said.

"I can't do this," Millie cries out.

Nancy takes a step forward towards her daughter.

Tom holds her back.

"Millie, you can do this. You are stronger than you think," he said in a loud voice. He turns to Nancy and whispers, "Alice knows what she is doing."

Nancy grips his arm. "This is killing me. I hate to see Millie so upset."

Alice and Millie edge toward the thick hibiscus and grevillea plants. "This is where the man asked you to help find his dog. You bent over to call the dog, and the man grabbed your head in a headlock, and you bit his hand. Stop for a moment," said Alice.

Millie is motionless, face ashen, hesitant to walk forward. "I'm scared."

"Breathe as I taught you." She watches Millie's face. "I know you are fearful. But we will do this together. I promise you nothing will harm you."

"I can't go any further," Millie said.

The psychologist parts the bushes and sits on the grass in front of the hibiscus plant. "Come and sit next to me," Alice said. "Sit here and look at the spot where it happened. I am here. Your mother and Tom are here. You are safe." Alice repeated.

Millie drops to the ground next to Alice.

They sit in silence until Millie relaxes.

"Millie, you are not the same girl who was attacked. You are older and stronger. You can protect yourself." Alice looks deep into Millie's eyes. "See the bushes. They have no power over you." Alice runs her fingers over the grevillea bush. "Don't let the attacker take over your life. You can overcome him and his legacy." Alice's voice is powerful.

Millie bites her lip, closes her eyes, pulls the hoodie over her face.

"Open your eyes," Alice said.

Millie opens her eyes.

"What can you see?" Alice points to the bushes.

"It's a bush," Millie said.

"Yes, it is a bush and has no power over you." Alice sweeps her hand over the bushes again. "Relax into the moment. Note the details. Look around you. Take in this moment. Listen to the sounds. We will stay here a while longer."

Millie studies the ants on the ground, runs her hand over the grass, flinches when a dragonfly flies past. She stares at the spot where she had been attacked those years ago. The fear and recollection of the attack swirl in her head. She cannot speak. After some minutes, the colour returns to her cheeks. Her older self has restored a sense of power over the situation with her younger self. The two identities merge and become one. She is stronger and unafraid of the memory of the assailant. Wonders, what happened to the horrible man who assaulted her? Has he been brought to justice? She turns to look at Alice.

"It's just a bush. It is a small green bush, and it can't hurt me. I gave it power over me and now I take the power back," said Millie.

"How are you right now?"

"I am not the same girl."

Alice heaves a sigh. It has come together. They get to their feet, dust down their clothes, walk into the sunshine. The sun has come out of the clouds.

"Millie, take note of the surrounding sounds, listen," said Alice.

Millie inclines her head, hears the rhythmic sounds of a swing going back and forth. The squeak of a round-about going around, children's rubber shoes clambering on a slide, feet scrape on wood chips. She hears loud shouts from a nearby soccer field, somewhere a dog barks. She sniffs the air, rotting food in the nearby rubbish bin, the smell of her own sweat.

"It's not as I remembered ....." Millie's voice has a positive lift.

"How is it different?"

"Not so scary." Millie shoves her hands in the pockets of her jeans, then after a moment pulls the windcheater's hood back off her head.

"Well done. You stared down your fears. The attacker has no power over you." Alice's face relaxes. "We will need a few more sessions to debrief and to make sure you are doing the relaxation exercises, and you will be fine."

～

Later that day, Alice Parker is alone in her office, drafts the report on Millie's Prolonged Exposure session. She gazes out of the window, moves away from the computer. She recalls another young girl who had been assaulted. The attack drove the young patient to suicide.

I was determined that Millie would live.

CHAPTER EIGHTY-SEVEN

It has been six months since the Exposure therapy. Nancy empties the canvas shopping bag on the bench of the Coburg flat: a cooked chicken, a block of tasty cheese, low-fat milk, Greek yogurt, four apples, a punnet of cherry red tomatoes, radicchio lettuce, cucumbers for a salad, and cereal. She rearranges the food cupboard to fit the shopping into the small space and places the other items in the refrigerator. Opens the windows, the curtains flutter, the small geranium plants on the window ledge flutter in the gentle breeze. It has been a tiring shift at work; she has plans to disappear into a nonsense television program.

She fills a hot water bottle with boiling water and presses it to her abdomen. Makes a cup of green tea, carries it towards the lounge room.

The one-eyed tabby cat materialises, sensing the possibility of a snack. Nancy nearly trips over the cat. Last month, Millie heard a small mewing sound coming from a rubbish bin, found a small, terrified cat under rubbish, brought him home. She named the cat Scabby as he had cuts and scars and signs of malnourishment. He hid under Millie's bed for a week, too fearful to come out. Later, enticed by hunger and curiosity, he decided the occupants were trustworthy.

Millie and Scabby have a symbiotic connection; he is a therapy cat, worth his weight in cat food. He accepted Nancy as soon as he discovered she fed him. Most days, he waits at the front door around the time Millie is due home from school and meows with excitement when he hears her key in the door.

Scabby follows Nancy, rubbing his purring body against her legs. She opens the door. Millie is watching TV. Josh, a friend, lounges on the floor next to her. Millie met Josh at one of Angie's parties. He is a resentful, gangly youth who picks at his facial acne, is older than Millie, has taken to hanging around the green flat when Millie is home. Nancy feels he is a bad influence on Millie but is reluctant to comment on Josh's lack of motivation to do well in his studies.

Scabby meows and jumps on Millie's lap.

"Why aren't you at school?" Said Nancy

"The teachers had a curriculum meeting and sent us home early," said Millie.

"Josh, shouldn't you be home studying for your exams?"

"I dropped out of school," he said.

"Can you go to your own home now? I need to be alone."

Josh does not leave.

"Did you find the letter I left out on the bench?" said Millie. "It looks like your tax return. Can we borrow $400? Josh needs it to fix his car."

"He can ask his father for the money or get a job."

Ideas of lying stretched out watching television forgotten, she returns to the kitchen, opens the fridge door, searches for the leftover stew from yesterday. It was in the back of the fridge; it is not there.

"Who ate my stew?"

"We can order ham and pineapple pizza," Josh materialises by her side.

"I am boiling two eggs for me. You can cook something for yourselves." She places two eggs into a saucepan of water, turns on the stove; opens a can of cat food, feeds Scabby.

The doorbell rings.

"Hi. Come in," Nancy said to the freckled red-haired youth on the front doorstep.

"Millie, it's Bill," Nancy said.

Josh and Millie appear at once at the door.

"You should bugger off," Josh said to Bill.

"Oh, yeah?" Said Bill.

"Let's go for pizza," Millie takes the arms of the two boys and leads them out.

She can hear the boys arguing as the three go down the stairs. She eats her eggs, Scabby by her side. Revels in the sheer magnificence of teenager life.

Since the Exposure Therapy, Millie is less fearful. Nancy understands it is early days, and something might slip her up, and Millie could revert to her old fears. But today she is enjoying the moment and is grateful.

"Things are good," she said to the cat.

He purrs his response.

CHAPTER EIGHTY-EIGHT

Clarissa and Robert find the perfect townhouse in Birdwood Avenue South Yarra. It is opposite the Royal Botanical Gardens with its thirty-five hectares of over 20,000 distinct species of native and exotic plants. They regularly walk in the lush gardens and visit The Herbarium. Robert bought the townhouse from a former client who had to move overseas in a hurry. The townhouse is four years old, well maintained, shares a wall with another townhouse. It has three bedrooms—one large bedroom for them, a smaller one for an office, and a bedroom so Millie can stay when she likes. The garden is established, with small shrubs, requiring minimal maintenance. Robert is up to his ears in debt again with the mortgage and splashing out on furniture.

They are like newlyweds, kissing and hugging. Clarissa is humming and singing. She told Robert she missed a period and might be pregnant.

Robert has resigned himself to being a father again.

CHAPTER EIGHTY-NINE

It is the start of a warm day. The gardener has mowed the lawns at Maxine's South Yarra house, the smell of green grass is in the air. Everything was as it should be when Maxine invited Robert and Clarissa for lunch. She purchased an elegant salmon quiche and cheesecake from the special bakery, made a garden salad

"I am curious to meet this person who Robert has lost his head over," she told a close friend.

Clarissa wore her best ladylike dress, a black dress with the least cleavage. Robert brought an enormous bunch of Australian native flowers, which included vibrant red waratah.

Robert said, "You must not comment on the surroundings. Maxine will think poorly of you if you do. Let me do the talking. Don't bring attention to yourself."

During lunch Maxine said, "Where did you go to school?"

"St Catherine's College," said Clarissa.

Maxine's friend's daughter had been a student at St. Catherine's College. This response met with her approval. She was interested to hear that Clarissa's father had once been on the Forbes wealth list. Robert did not mention that Clarissa's father was no longer on the list, as he had made too many risky investments and fallen on challenging times.

After lunch, despite Robert's instructions, Clarissa raved about the magnificence of the house. "I would love to live in a home as grand and beautiful as this house."

Maxine's face grew dark.

Robert caught Maxine's reflection in the mirror. She was not pleased.

"When we are married, we plan to have a large family," Clarissa said. "You will be a grandmother again." Maxine did not reply, grits her teeth, stares at the large painting of a relative on the wall, screws the linen napkin in her hand.

~

Maxine calls Robert that night. "You are making another dreadful mistake. If you marry Clarissa, she will bankrupt you."

Robert did not reply. If he upset Maxine, she would cut him out of his inheritance, as she did with his brother. Maxine is a wealthy woman. Robert knows how rich she is—he has managed Maxine's profitable financial portfolios. The house alone is worth $6 million, not counting the antique furniture and paintings. When his father left Maxine years ago, he had been financially generous towards Maxine.

Reginald started a new profitable business and remarried and has two stepchildren. Robert maintains contact with his father and catches up with him and his new family. Dean is closer to his father, manages one of his father's businesses.

Robert considered the day his brother and his mother had a falling out.

"You are a control freak," Dean had shouted at Maxine after a bitter argument. "No wonder dad left you."

"You'll never receive a dollar from me," Maxine said.

"I need nothing from you," Dean said.

But Robert wants his inheritance, a reward for putting up with Maxine's behaviour over the years.

CHAPTER NINETY

Robert hesitates before pressing the buzzer of Nancy's flat. He is unsure what to say, wears a nervous expression, clears his throat. He pulls a handkerchief from his pocket and wipes his face. After a few minutes, he presses the buzzer of the green flat.

"It is me, Robert. Can I come in?" He moves his feet from side to side. He closes his eyes. His tall frame hunched over.

Nancy gives a loud groan when she sees him. "Millie is still at school."

"I came to see you." He doesn't have his usual swagger and confidence, has a fearful look on his face.

She sees the expression- shows him into the kitchen. Her books and laptop are on the table, pushes them to one side.

He pulls a chair out. They sit facing each other, neither wanting to speak first.

"So, what is on your mind?" She said. "I hope you will not be badgering me about wanting to live with us again."

"Do you need any financial help?"

She gives him a curious look.

He hesitates, fidgets with his watch. "I am sure you

have noted that Millie's school fees are paid on time." Normally, his arrogance and size take over the small flat. Today he is smaller, has a look of defeat.

She is aware of his unease.

He avoids looking at her. "I have to make a confession; your studying was an excuse for leaving. It wasn't your fault the marriage ended." He looks vulnerable, childlike.

Anger brews up inside of her, "So, when did this amazing revelation come about?" Her arms crossed over each other as if in a tight knot.

"I had been unhappy in our marriage for a long time," he said. "Before you started the Masters..."

She frowns.

There is an uncomfortable silence.

"Clarissa and I are together again."

She blinks.

"Clarissa is pregnant," he said. The sentence is rushed.

The words jolt like a hammer to her brain. Only recently, he had begged to come back to the marriage, saying leaving was a terrible mistake on his part. Now back with Clarissa and a baby on the way.

"That was quick," she said.

"It wasn't the plan," he said.

"Have you told Maxine?"

"Not yet." He clenches his jaw.

She is relieved he would not be under her feet, begging to return to the family. "Millie used to beg us to have another child," she said. It did not seem to cheer him.

Robert up his ears with stinky baby nappies and baby vomit. It sounds like karma.

~

After Robert leaves, she peers out of her window onto the street. The sky has changed from blue to grey— the trees move with the rising wind. A dark-haired woman often sits on the bench in front of the tram stop. The woman has a disability and moves slowly with a walking stick. The woman often sips on a stubby of beer, drinks by herself on the bench. Two teenage boys often join her, they drink beer and laugh. After a time, the group gets up as one and boards a passing tram. Today, the young woman is there again, sitting on the bench alone. Nancy would like to help them all, knows what it is like to be broken.

~

School has finished, Millie and Angie ride the crowded tram home. Millie has been telling Angie about Tom.

"Do you like Tom?" said Angie.

"He is OK. But my dad is the best."

"Tom and I talk art. I might be an art teacher."

~

Nancy and Gloria are again at the hospital cafe, debriefing about their workday. The hum of conversations and ringing phones creates the usual noisy background. There are long queues waiting for hot beverages.

"Millie seems calmer, The Exposure Therapy must have done something," said Nancy. "Alice said it is too soon to see if it is a long-lasting change. But we are optimistic." She tugs at the gold chain around her neck, runs it over her teeth.

"We can only hope. Millie has been through a lot," said Gloria.

They sip their drinks in silence. "Have you been to Tom's house?" said Gloria. "It might be nice to see his home. Maybe he has a secret hidden there," said Gloria.

Nancy frowns.

When Tom and Nancy work similar shifts at the hospital, Tom winks, acts silly to make her laugh. She catches herself humming, looking at life through a softer lens. She knows Tom wants to be more than friends.

He rings most evenings. "What are you doing? I was thinking of you."

They talk, rehash the day.

She looks forward to his calls.

❧

It is quiet today at the accident and emergency department, there are no ambulances queues outside, only a handful of patients in the cubicles. A young boy of thirteen sits cross-legged on a chair in a cubicle, his mother lies on the trolley next to him, her hair covered in a black scarf. The woman shivers.

"Are you cold?" said Nancy.

She takes a warm, white cotton blanket out of the heated blanket box and places it over the shivering patient.

"This is heaven." The woman snuggles under the warm blanket.

Nancy takes the patient's blood pressure, temperature and pulse, adjusts the patient's intravenous line, gives the required pain medication, tidies the cubicle, it smells of antiseptic.

Dr Sam Edwards is in the cubicle with the patient, taking the patient's medical history. He is aware Tom and Nancy have become close. Sam leans over and whispers, "Have you been to Tom's house?"

Nancy frowns and steps back. "You are the second person who has asked me the same question."

"You should," he said.

❧

Two days later, on her day off, when she knows Tom is at home, she drives to Tom's home in Richmond, parks her car on the street. She carries a red geranium plant from her windowsill as an excuse to see the mysterious home for herself. She wears a blue dress and medium high heels, a light waft of Coco Chanel perfume around her body, knocks on the door.

Tom opens the door. "It must be my birthday. Here is my favourite nurse on my doorstep." He welcomes her with a long hug. "Come in, come in. What a pleasure to see you! What brings you here?"

She hands him the plant. "This plant has grown too big for my windowsill. It needs a new home. I think it might look good on your kitchen table."

Tom places the plant on the kitchen table. "The table and the plant have bonded."

She prattles on, giving details about watering requirements for geraniums and their need to see the sun. Nancy makes an excuse to use the bathroom and check the rooms of the house. Everything is neat, no dirty clothes on the floor, no scattered papers. It is a quiet, harmonious home, a place of refuge. Piles of medical books are on Tom's desk, a wooden bookshelf crammed with more books. She opens the back door to the garden, red and white camelia bushes surround a paved area.

"What do you think of the garden?" Tom joins her.

"I love your garden," she said.

"The garden was Sandra's domain. All I do is water the plants," he said.

On the return to the kitchen, she notices a canvas set up near an open window. She stares at the painting.

Was she looking in a mirror? He has painted a red-haired woman with dancing eyes. "Who is this?"

"My wife Sandra," his voice was low.

"We could have been twins." Their common features shock her.

"I have other paintings of Sandra." He points to three large paintings of Sandra hanging on the wall in the lounge room.

"You must have loved her very much." Nancy is unsure what to say. Her brain whirls, tries to make sense of the situation. She realises it was a mistake to have come today and stumble on his evergreen love for his dead wife.

"I find it relaxing to paint Sandra. She was a large part of my life. I still love her." He edges closer to Nancy. "It doesn't mean that I can't love you too."

The room is hot, the words *love you, too*. It was the first time he had said the words, unsure what to do next.

"Tell me about Sandra. Why was she so special?" Nancy said. She notices he appears uneasy, torn between telling or not telling the truth.

"I owe Sandra my life. She lifted me when I needed it," he said.

Nancy catches a whiff of lemon blossom through the open window. A child calls to another. She swallows hard. "I owe *you* a good deal. You opened a door for both Millie and me." She was uncomfortable, as though meeting Tom for the first time, overcome with embarrassment and shyness. "Your support of

Millie and her art has changed her life ... and mine. Your powerful presence in our lives these last few months has made us both happy." She trails off, unsure what to say next. "This is hard for me to say...." A red flush creeps over Nancy's face.

Tom's mobile phone rings. He mouths, "The hospital...."

She wants to stay, needs to run. "Better let you get back to whatever you were doing before I came," she said.

"Come again, you are always welcome here," he said, placing his hand over the phone.

She scolds herself on the way home.

How could I have been so stupid to go to his house?

When she returns to the flat, she rings Gloria and relays the story.

"He is only friends with me because I look like his dead wife."

"For God's sake, don't be a scary cat all your life. Do I always have to push you to get you going? Honestly, I despair you will ever grow a muscle. Grab Tom before another woman snaps him up," she said. "You know how to dim the lights on old Sandra. For your information, two nurses are quite impressed with our Tom. They gossiped in the tearoom who will date him first. If you lose your chance, it will be all over red rover for you and Tom."

CHAPTER NINETY-ONE

Nancy is in the green flat, moves back and forth from the kitchen to the hall and back. Scabby meows each time she passes. She picks him up and strokes his soft neck. Millie is staying at Angie's. They are having a slumber party, which means eating junk food and watching videos until next morning.

Last night, she had a vivid dream of Dianne again, recalled the childhood times Dianne had been there for her, especially when she was bullied at school. The dream disturbed her, was Dianne trying to get a message to her. She plops Scabby on her lap.

"Scabby," she said to the cat. "Life is short."

The tabby snuggles closer and seems to understand.

She stares at the window, not seeing it, gets up and rings Tom. "Why don't you come over for a meal tonight? I am trying out a new pasta recipe." She hesitates, unsure what to say. "Millie is staying at Angie's." Her voice shakes. "And... bring your toothbrush. Stay the night." The words fly out of her mouth unguarded. She bites the inside of her cheek.

"Overnight bag, toothpaste and toothbrush packed," Tom responds immediately.

"I finish at 8:00 p.m.—is that too late?" His voice has a lightness to it.

"That's fine."

"Why now?" he said.

"You can call me Nancy the dragon slayer," she said.

"I will call you Nancy the weird."

"Yes, that too," she laughs.

She clicks off, examines the flat. Runs to the shower, carefully washes her hair with the special shampoo. Changes the sheets, puts clean towels out, sprays perfume lightly on the pillows. Rummages in the pantry, finds the bottle of wine that was given to her for Christmas by a colleague. Places two wine glasses in the fridge, makes a platter of cheese, olives, and biscuits.

She searches for appropriate music; locates an old CD, *Hot August Night* by Neil Diamond. She plays the track "I am… I said." Her eyes bright.

Gloria was right. Sometimes you need to take the initiative.

CHAPTER NINETY-TWO

Aunt Stella stares at the cuckoo clock in her home, hoping the cuckoo will come out. She bites her finger; her lies will soon be revealed. She dials the number, clicks off, rings again. "Nancy, the time has come to tell you what you need to know." She takes a gulp of air. "Can you come to my place now?" Her voice hesitant.

"What has happened?" Nancy opens her mouth to say something else but changes her mind.

"Just a weak heart. It is time I told you the truth about your mother and father..." Aunt Stella's voice is strained, as though a long way away.

Nancy is silent for a long moment. "Can I bring Millie?"

"Of course."

She calls out to Millie. "We are going to Aunt Stella's. She has a secret to tell us."

"I love a mystery," Millie's eyes widen.

Twenty minutes later, they arrive at Aunt Stella's retirement home. The lights from the other residents' homes shine bright against the darkening evening light. Two women gossip on the footpath near Aunt Stella's house.

Nancy knocks on Aunt Stella's door.

Aunt Stella beckons them in. She is settled on her armchair facing the Television, switches it off as they enter. The room is cosy and warm, photos in silver frames, cat and dog ornaments in their place on the mantelpiece.

"My beautiful girls," Aunt Stella holds them tight in a too long a hug. "How I love you both. You may not love me after what I will tell you tonight. Sit." She points to the sofa for them to sit. "Bear with me. It is hard for me and will be a shock to you both." Her voice cracks, becomes faint, hard to hear.

Millie and Nancy glance at one another. Curious to know where Aunt's conversation is heading.

Aunt Stella sits at the edge of the armchair. She spreads the knitted multicoloured rug over her knees, tucks the rug under her knees; does this three times. "I have avoided telling you the whole truth related to your parents. There is a reason for this, I am aware of the upset it will cause." She stops, takes a breath. "I had a small heart turn yesterday and can't postpone telling you any longer. I don't want to take the secret to my grave." Aunt Stella frowns.

Nancy stands up, Aunt Stella motions her to sit.

They wait for her to continue.

"Your mother... my sister Elizabeth is alive," she said.

"What?" Nancy jumps up. "Are you sure? Where is she? Can I see her? Why have you lied to me all those years and said she had died in an accident?" Her face flames, a shout of fury.

Aunt Stella puts her hand up to stop Nancy from speaking. "Wait. This is hard. Please listen." She stares at the cuckoo clock. "Let me tell you a story. My sister Elizabeth adored your father, Sandy. They married too young and had more than their share of problems for a young couple. The strain on their marriage was enormous."

Aunt Stella spoke slowly, choosing her words carefully. She clasps her hands together for support, tucks the rug around her knees again. Her face is pasty white. "Elizabeth became pregnant with you, just as Sandy lost his job. Although they were delighted to have a baby, they struggled to make ends meet. They managed for a while on the money Elizabeth brought home from working in the laundry. She hated the work, was a terrible job, but it kept them with food on the table and rent paid. Elizabeth became strange over this time."

Aunt Stella takes a long sip of water.

"Elizabeth started blaming Sandy for many things, that he didn't have a job, that she had to work in a place she detested. The laundry was hot and steamy, her hands rubbed rough with scrubbing other people's dirty clothes and sheets. She had been on her feet all day and was pregnant."

The room is silent.

"Nancy, your mother is alive. But Sandy, your father is dead." She wills herself to keep going.

"Can I meet Elizabeth?" said Millie.

"Wait until I finish before I answer that question." Aunt Stella takes another sip of water. "After you were born, Elizabeth became mentally ill. Ruth and I tried to get her help. Sandy took her to a doctor who prescribed medication. But she hated the medicine and stopped taking it. She heard voices that ordered her to kill Sandy. No matter what we said to her, she fixated on the idea she had to kill Sandy to save your life."

Nancy's mouth drops. She breaks out in a sweat.

Aunt Stella gulps down her drink. "Elizabeth had strange delusions, which were untrue. One was that Sandy was persecuting her, Elizabeth's speech became disorganised, she repeated words compulsively, she was distracted, spoke strange words. It was an awful time for us all. She became a recluse, refused to go out. We were all concerned. Her mental state was a worry."

Aunt Stella did not speak for a long time.

"Poor Sandy took the brunt of Elizabeth's anger. He did most of the care for you as a baby and refused to leave as he loved you and Elizabeth."

Aunt Stella eyes the corner of the room.

"One night, while Sandy slept, Elizabeth took a large carving knife and stabbed Sandy in the chest. He staggered next door and told the neighbour to ring the police. The neighbour raced over to find Elizabeth psychotic, mumbling to herself. She was sitting in a chair holding the knife, fresh blood covering her hands and dress."

Aunt Stella turns to Nancy. "You were asleep in your cot, safe. By the time the ambulance came, Sandy had died." Aunt Stella blew her nose.

Nancy gasps, jerks her head back, touches her throat, cannot make sense of the words. She has no way of protecting herself. Buries her face in her hands.

"The police came... Eventually, the courts found Elizabeth unfit for trial because of mental illness under the Sentencing Act." Aunt Stella stares at Nancy. "They gave her a Custodial Supervision Order and sent her to a secure correctional facility."

Nancy is mute. There are no words she can say. She scans Aunt Stella's room. The cuckoo clock is on the wall. The pictures, small ornaments in the room once familiar, now seem bewildering and foreign to her. Her brain cannot comprehend what Aunt Stella has said.

"When Elizabeth was in the correctional facility her only concern was you." 'Where is my little Nancy?' Elizabeth kept saying over and over. 'Why have they taken my little baby from me? The baby needs to be fed... she will be hungry.'

"It was heartbreaking to hear her distress," said Aunt Stella. "The doctors feared Elizabeth might harm you and told us we must keep the baby away from her."

Aunt Stella stops.

Nancy's sobs punctuate the silence in the room.

Millie is silent.

"The other day, you asked me where I go on

Wednesdays. I visit Elizabeth and keep her up to date with what is happening with you and Millie."

Nancy gasps.

"I see Elizabeth every week when she can have visitors. Ruth used to come with me before she moved to Queensland," she said.

Nancy lets out a loud moan.

Millie remains silent.

"Will you find it in your heart to forgive me for not telling you?" Aunt Stella said.

There is a long uncomfortable silence.

"Elizabeth is still mentally unwell. She continues to hallucinate and has weird delusions, despite the strong medication," she sighs. "Her behaviour can frighten, she argues with people no one else can see, mutters to herself.. she can be aggressive." Aunt Stella picks fluff from the rug. "She has punched the nurses several times... I am not frightened of her. Elizabeth has missed so much, all those years of not being part of your life. It is not her fault she is the way she is," Aunt Stella wipes her eyes.

Nancy has her hands clasped over her ears, rocks back and forth.

"I intended to tell you the truth, but it was never the right time. When you were a child, you wouldn't have understood. I didn't want to ruin your childhood. Elizabeth's psychiatrist told us to allow you to have a happy childhood, as the news of your mother being a murderer would upset you. He suggested telling you when you were an adult. You went off to university and enjoyed life fully. I didn't want to spoil that pleasure. Then you met Robert and were so happy, got married and had a baby. Why upset your happiness? Then the problems with Millie's assault and Robert leaving..."

Nancy still has her hands over her ears.

"I can see by your reaction to the news that the psychiatrist was right," she said. "Elizabeth did not mean to kill your father. She was a sick woman. You can forgive her," her voice breaks.

Nancy takes her hands from her ears; she can see the pain in Aunt Stella's face but cannot speak.

The cuckoo bursts out of its little house, chirping the hour.

"You wanted to know where your parents were buried, to place flowers on their grave. It sounds a simple request to you. But it is not. We buried Sandy in the Moama cemetery. Elizabeth is buried in the mental health facility, alive but lost to us."

The significance hit Nancy. To be alive and buried in a mental health facility was too hard.

"I intended to tell you earlier. I didn't want to layer this on you. But now you are stronger. I believe you can cope with the truth." Aunt Stella's eyebrows gather inward, rubs her chest.

"When can I see my grandmother?" said Millie, puts her arms around Aunt Stella, holds her tight.

Nancy rocks back and forth repeatedly. She unclasps her mother's vintage gold chain with the handmade individual links from her neck. Throws the chain in her bag.

CHAPTER NINETY-THREE

The correctional facility waiting room has no windows. Nancy is worried if the power were to go off, it would plunge all in the waiting room into darkness in the airless black hole. She recalls reading of the attack of 9/11 in the USA, and the trapped people underground. They were stuck in the basement when the building collapsed and were entombed in darkness, with no escape. The room smells of stale bananas and rancid sandwiches from the overflowing rubbish in the bin in the corner. Hard fluorescent lights hang overhead. The place reminds Nancy of movies where police interrogate innocent people. There are old, faded prints of thoroughbred horses on the wall. The chairs are of hard metal with a spongy seat cushion as an afterthought. The seat is in the wrong proportion for Nancy's body. She moves forward, is trying to find the proper equilibrium between putting her feet on the floor and sitting back on the seat. Nancy spots a loudspeaker on the wall, reads the Emergency procedure sign underneath.

Evacuation points information in case of emergency.
Nancy watches Aunt Stella to learn how to behave

in this strange environment. Aunt Stella has a slight flush on her cheeks.

It has taken forty-five minutes for Aunt Stella and Millie to be cleared by security to the waiting room. The team checked them for drugs and contraband and their permission papers and identifications checked.

Aunt Stella sits, leans forward over her walking stick, a bunch of pink carnations next to her.

Nancy is afraid to open this pandora's box to the past.

Millie paces around the room and looks at the paintings on the wall. "This is exciting," Millie seems unperturbed.

Nancy's stomach churns, she wants to be sick, has no plan how to manage this strange situation. She feels like a fly on the wall looking down, out of her depth, unsure what to do or say, keeps her eyes on Aunt Stella.

"Don't expect too much," Aunt Stella said. "Elizabeth can be unnerving."

The door opens, a short, plump, grey-haired woman enters. She wears a plain brown dress with a black cardigan, walks with a stoop. There is a family resemblance. Nancy can see it straight away. She resembles Aunt Stella but appears years older.

A nurse follows behind.

"Stella," said the woman, throws her arms around Aunt Stella. They hug for a minute. "You came," said Elizabeth. "I have been counting the hours until your visit." She looks at Nancy and Millie. "Who are the strangers?" Elizabeth points to Millie and Nancy.

"The time has come. No escaping it. Today is the day to reconnect with your daughter Nancy and to meet your granddaughter Millie," said Aunt Stella.

Elizabeth freezes, pulls back, terror in her eyes, turns to the nurse. "I want to go back to my room."

"I am here, and so is Stella," said the nurse.

Elizabeth dashes for the door and turns the handle.

Millie shouts, "Grandma." "I brought you these." Millie collects the carnations and thrusts them into Elizabeth's arms.

Elizabeth holds the flowers, smells them. "Who told you pink carnations are my favourite flowers?"

Nancy notices Millie has the same thick brown wavy hair as this woman.

"Come and sit next to me," said Millie. "I waited a long time to meet you." Millie takes Elizabeth's hand, and they move to the hard seats.

Nancy is frozen.

This is my mother.

She cannot process the information. It is as if she is watching the scene from far away, an observer at a play, cannot interact, unsure what will happen next.

Aunt Stella opens a plastic Tupperware container. "Your favourite, lemon slice...." She offers a piece to Elizabeth. "And here is your cup of tea." She pours steamy tea from a thermos.

Elizabeth holds the cup, turns her head back and forth between Millie and Nancy.

Aunt Stella, sensing her distress, chatters amiably.

"I told you that Millie has grown; isn't she a

beauty? She looks like you at the same age, except you had pigtails. She's an artist. Nancy still works as a nurse, as I told you."

Elizabeth turns to face Nancy. Neither can acknowledge each other.

Taking the cue from Aunt Stella, Millie tells Elizabeth about her cat. "We recently added a new member to our family, a rescue cat. His name is Scabby. I found him in a garbage bin."

"Your hair is the same curly brown hair as mine." Elizabeth touches Millie's hair. "My husband had red hair," Elizabeth said.

"My hair is red," Nancy squeaks, finding her voice.

Elizabeth looks intently at her as if she just saw a ghost.

A heavy silence.

The nurse said, "I will leave for a few minutes and give you private time. Press this button if you need any help. I am next door."

"Stella tells me you're divorced," said Elizabeth.

This comment is unexpected. Nancy coughs over and over as though she has a fishbone stuck in her throat. Aunt Stella and Millie stare at Nancy, hoping she will speak.

"He... left me for another woman. Then he wanted to come back. Now has gone back to the other woman." She makes little sense.

"Never take him back," said Elizabeth, shakes one wrinkled finger for emphasis. "Stella has told me how he deceived you. Let me look at you." Elizabeth places a warm hand on Nancy's face. "You are crying. No need to cry," she said. "I remember you asleep in your cot, such a peaceful baby, never any trouble."

"I told you she would come." Elizabeth jerks her face to the ceiling, shakes a fist. "You kept saying no, but she did."

Nancy peers up at the ceiling. No one was there.

"Stella keeps me up to date with your lives," Elizabeth said.

"You are lovely." She places a wrinkled hand on Nancy's face again. "Stella has done a wonderful job of being your mother while I was here." She pats Nancy's head. "I am not sure what to say to you to make up for the lost years."

Nancy sobs.

"Drink your tea, Elizabeth, while it's hot," said Aunt Stella. "The nurse will be back soon."

The normality of the action brings Nancy undone. She cries into her hands.

The nurse returns. "Enough excitement for one day," takes Elizabeth by the arm.

"Can we come back to see you?" said Millie. Her lovely open face and gentle manner makes Nancy cry again. Millie acting like an adult while she is babbling nonsense.

"Please come back with Stella next Wednesday," said Elizabeth.

"I want to show you my art. I am having art lessons," said Millie.

"We have regular art therapy here as well. Our

373

instructor has been sharing her art tips. She draws with charcoal," she said. "If you bring your paintings, I will show you mine. We can compare styles. I have copied Picasso. His abstract work appeals to me."

"Elizabeth, it's time to go back." The nurse links an arm around her.

They walk out together.

"Now you know the story," said Aunt Stella.

"Perhaps you can understand why I couldn't tell you."

CHAPTER NINETY-FOUR

The streetlights enhance the blackness of the night outside the Coburg flats. Cars go past, shining brightly on the roads.

Nancy tightens the cord of her dressing gown; she sits at the chrome edged table. She holds the snapshot of her parents. This time looking at the photo with revulsion as she tries to comprehend the recent events. Aunt Stella finally told her the true story related to her parents, they visited Elizabeth at the correctional facility and on the surface she appeared to be an unremarkable old woman. Nancy has been awake all night, mulling over the complexities of the situation. She gets up, paces back and forth in the hall, goes to the window that overlooks Sydney road.

Her mother killed her father.

All those years of yearning for a kind mother, she has come to the ugly truth: she was not the saintly woman of her imagination, but a murderer. She punches a cushion over and over in frustration.

Scabby meows indignantly.

I want to scream.

She bites her tongue, not wanting to wake Millie and add to her stress.

I wish I had never badgered Aunt Stella for the truth.

She rubs her eyes; it is so unfair; her life had started to be manageable. She and Robert were learning to be nicer to each other, which was good for Millie. The Exposure Therapy had been helpful for now. Millie had changed from a terrified young girl to becoming a more self-confident adolescent. She had Tom in her life. Now her life is again in chaos.

How to process that her mother murdered her father?

Nancy moves into the small living room, sits down with Scabby next to her, he nudges his fluffy head against her body. She goes back to the kitchen, then to her bedroom, lies on the bed and stares at the ceiling.

Tom has explained what happens in the brains of patients with chronic paranoid schizophrenia. The rational health professional part of Nancy acknowledges this—but the small child inside does not.

There is no way I can function at work today.

She finds her mobile, clicks in the ward number. "Night staff... I won't be able to come to work today. I am unwell. Can you inform the morning staff? I was to start work at seven."

"You sound terrible," said the night duty Nurse Unit Manager.

They will be short staffed, hopefully they can call someone from Nurse bank to fill my shift.

Scabby rolls into a ball, falls asleep on her bed. His tan and white chest rises and falls in time with his snores. She strokes him.

"It wouldn't worry you if your mother puss was a murderer."

～

The following Wednesday, Millie wakes at seven and goes into her mother's bedroom. Nancy is in bed reading.

"Are you coming with Aunt Stella and me to visit Elizabeth today? I have a day off from school because of a school meeting," said Millie.

"Next time," said Nancy.

Later that day, Millie catches the tram to Aunt Stella's. She is more confident since the In vivo Exposure Therapy and is able to navigate public transport by herself.

Aunt Stella is waiting, dressed in her street clothes and overcoat, holding a bag with the thermos and sweet treats. "Where's Nancy?"

Millie shakes her head. "She is having some sort of meltdown."

"I knew it would be a horrible shock for her."

They catch the bus to the correctional facility for the Wednesday appointment to visit Elizabeth.

～

Later that afternoon at the green flat, Scabby meows as soon as he hears Millie at the front door.

She picks him up. "Did you miss me old furry face?" The cat purrs.

"It was better this time," Millie said. "Elizabeth was friendly. We talked about art, and she likes my art folio. I loved hers. We discussed art and artists... Like I do with Tom." She stands in front of her Mother. "Elizabeth does great charcoal sketches. Gran asked after you. I said you were busy with work and would visit soon." Millie stares hard at her mother.

Nancy glares at Millie. "She's not your Gran."

"Don't be dramatic. She is my Gran," Millie said. "Gran told me she has been waiting to see you all her life and wants to make up for the lost time." She takes a banana from the fruit bowl, takes a bite.

Nancy gets up, rinses her cup, uses a sponge to wipe the kitchen sink in long laborious movements, over and over.

"Did you know Gran Elizabeth has a baby photo of you tucked in her cardigan pocket? The photo is old and faded," Millie said. "She told me she always keeps it with her and kisses it often."

Nancy looks up, finds it hard to believe that Elizabeth would miss her.

~

Nancy calls Gloria. "I cannot get my head around that my mother is a murderer," she said.

"For God's sake, Nancy. Elizabeth was psychotic when she killed your father. Can't you see this? Life is unscripted and chaotic," Gloria said. "But I have to admit you take the cake for crazy. You probably carry the crazy gene too."

"This is no laughing matter," said Nancy.

"When you get to know her better, perhaps you can take Elizabeth out on day leave," said Gloria.

"You have to be kidding," said Nancy.

Tom agreed to go with Nancy for moral support when she next visited Elizabeth—the word mother still sticks in her mouth. She cannot say it.

The next Wednesday, Aunt Stella, Tom, Millie, and Nancy drive to the correctional facility. Millie takes a day off from school. Tom parks his car and they all go through security and wait in the windowless waiting room. The rubbish bin is empty of rubbish, the room is cold and intimidating.

Tom puts his arm around Nancy's. "It will be all right," he said in a gentle voice.

There is fear in her eyes, she is out of her depth, is used to being in control, but has no control over the current situation.

A few minutes later, the door is tossed open. Elizabeth enters the waiting room, followed by the same nurse. Elizabeth moves to Millie and Aunt Stella and puts her arms around them. "I have been up and dressed early, watching the clock tick to the time to see you," Elizabeth smiles.

Nancy feels she is walking on quicksand and could fall through the sand and disappear forever.

"Hello Nancy," said Elizabeth. "Millie tells me you have been busy at work and couldn't see me."

Nancy nods and does not speak.

"Who is this?" Elizabeth points to Tom.

"I am the man who is there for Nancy and Millie," Tom said.

Elizabeth sighs, "I wish I had a man to be there for me."

"Tom used to be an art teacher. He is a doctor now," said Millie.

Tom and Millie appear to have a relaxed conversation with Elizabeth. The conversation centres around art, it has become a universal language for those interested in art. Nancy cannot join in, feels an outsider again, a person out of step with the rest of the world.

I have to say something...

"If we can get permission, would you like to go out for a few hours' day leave with us?" Nancy said. "It must be hard stuck inside here all the time." She moves closer to Elizabeth.

They turn to stare at Nancy.

"It can be arranged," Aunt Stella said. "Earlier, when I was fitter, Ruth and I received permission to take Elizabeth out on day leave. We had to take a nurse with us."

Elizabeth claps her hands and shouts. "I want a picnic—on a rug, on the sand by the beach... the beach...." She does a little skip on the spot. "It has been years since I've been to the beach."

Tom squeezes Nancy's hand.

"The beach it is. I will get the details for the procedure for permission for day leave on our way out," said Tom.

Millie whispers in Nancy's ear, "A great idea, mum."

Nancy closes her eyes.

What have I got myself into?

On a warm, moonlit Saturday night, Tom and Nancy walk hand in hand after eating at a Turkish restaurant on Sydney Road. They enjoyed a meal of Mezes, Gozleme and baklava.

A male voice calls from the street. "Tom, is that you and Sandra?" Then, realizing his mistake, he said. "I could have sworn you were Sandra for a moment."

Nancy searches Tom's face.

He avoids her gaze.

"Are you only friends with me because I remind you of Sandra?" she said.

Tom looks awkward, unsettled. "It may have been an unconscious attraction at first." He looks into her eyes. "But I know you are Nancy, not Sandra."

The air has lost its warmth, is chilly, looks like it will rain. Tom's car stops at Moreland Road, they wait for the tram to move forward before driving on. Tom glances at Nancy. She does not meet his eyes. When they reached the flat complex, she said, "thanks for the meal. I may turn in as I'm tired."

"See you around."

"Yes, see you around," she said.

~

Once inside the green flat, Nancy rings Gloria.

"I am such a fool. I allowed myself to fall in love with someone who loves someone who is dead."

Gloria listens for a brief time. "Tom is a great human, is protective of you and Millie, blends into your life. It is not like the fairy tales. We are all imperfect."

"I don't want to be hurt again," said Nancy.

"You need to take a risk in life, allow others to be flawed," said Gloria.

"Easier said than done," Nancy said.

CHAPTER NINETY-FIVE

Nancy was showered and dressed in her work scrubs, about to take Millie to school and drive to work for her nursing shift when the first phone call came. If she had known what was in store, Nancy might have ignored the call and let the phone ring out.

"Is this Nancy Dunfield?" A deep male voice said.

"Yes, who is this?" She is guarded, does not recognise the voice.

"Sorry to ring so early, Mrs. Dunfield. This is Detective Simon Hamilton from the Brunswick police station. I have news for you and your daughter." He pauses, knowing his words would be stressful. "We have charged a man who assaulted a young girl in a park near your home."

"Oh, no" She covers her mouth.

"The young girl will be all right... The DNA evidence shows the man is the same person who assaulted your daughter."

Nancy gasps. "Oh, my God ..."

"Are you all right, Mrs Dunfield?... I know this is a shock for you."

She places her car keys on the table.

"Mrs Dunfield...," the police officer said.

"I am here. Keep going," she quietly closes the kitchen door, so Millie cannot hear.

"From the DNA and the description from your daughter and Mr Brody, we are pretty sure we have a match."

"Thank goodness the police have caught the criminal. Can you tell me the condition of the girl who was assaulted...?"

"The girl will be all right. She was brave, kicked him hard in the groin, while he was doubled up in pain. She escaped and called the police," he said. "The assailant was caught on CT camera; we sent a squad car out quickly and found him cowering behind a car and arrested him." He shuffles some papers. "Your daughter was in a worse situation, as she was beaten badly. How is Millie?"

"Millie has improved, the assault left her with PTSD, we have turned the corner at last. The counsellor who has been working with Millie has been wonderful."

"Good," he said. A pause. "The reason for this call today is to see if it would be possible to bring Millie to the police station today. We want her to look at some photos of a few suspects and see if she can identify the man who assaulted her. Her cooperation will assist us in stopping this man who has been preying on young girls in the neighbourhood."

Nancy holds her breath. It has been some time since the attack. Will the identification procedure rekindle the pain and anxiety once more for Millie? Will it trigger PTSD again?

"Can I ring you back after I speak to Millie's psychologist? The identification may stir up negative aspects in Millie again."

"Often, the identification and charging of the assailant often brings closure to the people involved." He gives details where Nancy can connect with him.

She places the phone on the table.

Scabby senses something is going on, jumps on the table, meows for Nancy to notice him. She strokes the cat.

Nancy texts Alice Parker, who rings back and suggests she is available to speak with Millie if she needs help.

The door opens, an annoyed Millie stands in the kitchen, dressed in her school uniform. "Who are you talking to and why is the door shut?"

"Sit down. I have something unpleasant to tell you."

Millie gives Nancy a wary look.

She relays the message from Detective Hamilton, expecting Millie to cry and be distressed.

Instead, Millie's reaction is one of white-hot anger. "So, they have caught the bastard. Good!" She pounds a fist in her hand. "Bring on the identification. I will do anything I can to make sure the bastard is stuck in jail for the rest of his life."

It is not the response that Nancy expected.

"Do you want to speak to Alice first before we go for the identification?"

"No. I don't need to speak to Alice. I want to see this vile man locked up for what he did to me and the other girls."

∼

At the allocated time, Nancy and Millie arrive at the Brunswick police station for their appointment with Detective Hamilton. The station is a clean, pleasant place- the walls covered with community information and faces of criminals. Three men queue at the counter, Nancy and Millie join the queue. The station is busy, men and women in police uniform open and shut the doors behind the counter. The phones are constantly ringing.

Millie fidgets, is impatient.

"We have an appointment with Detective Hamilton," said Nancy to the policewoman behind the office grill at the counter, giving their names.

They are ushered into a small bright office at the back of the police station. Detective Hamilton is a tall, muscular man with dark hair and a thick black moustache. He talks to Millie about her school and interests and has a photo of a black and white cat on his desk.

"What's your cat's name?" said Millie.

"Her name is Persian. The kids named her. She is

a rescue cat and has been perfect for our son who has autism," said Detective Hamilton.

Millie tells him the story of Scabby and where she found him.

"Cats are great communicators," he said. "Persian has trained us to feed her at the right time," he said.

Nancy chews her lip.

"Millie, here is your chance to gain revenge on the man who hurt you so badly and almost destroyed you," he said. "We need consent from you and your mother. You will be asked to view an album of photos. I want you to examine each photo carefully and identify the person who attacked you. Can you do that?"

"I have been waiting for years to get him." Millie opens the book of suspects, scrutinises them intently, points to the man. "He is the man who assaulted me, tried to rape me, hit me, and attempted to end my life. His face is etched in my mind. I can never erase his face."

"Are you certain that is the guy?" said Detective Hamilton.

"That is the man, it is him... it is him...it is him." Her eyes wide, her body straight, voice loud. "If you can throw this man into jail, the world will be a safer place." There is a triumphant look on her face.

"At last, he will be brought to justice."

CHAPTER NINETY-SIX

The second phone call came later the same day. Nancy and Millie had returned from the police station and were sitting at the chrome table discussing the identification.

Nancy's mobile phone rang. "Mrs Dunfield, this is the retirement village manager. I have sad news," said the caller. "Are you sitting down?"

Nancy's heart races.

"I am sorry to have to inform you that your Aunt Stella has died. One of her friends knocked on her door today, when she did not answer, called the supervisor. They found her in her bed. The doctor came and verified that she had died."

"Oh, no." Nancy places her hand on her neck, shakes. "It is not possible. We had lunch together the day before. She was her usual self."

Millie puls at her sleeve. "What is it?"

"Aunt Stella has died."

"Poor Aunt Stella," Millie said.

They drive to the residential village. Aunt Stella's unit blazes with lights. The supervisor opened the door for them.

Did Aunt Stella have a premonition that she would die?

❦

The sun shines bright on the day of Aunt Stella's funeral. Tom arrives early at the Coburg flat to drive Nancy and Millie to the small chapel at the retirement village.

"Can you check my eulogy?" Nancy said in a quiet voice.

He glances through the words. "Perfect. I can read the eulogy at the service for you if you like."

"Thank you. I don't think I can..." she said.

The retirement village chapel is packed with Aunt Stella's friends. Many are residents from the retirement village, others are friends throughout her life. Aunt Stella's thin body lies inside the plain wooden coffin in the chapel. Noises filter around Nancy, people talk, the organ plays. She inhales the heady scent of white gardenias arranged on Aunt Stella's coffin. The day has an unreal quality. A nurse is with Elizabeth, who weeps quietly into her handkerchief, Gloria is with her giving support.

Tom reads Nancy's eulogy, she uses some lines from Mary Elizabeth Frye's poem: "I do not sleep. I am a thousand winds that blow. I am the diamond glints on snow..." he stops, looks straight at Nancy.

She nods.

He reads Nancy's notes of gratitude for Aunt Stella being her mother and her humour and kindness.

Nancy feels as though she has been cut into tiny fragments of pain and is unsure how she will survive without Aunt Stella.

Farewell, Aunt Stella. Thank you for being my mother.

CHAPTER NINETY-SEVEN

Six months have passed since Aunt Stella's death. A strange normality has crept into Nancy's life. She has lost her lifelong confidant and support, found it heartbreaking to go through Aunt Stella's possessions and markers of her life. Everything feels unreal to Nancy.

It is evening at the Coburg flat. Millie is stretched out on her bed and is speaking on the phone to Angie.

"It has been a crazy time," said Millie. "I am not sure where to start. Scabby is next to me. He senses I am miserable and has snuggled into my lap."

"Do you want to come and stay with me?" said Angie.

"I better stay here with mum, she is quite jittery," said Millie.

"I can't believe what has happened in the last few months... First the police station and the identification process. The evil man deserves to be locked away forever."

"I am glad they caught him. You won't have to look

over your shoulder to see if he is around anymore," said Angie.

"I am sorry your Aunt Stella has died," said Angie.

"Mum and I are heartbroken. We miss her so much. Aunt Stella has always been in my life. When we lived in East Brunswick, Aunt Stella often stayed with me when mum and dad went away- they liked each other in those days. Then it changed, not sure who started the arguments; my parents were always at each other's backs... I hated them fighting," said Millie.

"My parents still argue over stupid things even though they don't live together," said Angie.

"Aunt Stella's retirement village was an escape for me. The oldies used to make a fuss of me," said Millie.

Angie tried not to interrupt; aware Millie needed to talk.

"I used to swim in the retirement village pool. Aunt Stella sat on the edge, chattering with the other residents as I practised my freestyle stroke. Sometimes I stayed overnight at Aunt Stella's—her sofa opens up to be a comfortable bed. We used to play board games, Cluedo, Monopoly and Pictionary. She told me about her fiancée who died," Millie said.

"In the last two years, it has been one thing after another. The assault, dad leaving to live with Clarissa, selling our home, shifting into this place. All those sessions with Alice... Finding Gran Elizabeth, and Aunt Stella dying," Millie strokes the cat. "Can you hear that?" Millie places the mobile close to Scabby, who is purring in his sleep.

"He sounds like a truck revving," said Angie.

"Where was I? Oh yes. I hated it when dad left us to live with Clarissa. Mum freaked when he went. Do you remember how worried I was? When I returned from school, she was often still in her pyjamas?"

"Things are better with your mother and father now," said Angie.

"Yes, they get on, sort of. Clarissa and dad are happy. And mum has Tom."

"I would like to meet Tom," said Angie.

"You will," said Millie.

"I hope you will take me to meet your Gran," said Angie.

"You will love her, although she is odd. The three sisters had the same wiry, flyaway hair tied in a bun. Aunt Stella was more outgoing and needed a walking stick. Gran Elizabeth is quieter, an artist like me."

A knock was heard on the door. "Dinner will be ready in 20 minutes," said Nancy.

"Won't be long. I am talking to Angie." She returns to the phone.

"I remember Aunt Ruth. She was nice to me, different from her sisters, not as chatty as Aunt Stella. When Aunt Ruth moved to Queensland with Uncle Jack, I loved staying with her in Maroochydore. The Big Pineapple was my favourite."

"I have been to the Big Pineapple," said Angie.

"Aunt Ruth adored her birds. She fed the magpies and kookaburras who lined up on the balcony. They had no fear of her. She treated them like her family, especially after Uncle Jack died. Now both aunts are dead. Aunt Stella and Aunt Ruth might be together on the other side. There is only Gran Elizabeth alive of the three sisters."

"I need to go now. I will talk to you later. Mum is calling me for dinner," said Angie.

"Mine too," said Millie.

~

After dinner, the girls resume their conversation.

"Aunt Stella left mum the retirement unit in her will. Mum plans to sell it and buy a house. It will be a small house, not as flash as our East Brunswick home. I know she is desperate for a garden," Millie said. "We will need a truck to move all the plants mum has throughout the flat."

"I like the plants in your flat," said Angie.

"Scabby will come with us when we move. He is part of the family. I am his favourite human. He sneaks onto my bed in the morning and purrs. If I do not wake, he pats my face. I pretend to be asleep. He jumps on my chest and stares at me, making funny cat noises. It makes me laugh."

There is the clatter of falling books at Millie's flat.

"What was that?" Angie said.

"Just some books fell over. This flat is so small if I turn around, I bump into something... Good news. Dad told me Clarissa is pregnant. At last, a stepbrother or stepsister..." she said. "I rang Maxine to tell her that

Clarissa was pregnant. She was furious as dad had not told her."

Millie places Scabby on the floor.

"I am glad you get on with Clarissa. I hate my mother's partner; he is a creep," said Angie. "Have you always called Maxine by her Christian name?"

"Maxine asked me a long time ago to call her by her Christian name. She hates being called Gran," Millie said. "I told Maxine the news about Gran Elizabeth. She asked if I was safe around her."

"Hang on a moment. I need to answer the door," said Angie. She returns a few minutes later.

"A late delivery for mum," said Angie. "My mother is addicted to ordering clothes online. And then tries to return them when they don't fit." She gives a giggle.

"I told Maxine that Gran Elizabeth is an old lady, couldn't kill a fly now. She has suffered enough with her mental illness." Millie gets up and closes the curtains, switches on the bedside light. "Maxine asked me how mum is coping with a murderer for a parent. I told her mum was not coping. You know I expected mum to throw herself into Gran Elizabeth's arms, having a mother at last. That sort of thing."

Millie makes shadow puppets against the lamp's light.

"I would be freaked if I found out my mother was a murderer," said Angie.

"Yeah, I guess you are right..." said Millie.

"I asked Maxine if she would like to meet Gran

Elizabeth. I told her that Gran Elizabeth is a bit crazy and talks to herself," said Millie.

"What did she say?" said Angie.

"She asked me when I was planning to visit Gran Elizabeth next and she would come with me," said Millie.

"Maxine has changed," said Angie. "I remember you telling me she was snobby."

"Yes, posh and haughty.... So much has happened in the last few years. Even Maxine has amazed me."

Nancy sticks her head inside Millie's room. "Are you girls still talking? Have you completed your homework?"

"I will do it as soon as I finish talking with Angie," said Millie. She returns to the phone.

"Here is when it gets weird. Maxine mentioned she had some confidential knowledge to share with me, and you know I adore secrets."

She gets up and closes the door.

"Maxine said since lots of secrets are popping out, she had a secret so big that not even dad knows. I hassled her to tell me the secret."

"What was the secret?" said Angie.

"I asked Maxine whether she had ever killed someone. She said she wanted to. Later, she told me that her parents were both alcoholics and abused her."

"You have so many odd people in your life," Angie said.

"I am keeping a diary to record it all, so I don't forget," said Millie.

"So how did Maxine and Gran Elizabeth get on when they met?"

"They got on fine. The knowledge that Gran Elizabeth had been a murderer did not repulse Maxine. She told me how she used to keep a knife under her pillow to protect herself from her parent's drunken friends who tried to molest her."

"That's frightening," said Angie.

"I learnt Maxine has been paying for my school fees, not dad. She did it without telling mum. Dad was supposed to pay the fees, but since living with Clarissa, he has no money."

"I am glad she paid the school fees, so you didn't have to change schools," said Angie.

"Me too."

"Hang on, I have to do something," Angie went outside and came back with a bag of potato crisps. "Go on, I am listening."

"Maxine asked if she could see Gran's art. She went back to her room and returned with charcoal images of sad faces. It impressed Maxine, I could tell. She offered to organise an exhibition of her work. Maxine belongs to a committee that promotes struggling artists, raising money, that sort of thing."

"More artists..." said Angie.

"My world is swimming with art and artists... I told Maxine about Tom's friend with dyslexia. She was interested to hear Tom had been an art teacher before he became a doctor."

Angie stopped eating. "How is your mother going with Gran Elizabeth? Is she still scared of her?"

"Sort of, last Wednesday, mum came with me to see Gran Elizabeth. They are attempting to talk more, but the conversation seems forced. I did most of the talking." Millie looks at her watch. "I better finish my homework."

"Me too," said Angie.

CHAPTER NINETY-EIGHT

Millie and Angie are on the tram going to school; as usual, the tram is a noisy conglomeration of students, exchanging seats, making a racket.

"How did you go taking your Gran out for the day?" Said Angie.

"No problems. Tom got permission from the authorities to take Gran out for two hours. A nurse had to come with us," said Millie. She turned around to face a grinning boy, tapping on her shoulder.

"Stop that," she said to the boy.

"We organised a trip to St Kilda beach. Tom had to work at the last moment and couldn't come with us. Mum was not happy about Tom not being there, she wanted to cancel the outing. In the end mum packed a picnic lunch, rug, and cold drinks; we picked up Gran Elizabth and a nurse."

"Hi," said Millie, waves to a friend.

"Mum was strange, a funny type of quiet and withdrawn. I am not sure why. It had been her idea to take Gran out," Millie said. "But the nurse chattered with Gran Elizabeth, and I did, of course. She acted like a little kid, excited to be let out and spend the time at the beach."

"A good day all round," said Angie.

"Gran went on about the softness of the sand. She took her shoes and socks off and paddled around the water's edge. Then a dog bounded over and sniffed Gran. She let out a yell, 'Help me.' She was very scared."

"I ran up and said he was just a pup," said Millie. "She had forgotten how the outside world works. The nurse and I calmed her down."

The tram lurches to a stop, Millie and Angie hitch their back packs on to their shoulders and move off the tram with the other students in similar uniforms.

"On the drive back from the beach, Gran Elizabeth started mumbling silly things to herself. She had a faraway gaze in her eyes. Now and then she yelled to an invisible person as if they were in the car. Creepy... I sat in the back seat next to Gran, the nurse on the other side, mum in the front, driving. I glimpsed mum's worried eyes in the rear-view mirror."

The nurse patted Gran Elizabeth's hand. "You had your wish, to have a picnic by the beach."

Gran Elizabeth said. "I hope we can go to the beach again soon."

"Of course we can," the nurse said.

~

Millie and Angie join the hundreds of girls streaming through the school gates.

"How are things with you and Josh?" said Angie.

"I broke up with him. He is too immature for me." She whispers in Angie's ear, "I want to do well in my exams, go to university, be a psychologist like Alice. Josh has no ambition. Wants to goof off and do nothing," said Millie.

"Pity, Josh was a hunk," said Angie.

"Yes, a hunk with no brains." Millie pulls a face.

"When I told Tom I had been thinking of being a psychologist, he said it had was a great idea. He said that my experience with PTSD and Gran's mental health issues will make me a compassionate psychologist."

"I hope so," said Angie.

They place their backpacks in the school lockers, take out textbooks, and writing materials for the next lesson.

"Next month, Gran is moving into a community house with three other women and a supervisor. I have been working on a painting of a beach scene for her room."

"How are things with you and Clarissa?" said Angie.

"Clarissa and I have become friends. I am so pleased to have a baby sister or a brother. I told Clarissa I could babysit any time."

"Are you going to their wedding?" said Angie.

"They invited me," said Millie.

"It sounds as though things are going extra well for you," said Angie.

"About time...." Millie said.

The two friends hurried down the corridor as

the school bell rang to herald the commencement of classes.

CHAPTER NINETY-NINE

The Coburg flat. Millie is in her bedroom writing in her personal diary, as Alice has suggested.

Millie's diary entry:

Before she died, Aunt Stella gave us photos of Sandy and Elizabeth that mum had never seen. Gran Elizabeth was beautiful with dark hair. Sandy was skinny, with red hair and freckles. Aunt Stella had told us where they buried Sandy in Moama, which is between New South Wales and Victoria.

Mum and I decided to visit the cemetery where Sandy was buried. We stayed in a local motel and had a good look round. We explored the Murray River, visited the Port of Echuca, and even had a ride on a paddle steamer PS Emmylou.

Mum showed me the farm that once belonged to Aunt Ruth and Uncle Jack. Whoever bought it had knocked the house down and build a two-storey house in its place. We located Mum's old school; it is not a school anymore. The old wooden building is now a drop-in centre for the Country Women's Association.

'This once was our classroom,' mum said and pointed to a room to where five women were sewing. Later, mum pointed out Dianne's house.

We found the Moama cemetery in a quiet part of town. It took us a while to find Sandy's brass plaque on the lawn cemetery. The plaque had his name, birth date and death date. He died over forty years ago. A yellow rose bush hovered over the plaque. It was silent at the cemetery; a few old men and women were there when we were there. Mum and I placed a posy of yellow daisies on his plaque.

Another missing piece of the family puzzle found.

I wonder if Sandy made bad dad jokes. Was he a nice person?

It is unusual to cry for a person you never met. Mum and I did.

At the cemetery, I blurted out, "My name is Millie. I am your granddaughter, and I am sorry that Elizabeth killed you."

Mum bent over and kissed the plaque, her face red and puffy. I have never seen her so upset. I placed my hand on her shoulder. "Mum...."

'Thank you, Sandy, for my life. Be safe wherever you are,' said mum.

CHAPTER ONE HUNDRED

It is late in the afternoon, Gloria and Nancy are at their usual place at the hospital cafe after work, catching up on gossip. Around them, the usual hectic activity, people check their phones; others read or talk. A thick set man with a long brown pigtail draped over his back chats to the long queue of customers at the coffee shop.

Nancy said. "I have good news. I just had a phone call from my supervisor. He told me he passed my thesis. That means I will now graduate with my Masters." Nancy did a high five. "I did it, Gloria. I did it." Her eyes shine.

"Well done," Gloria gives her a hug. "To finish your Masters is a monumental event, considering what you have been through. I am proud of you."

"Tom said I should do my PhD and teach. It sounds good. A change of career path," Nancy said.

"Studying has changed you," said Gloria.

"Honestly Gloria, I am stoked." Nancy said. "So much has happened in my life since Robert left. I am gaining the ability to trust people. They will go on in their way, no matter what I want. And I am learning the skill of stepping back and not trying to control things. I don't hold anger or resentment towards Robert anymore. He did me a favour by leaving. Despite Robert's failings, he is still Millie's father."

"He will always be a monster in my eyes, a self-obsessed, stupid man," said Gloria.

"I am learning to adjust to change. It occurs rightly or wrongly, bought by deliberation or a stroke of luck," Nancy said.

"Is it philosophical Nancy I am speaking to today?" Said Gloria, her head to one side.

"I am waffly... I wonder what the secret to life is. Is it accepting everything? I am sad for those who died that I loved and loved me: Aunt Stella, Aunt Ruth, Uncle Jack, Dianne, and Sandy. They left an essence of themselves, as lavender you can smell somewhere in your brain, even when the lavender is not there. It is easy to say each person lives in their own time. But how hard it is to trust and let go."

"All this insight because you have passed your degree." Gloria raised her eyebrows.

"I still worry about Millie, but you were right. She has to live her life. I will die one day, and Millie has to learn to survive her way. I hope I have given her enough knowledge and strength to deal with any future stressors in her life."

CHAPTER ONE HUNDRED AND ONE

Gloria's house in Moonee Ponds. Gloria moves the colouring books and assorted pencils and pens further down the kitchen table.

Nancy and Gloria are discussing Robert's wedding with Clarissa.

"Baby James was born a month before Robert and Clarissa's registry office wedding. It surprised me they had a registry wedding," Nancy said. "I was sure Clarissa would have been a 'Bride Godzilla,' wanting all the wedding trimmings."

Gloria gathers the pencils that have fallen on the floor.

"They invited Millie to the registry wedding. They invited me to the luncheon after, but I didn't go. New wife and old wife together would be awkward."

Gloria stares under the table, Betsy is chewing on something. "Bad dog. You ate a crayon." The dog growls at her when she tries to remove the crayon from her mouth.

"Go on, I'm listening."

"Apparently, James screamed throughout the

wedding service. Millie said that Maxine rocked the baby while Robert and Clarissa took their vows."

"I hope Robert is a better father to James than he has been with his daughter." Gloria said.

"Millie is besotted with baby James. She finds any excuse to go over to Robert's place to be with him."

"You must be proud of your Millie. She has blossomed into a beautiful human," said Gloria.

"Millie can do what I cannot. I am learning through her to accept life on its terms. Elizabeth killed my father, mental illness or not. The truth is she unnerves me, fluctuates from being normal to bizarre. Her mental illness is always just under the surface. The hallucinations and voices she hears are off-putting to me. It is worse when the person who has a mental illness is a member of your own family. Not so easy to rationalise when there is too much interwoven emotion."

"Elizabeth must be missing Stella. I sat next to her at the funeral. The poor woman seemed terribly upset," said Gloria.

Nancy was quiet.

"In a lucid moment, Elizabeth has been remorseful about Sandy's death. I told Elizabeth that Millie, and I travelled to Moama to lay flowers on Sandy's plaque. Elizabeth surprised me. She said she wanted to ask Sandy for forgiveness," said Nancy.

"Sandy has forgiven you. You need to forgive yourself; I told her."

CHAPTER ONE HUNDRED AND TWO

Nancy and Tom are again wedged next to each other in the hospital staff room. Tom munches on a salad roll. Nancy nibbles on her cheese sandwich. Steaming cups of coffee are in front of them. The buzz of twenty conversations surrounds them.

"How did Elizabeth's move into the Community house go?" said Tom.

"It is hard to restructure your life at Elizabeth's age. She keeps forgetting where her bedroom is but is managing. There are three other women with her, and a nurse monitors them," said Nancy.

"Gloria and I developed a small garden for the community house. We dug the soil, added compost and fertiliser, planted a mass of pink fuchsias. They are hardy plants and will survive a measure of neglect. The little square of a garden will be bright with flowers. Gloria has never been interested in gardening. But she came to help me."

"Gloria chattered to Elizabeth as if they had known each other for years. It is a skill I wish I had..." she sighs.

"You do fine," Tom said.

"I gave her a bird feeder, added seeds. I hope the

local birds come. Elizabeth reached out to hug me. This time I did not pull back. I am learning to adapt to her changing moods. When she is afraid, she reverts to talking to herself and people no one can see," Nancy said.

"Elizabeth said she has been born again. Gloria, and I both agreed this was true."

CHAPTER ONE HUNDRED
AND THREE

The Master's graduation ceremony was held at the university in Parkville. It was a decorous affair, the graduating students, dressed in black gowns with bright blue silk sashes and black caps, lined up in the procession. The university hall was a grand room with a veneered interior with a curved sweeping veneer overhead, an impressive glass wall with a stained-glass mural. A textured brick wall has a copper structure of The Trial of Socrates.

The vice chancellor called out each student's name as they hurried to the stage. Nancy had a stupid grin on her face when they called her name. She shook the vice chancellor's hand and collected her award, turned and faced the flashing cameras.

I wish Aunt Stella were here.

In the main lecture hall, the university arranged an afternoon tea with sandwiches and cake for the graduates and their families. The room buzzed with exuberance and joy, a crush of students and relatives. The graduating student held their awards as they lined up to have their photographs taken. Nancy's colleagues, Rebecca and Marlene also graduated.

The possibilities for Nancy are now endless. She could continue studying for a PhD, be an academic, and teach nurses.

CHAPTER ONE HUNDRED AND FOUR

Gloria stirs her coffee; she and Nancy are at The Boathouse Restaurant next to the Maribyrnong river. They watch two girls paddling a canoe down the river. Gloria's sons run from one climbing frame to another at the nearby playground.

Nancy swats a fly from her plate at the restaurant next to the river. "Did I tell you Maxine sold her expensive home and moved to a classy third-floor apartment in Prahran?" said Nancy.

"Your mother-in-law has become a human," said Gloria.

"She put on snooty airs as a defence mechanism," said Nancy.

"We are all full of contradictions. What you see is not what we are," said Gloria.

"I cannot get my head around the idea that Maxine plans to hold an exhibition of Elizabeth's charcoal drawings. Personally, I credit the change in Maxine with Millie. She brought Maxine into Elizabeth's orbit. Although Maxine is still not a babysitting nanna, she appears to enjoy James."

Timothy came rushing to Gloria. "Snake, snake ...."

Gloria and Nancy jump up and follow Timothy. He points to a small grass snake asleep on the path.

"I better collect my boys before they poke sticks at the snake," Gloria said.

~

Maxine invited the family to her new apartment. Robert and Clarissa and the baby were there. Nancy and Tom collected Elizabeth from the community house. Maxine's son Dean and his girlfriend came, but not her ex-husband and his wife.

Nancy wore the antique gold chain that Aunt Stella gave her. The gold shone. She touched the chain, a connection to her parents. In a strange way, it helped her bridge the gap from the past to the present. The chain was a tangible aspect that showed she came from two people who loved her and each other.

"I am so glad to see you wearing the chain. Sandy gave it to me when we were married," Elizabeth said.

It was a pleasant lunch, elegant canapes, cheese puffs and fruit. A Spanish server served the food and drinks.

Robert seemed tired; a new baby does that.

"My boss Nick had a heart attack and is on leave. I am managing the administration part of the business while he is away." He glances at Clarissa, who is speaking to Dean and his girlfriend. "Clarissa complains I am spending too much time at work, coming home late," he said.

"Sounds familiar," Nancy said.

There were champagne toasts for the baby James, Elizabeth, Millie—even Nancy—for graduating.

"What amazing stories in this room," Tom said. "All of them crisscrossing each other to arrive at this moment."

He whispers in Nancy's ear. "I want your story and mine to join up and we can be together," he squeezes Nancy's hand tight.

She squeezes back.

POSCRIPT

Ruth's story

Ruth woke from a fitful night's sleep, tossed from side to side, finding it hard to settle. She ran her hand through her short, grey hair. Something was wrong; she had been unwell for a week and had seen the local doctor two days earlier. The doctor informed Ruth that the diagnostic tests were normal, nothing to worry about.

"You're fit for your age; cognition is good and still independent. No need to worry—no nursing home needed yet. You probably will outlive me." The doctor grinned at her joke.

Ruth was unconvinced.

At 7:00 a.m., Ruth's day started like any other. The Queensland morning light slipped through the open chink in the curtains and shimmered on Jack's photo on the dressing table. She loved the picture—Jack's dark hair edged with grey, slicked back, wearing a blue cotton shirt she bought him for Christmas.

"Jack, you look like a movie star," she had told him when he was alive.

"More Boris Karloff," he said.

Ruth was reluctant to get out of bed.

"Hello Jack, I dreamt of you again last night," she said to his photo.

Ruth stretches arms up in the air, sorts the two pillows, makes a tower, and leans on the pillows semi-upright, listening to the radio by her bed. The weather report has forecast another sweltering day in Buderim. "I must water the potted plants," she yawns. "And check if Bonnie needs any chores done." Neighbour Bonnie had recently returned from rehabilitation for a fractured hip. Ruth had been popping in each day to see if she needed help.

Ruth sleeps in the spare room in the single bed since Jack died. It is less lonely than the main bedroom, with the double bed and the white princess ruffle quilt and two soft toy dogs. She glances at the wall. The crack in the plaster has grown larger.

I should call a plasterer.

A loud screeching erupts from the front door.

"Wait on. I'm coming."

Ruth and her husband Jack had long ago cleared the scraggy bits of the jungle of weeds and overhanging tree vines next to their home in Queensland and it became a lush, tropical garden, an oasis for native birds. Ruth pulls on the faded red chenille dressing gown, slips her feet into Jack's old black slippers, shuffles into the kitchen. Peers in the Kelvinator refrigerator, takes a handful of mince from the yellow tub in the fridge, places the meat on the yellow plastic lid on the front step. Two anxious black and white magpies are waiting on the step; a flutter of wings and the mince vanishes.

"Are these your babies?" She spots two shy baby magpies hiding under the rosebush. She gives the magpies the last of the meat and closes the wire door. Loud carolling of thanks came from the two older magpies.

Ruth smiles.

At 8:00 a.m., she returns to the kitchen, measures two cups of pure water collected from the water tank: tips the water into the electric kettle. She locates the half-used tea bag, dangles it over the red and white spotted cup. The kettle boils. She empties the boiling water onto the tea bag, waits five seconds, and retrieves the bag. Ruth can stretch one tea bag for three cups. Toasts two pieces of white bread, smothers it with butter and a lick of strawberry jam. Carries the breakfast on a wooden tray and places it on the table at the back veranda. Ruth inhales the fresh frangipani scent.

I need to make a shopping list.

Ruth writes in perfect cursive script; one carton of strawberry yoghurt, six eggs, half a loaf of white sliced bread, The New Idea magazine, one kilo of animal mince for the birds, four sausages, three corned beef slices, a mango, and two Lady Finger bananas. Ruth can carry the lot in her wicker basket.

At 9:30 a.m. Ruth climbs into the ten-seater yellow retirement bus to the Maroochydore shops.

"Morning, early bird," said Ben, the driver. He waits for Ruth to sit before starting off.

"It's a beautiful day," she said.

She returns to the village at the usual time, checks on Bonnie. Her daughter Marion had arrived from Melbourne, so Ruth did not stop. She unpacks the shopping, has another cup of tea, using the same tea bag she used earlier from breakfast.

At 1:00 p.m., lunch is a corned beef sandwich with relish, cut up into four neat pieces. She watches the midday movie *Cat on a Hot Tin Roof* with Elizabeth Taylor in the lead role. Ruth and Jack had seen the movie when they lived in Victoria; they had slipped into the cinema behind Jack's mother's back. His mother had disapproved of Ruth because she was not Roman Catholic and refused to accept the idea of Jack and Ruth getting married. And pretended to be persistently ill whenever the topic came up. Ruth and Jack waited until she died before getting married. By then, Ruth was too old to have children. They bought a small farm near Moama, asked Aunt Stella to come and live with them and later Nancy came when she was a baby.

At 2:30 p.m., the mailman delivers a card from Nancy. The card informs Ruth of the good news that Nancy and Millie plan to visit next month. They will sleep in the main bedroom with the princess ruffle quilt and toy dogs. She places the card next to the phone on the side table.

She eyes the pile of dirty clothes in the laundry basket.

I should throw the clothes in the washing machine. The clothes will dry in a flash in this hot weather.

At 2:40 p.m., the world news on the radio declares a financial meltdown in the United States of America. A bomb exploded in Iraq, killing civilians.

At 3:00 p.m., the man from the council came to mow the nature strip. He lifts the mower from the back of the old green Holden utility, starts the machine, filling the air with roaring and spluttering.

At 3:20 p.m., the ten-seater yellow bus again takes residents to the Maroochydore shops. Mrs. Jones, another resident, hurries forward and climbs the bus steps.

"Good afternoon, wonderful day," said the driver.

"You wouldn't say that if you had my arthritis," she said and heaves herself on to her seat.

At 3:22 p.m., one hungry kookaburra waits on Ruth's back veranda.

At 3:24 p.m., Ruth dawdles down the wooden steps to the basement where the washing machine is housed. The phone rings, but Ruth does not hear it.

At 3:25 p.m. She clings to the rails in order to steady herself. She carries a green plastic basket on one hip. It contains blue and white striped sheets, matching pillowcases, and two towels. A blue cotton nightie, tea towels with pictures of Alsatian dogs, bras and pants, a pink shirt, pair of white slacks.

She stops to glance at the pink hibiscus tree at

the bottom steps. "At last, you have flowered," she said aloud. "I worried I had pruned you too hard." She edges past the creeper which has twisted around the rails, trailing bright buttery flowers. Another two kookaburras fly in and take their usual positions on the wooden veranda. They leave white marks on the rails as they jostle for position. They have no fear of Ruth, open their beaks wide for the animal mince.

"Won't be long," Ruth shouts to the kookaburras. She loads the dirty clothes and adds detergent and fabric softener in the washing machine but didn't start it. She feels dizzy.

Ruth falls at 3:30 p.m. on the warm spring Wednesday afternoon. The kookaburras wait above, screeching and pushing on the rails, the motor mower running outside. Ruth drops on the concrete laundry floor and passes out. Her heart slows until the brain starved of oxygen switches off, a television fading into black. It might have taken several minutes for Ruth to die. Nobody witnessed her fall. She had bypassed the nursing home relocation shuffle, transitioned in the laundry. She died as she had lived, never making a fuss, never demanding special attention.

Many years earlier, in the town of Gilgandra, Ruth had been born to a young, loving mother who developed a progressive brain tumour during her pregnancy. The tumour rendered the young mother blind at Ruth's birth. She had two other small daughters—Stella, then aged two and Elizabeth, four. Ruth was the baby. The young mother sought to experience motherhood in its fullness, even in her sightless world. Baby Ruth was an adored child. Her sisters blew raspberry kisses over Ruth's soft arms. The young mother asked the husband to erect a rope starting at the back door to the clothesline to hang out the baby's clothes.

She managed the three steps, starting at the rear entrance, carrying a basket of baby clothes. She gripped the rope, still holding the basket until it came to the clothesline. The young mother carefully hung the clothes, taking wooden pegs from the pocket of her apron. Later, she placed the wriggling baby to her breast and traced gentle fingers over the baby's tiny face, felt the suckling chin, determined lips, and moving cheeks. She told the baby although she might die soon; she planned to be always nearby.

The young mother died when Ruth was twelve months old.

The young father tried but could not nurture the baby and the two older daughters. He had no choice but to be send baby Ruth, dressed in a white bonnet and matching crocheted dress and shawl, to live with an older sister of the young mother.

The older woman, burdened with the responsibilities of her own three children, had little time for warmth and affection for Ruth or any of her own children. She held onto righteous anger, religiosity, and rules. These rules extended to Ruth and the entire family—mandatory church attendance twice on Sundays and no laughing or playing on Sundays. The children's behaviour checked with beatings from a black strap hung on the kitchen door. There were rules related to cleanliness, food preparation, chores. "Only speak when spoken to." She reminded Ruth that she had taken her in out of kindness. Ruth's father and sisters, Stella and Elizabeth, stayed connected as they could. The father could only afford the train fare to visit Ruth twice a year. When Ruth was ten, she returned home to be with her father, Stella, and Elizabeth in Moama.

Ruth died at 3:30 p.m.; made no sound in the warm, scented afternoon air. She made the journey on her terms. Died by the washing machine, connected to an invisible rope leading to the young mother's open arms.

THE END

If you liked this book, please write a review on KDP.
Thank you.